COVER-UP

BOOKS BY JOHN FEINSTEIN

THE SPORTS BEAT

LAST SHOT: MYSTERY AT THE FINAL FOUR
VANISHING ACT: MYSTERY AT THE U.S. OPEN
COVER-UP: MYSTERY AT THE SUPER BOWL
CHANGE-UP: MYSTERY AT THE WORLD SERIES
THE RIVALRY: MYSTERY AT THE ARMY-NAVY GAME
RUSH FOR THE GOLD: MYSTERY AT THE OLYMPICS

NEW SERIES

THE TRIPLE THREAT

THE WALK ON

FOUL TROUBLE

JOHN FEINSTEIN
COVER-UP

MYSTERY AT THE SUPER BOWL

A YEARLING BOOK

Text copyright © 2007 by John Feinstein
Cover design by Christian Fuenfhausen

All rights reserved. Published in the United States by Yearling, an imprint of Random House Children's Books, a division of Random House LLC, a Penguin Random House Company, New York. Originally published in hardcover in the United States by Alfred A. Knopf, an imprint of Random House Children's Books, New York, in 2007.

Yearling and the jumping horse design are registered trademarks of Random House LLC.

Visit us on the Web! randomhouse.com/kids

Educators and librarians, for a variety of teaching tools, visit us at RHTeachersLibrarians.com

The Library of Congress has cataloged the hardcover edition of this work as follows:
Feinstein, John.
Cover up : mystery at the Super Bowl / John Feinstein — 1st ed.
p.   cm.
Summary: Fledgling fourteen-year-old sports reporters Susan Carol and Stevie investigate suspicious activities at the Super Bowl after Stevie gets fired from his co-anchor job on a groundbreaking teen sports show.
ISBN 978-0-375-84247-4 (trade) — ISBN 978-0-375-94247-1 (lib. bdg.) — ISBN 978-0-375-89071-0 (ebook)
[1. Super Bowl—Juvenile fiction. 2. Journalists—Fiction. 3. Super Bowl (Football game)—Fiction. 4. Football—Fiction. 5. Mystery and detective stories. 6. Journalists—Juvenile fiction. 7. Football—Juvenile fiction.] I. Title.
PZ7.F3343Co 2007 [Fic]—dc22 2007022015

ISBN 978-0-440-42205-1 (pbk.)

Printed in the United States of America
23   22   21   20   19

*This is for the real Ed Brennan,
who taught me how to compete as a teenager.*

Once again I have to thank my editor at Knopf, Nancy Siscoe, who has a remarkable knack for making a writer feel good about being edited—a rare quality, I can assure you. Thanks also to Nancy's assistant editor, Michele Burke, and to all the marketing people at Knopf who have worked so hard to make people want to read more about Stevie and Susan Carol.

I'm not certain I would have written one book in my life, much less twenty-two, if not for my agent, Esther Newberg, who still has the enthusiasm of a teenager twenty-two years after we first began working together. Thanks also to Chris Bauch, who first thought writing kids' mysteries was something I should try and who reminds me more of Esther every day. Kari Stuart keeps both of them in line most of the time.

I also owe a debt of gratitude to all my friends with the Baltimore Ravens, who gave me the chance to see how an NFL team works from the inside. Many of them appear in cameo roles throughout the book. Thanks also to colleagues Mark Maske, Sally Jenkins, and Tony Kornheiser and Michael Wilbon, as well as Sean McManus, Jim Nantz, and Lesley Visser from CBS.

The best part of doing this series has been the involvement of Danny and Brigid—Stevie and Susan Carol's real-life alter egos. What's most scary is that, as in the books, they are both smarter than the adults in their lives. Special thanks to all my friends who have provided encouragement and support during the past year.

1: CUT FROM THE TEAM

"DAD, I THINK THEY'RE HERE."

Stevie Thomas was staring out the front window of his house, which offered a view of the entire street. He had been sitting on the couch, ostensibly reading a book, but he had read exactly one page in an hour because he kept looking out the window. He was too nervous to focus on the descriptions of igneous, sedimentary, and metamorphic rocks in the earth science book that was spread out on his lap.

Now, finally, he saw a black Town Car turn onto Pelphrey Lane and he was pretty certain it'd be stopping at his door.

"I'll be right down," Bill Thomas called back from upstairs. "Offer them something to drink."

His dad had left his law office early to be home for the

six o'clock meeting. Stevie's mom and little sister, Katie, were at an ice-skating lesson.

Stevie knew something bad was about to happen—even though his dad insisted he was jumping at shadows. The call had come from USTV on Monday.

"We'd like to get together with you and your dad before you leave for Indianapolis," Tal Vincent, the producer of *Kid-Sports*, had said to Stevie on the phone. "No need for you to come down here. We know you've got school. Mike and I will come to you."

To Stevie, that was a sign something was very wrong. "Mike Shupe doesn't fly to Philadelphia to meet with the co-star of a show unless it's something really important," he had told his dad. "I think they're canceling the show."

Mike Shupe was the executive producer of USTV's original programming unit. He was the creative force that had made USTV a serious rival to ESPN in the world of all-sports cable television. It had been Shupe's idea to have two teenagers host a weekly show on USTV aimed at teenage viewers. And it was Shupe who had convinced both their parents that Susan Carol Anderson and Stevie were made to star on *Kid-Sports*.

Stevie and Susan Carol were both only fourteen. But they had stumbled into something resembling stardom by helping solve two mysteries: one at the Final Four in New Orleans when a star player had been blackmailed to throw the national championship game; the other in New York at the U.S. Open tennis tournament when a glamorous Russian teenage star had disappeared just before her first match.

Stevie and Susan Carol had earned the chance to cover the Final Four by winning a writing contest sponsored by the U.S. Basketball Writers Association. The aspiring young sportswriters had gotten off to a rocky start: he was an opinionated northern kid who liked the Big East and the Big Five. She was an equally opinionated Southern girl who worshipped at the altar of Mike Krzyzewski and Duke. She was also annoyingly tall—at least five foot eight to Stevie's five four.

But she had turned out to be very smart and, too tall or not, very pretty. By the time they met again at the U.S. Open, Stevie had a full-blown crush on her. Plus, they made a great team. Together they had proven that Nadia Symanova's kidnapping had been a well-planned hoax. And by the end of the week, Susan Carol admitted that she really liked Stevie too. Well, her goodbye kiss had said so anyway.

That adventure had taken its toll, though. Stevie had been beaten up by a couple of thugs. But Susan Carol had it worse. It turned out her uncle Brendan had been a part of the hoax and was likely to end up in jail.

That may have been why her father had declared future big-time sports events strictly off-limits. Stevie's parents hadn't been thrilled with the goings-on in New York either. Which was why all the parents had balked when Mike Shupe called to say he wanted to make their kids into TV stars.

Even Susan Carol hadn't been too excited about the idea: "We're writers, remember?" she had said to Stevie on the phone. "TV is for pretty people who read from a teleprompter."

"Well," Stevie said, "you're pretty and I know how to read."

"Shut up, Stevie," Susan Carol laughed.

But Shupe was persistent. He had visited both families in their homes. He had offered a *lot* of money. "Even if the show only lasts a year," he had said to Bill Thomas, "you will have paid for Stevie's college education."

Stevie's dad had laughed at that one. "Obviously, you don't have kids, Mr. Shupe," he'd answered. "If you triple what you're offering, you might be right about paying for college."

Shupe hadn't tripled the offer—but he *had* almost doubled it. And he arranged it so the half-hour show would be taped on Friday afternoons—neither kid would miss any school. Stevie would go to a TV studio in Philadelphia, Susan Carol to a studio in Fayetteville, North Carolina. They would discuss the sports events of the week on a satellite hookup. They would respond to e-mails from other kids, and occasionally they would interview a guest.

Bill Thomas and Don Anderson had spent a lot of time talking on the phone. Finally they decided to let the kids try it—for one year. If it affected their schoolwork at all, if the parents weren't comfortable with how it was affecting them or their lives, the show would be over.

Deal, said Stevie and Susan Carol.

Deal, said Shupe.

The show had debuted on the first Saturday in November. The reviews were very good: people marveled at how much Stevie and—especially—Susan Carol knew about sports. Both of them became stars at their schools, and Susan Carol, who looked a lot more like eighteen than fourteen, was flooded with mail from love-struck teenage boys. Stevie even got some mail from love-struck teenage girls.

He loved every second of it. Susan Carol wasn't as sure. "What if you fall for some ninth-grade girl at school?" she asked him one night.

"Oh, come on, Scarlett," he said, calling her by the *Gone with the Wind* nickname he'd put on her at the Final Four because of her Southern accent and ability to charm almost anyone into doing anything. "If anyone should be jealous, it's me. What boy in the *country* doesn't want to go out with you?"

She paused. "But I don't want to go out with any of them."

"Well, neither do I," he said—although he had to admit Andrea Fassler was pretty hot. She was also a couple inches shorter than Stevie.

USTV had lived up to all its promises—not asking the kids to do anything more than the show and an occasional promo for the show—until just before Christmas, when Tal Vincent had called to say that Shupe and "everyone at the network" thought it very important that the show be done on location for the entire week before the Super Bowl. All of USTV's personalities would be there for the huge pre-championship media blitz.

Both fathers had immediately said no. USTV had

responded by offering the following week off, plus a financial bonus if the kids went. Naturally, they both wanted to do it. This was the Super Bowl! The biggest sporting event of the year. Ninety-five million people watching!

"Tell you what," Bill Thomas said to Stevie. "If you get permission from all your teachers—I mean *all* of them—you can do it. If one of them says no, it's no."

"Can you get Reverend Anderson to make the same deal?" Stevie asked. He was certain Susan Carol would have no trouble getting out of four days of school—she had never gotten less than an A in her life. Stevie's grades were okay—mostly B's.

"See what *your* teachers say, then I'll talk to Don," his father said.

Much to Stevie's surprise, not only did every teacher say it was okay, but they all thought it was a *great* idea. When Stevie told his dad, he had shrugged and said, "All right then, it's fine with me."

His mom wasn't quite so sure. "Do you remember what happened the last two times we let the kids go to an event like this?" she said.

"I know, I know," his father answered. "But they're going to be surrounded by people constantly. What trouble can they possibly get into?"

Susan Carol's parents had also relented, and so it was all set for both kids to fly to Indianapolis the Monday before the game. The best part of the deal, as far as Stevie was concerned, was that he would get to spend most of a week hanging out with Susan Carol—whom he hadn't seen except on a TV monitor since September.

"What I don't understand is why you have to be out there on Monday when the game isn't until Sunday," his dad had said.

Stevie had laughed at that question. "Are you kidding?" he said. "First of all, the teams come in on Sunday. They practice every day—"

"The practices are open to the media?" his dad had said, interrupting.

"No, they're not. Except to a couple of pool reporters in case someone gets injured or there's a fight or something. But the players and coaches are available to the media Tuesday, Wednesday, and Thursday in the morning. Come on, Dad, you've seen TV tape of the media surrounding players during Super Bowl week. You don't live on Mars."

"Okay, fine," Bill Thomas said. "What else is such a big deal?"

"*Everyone* in sports is there. Actually, everyone is there—period. If someone is launching a movie, they show up to be interviewed because there's like a million media people there and they're all looking for something to talk about. If someone has a book out—they're there. Running for office? Go to the Super Bowl. Then there are the parties—every night there are parties everywhere. . . ."

"Just how do you know all this?"

"Dad, I do know how to read. It hasn't been that long since the Eagles were in the Super Bowl. I read every word in the *Daily News* and the *Inquirer* that week. I even read a story on the fashions the Eagles' wives were going to wear to the game."

Bill Thomas had his hands in the air, waving them to make his son stop. "Okay, okay. I get it." He smiled. "Just your luck the Super Bowl is in a place even colder than here."

The NFL liked to take the Super Bowl to a cold-weather city about once every five years and had decided to go to Indianapolis instead of Detroit because of the new domed stadium the Colts had opened a year earlier.

"Dad, it's the Super Bowl," he said. "If they held it in the Nome Dome, I'd be there."

✦　✦　✦

So it was all set. Then, out of the blue, came the call from Tal Vincent.

Stevie knew his fear that the show was being canceled was probably silly. The ratings had been very good right from the start. He had called Susan Carol to see if anyone had asked to meet with her. The only call she'd gotten was from USTV's PR guy, who wanted to set up interviews for her during the week in Indianapolis. Stevie had heard nothing about that.

"Either he's going to call you later or he's just figuring whatever I do, you'll do too," she had said.

"Or it could be there's just a lot more demand for you than me," Stevie said. "You're the glamorous one."

"Stop it," she said. "Call me as soon as the meeting's over."

Now the doorbell was ringing, and as Stevie went to answer it, he was filled with dread.

"Stevie, how are you?" Mike Shupe said as he came in the door. It was snowing lightly, and both Shupe and Tal Vincent brushed flakes from their hair. Stevie, remembering his manners, offered to take their coats.

"Don't bother hanging them up," Shupe said. "You can just toss them on a chair." Stevie did as instructed, then led them into the living room, which was the neatest room in the house because it was the least used. Both men accepted his offer of a drink, saying that a Coke would be just fine.

While Stevie was in the kitchen pouring the sodas, he heard his father walk in and greetings being exchanged. He brought the drinks back in, then realized he should have poured one for himself. His mouth was dry.

"So," Bill Thomas said, no doubt sensing that Stevie couldn't take much small talk, "what brings you two to Philadelphia on a snowy winter night?"

Vincent turned to Shupe, who crossed his legs, trying to look casual, Stevie thought. Shupe nodded and cleared his throat.

"The show has been great," he said. "As you both know, the ratings are quite solid, especially for a once-a-week show we're still building in terms of promotion. Stevie, you've done everything we've asked."

"I sense a 'but' coming," Bill Thomas said, as if reading his son's thoughts.

Shupe leaned forward and took a long sip of his Coke. He put it back on the coaster in front of him and shook his head as if greatly pained by what he was about to say.

"This has been a really tough decision to come to," he said finally. "But everyone agrees we have to make a change."

"What kind of change?" Bill Thomas asked.

This time it was Shupe who looked at Vincent. The producer said nothing. Clearly, this was Shupe's show.

"As you guys both know, we do a lot of market research, a lot of viewer polling on all our shows. . . ."

"Mike, get to the point," Bill Thomas said.

Shupe nodded. "We're bringing in a new co-host."

Stevie and his father looked at each other. At first, Stevie was confused. "You mean there will be three of us?"

Shupe was shaking his head. "No, Stevie. I'm really sorry. We're replacing you."

Stevie hadn't been jumping at shadows.

"What about Susan Carol?" Stevie asked, no doubt a split second before his dad.

Shupe laughed, which was interesting since Stevie didn't see a lot of humor in what was going on at that moment.

"If her parents would allow it, we'd make her a *Sportsnight* anchor," he said, referring to the network's nightly news show. "Everyone loves Susan Carol. She may be more popular than Chris Berman right now."

Berman was ESPN's best-known anchor, famous for silly nicknames and bluster. Stevie liked Susan Carol more than Berman too. And it didn't surprise him that she was more popular than anyone else on-air at USTV. But that wasn't the point, he guessed.

"Let me make sure I have this straight," Bill Thomas was saying, his voice calm but filled with the kind of quiet anger Stevie had only witnessed a few times in his life. "You're firing Stevie because you have some surveys or something that say he isn't as popular as Susan Carol?" Shupe started to say something, but Bill Thomas put a hand up to stop him. "Let me finish. You came into my house four months ago and pleaded with us to try this for a year. Now, three months in, when, by your own admission, Stevie has done everything you've asked, you're firing him because someone in marketing is telling you he doesn't have enough sizzle?"

If any of this bothered Shupe, it didn't show on his face. "Look, Bill, television isn't always a fair business. . . ."

"Does Susan Carol know?" Stevie said, breaking in because he had a sudden desire to get out of the room as soon as possible.

"No, not yet," Shupe said. "We wanted to tell you first."

"She'll quit," Stevie said. "She won't do the show without me."

Shupe smiled, the kind of smile people smile when they know something you don't. "That will be her first instinct," he said. "We know she's very loyal to you, Stevie. But we think once she meets her new partner and finds out that we're going to honor your contract for the rest of the year—"

"*Honor* his contract?!" Bill Thomas said, his voice now raised. "You're legally *obligated* to 'honor' the contract. Don't make it sound like you're doing him a favor."

Stevie knew he had tears in his eyes and he didn't want

them to see him cry. He stood up, wanting to get out of the room. "You know, Bobby Kelleher was right about you guys," he said.

"Kelleher?" Shupe said, the sick smile still on his face. "What was he ever right about?"

"He was right when he told Susan Carol and me that no one who works in TV has a conscience, and that TV work is shallow and meaningless anyway."

"But quite lucrative," Shupe said, standing up. "That's why so many print guys have come to work for us."

"Not Kelleher," Stevie said. "He turned you down."

Shupe laughed. "That's because he's a lot more arrogant than he is bright. Stevie, we really have no choice. I'm truly sorry about this."

"No, you're not," Stevie said. "You can go to hell."

He glanced at his father to see if he was at all upset with him for using that kind of language with an adult. Shupe looked at Bill Thomas too, as if waiting for him to admonish his son. Everyone was standing now.

"You heard him," Stevie's father said. "You can start your trip by getting out of our house."

The two TV men looked at each other. They picked up their coats and walked out the door without another word.

2: TV TIME-OUT

STEVIE WATCHED Shupe and Vincent get into their waiting car and kept watching as the car slipped down the street and turned the corner, out of sight. His father stood next to him.

"You want to talk?" he said.

Stevie shrugged. "I need to call Susan Carol."

"Let's talk about that for a minute."

"Why? What's there to talk about?"

Bill Thomas walked over to the couch and sat down. Stevie remained by the window, wondering what could possibly be on his mind. He had a knot in his stomach that he guessed was a combination of anger, humiliation, and frustration. Part of him wanted to cry—but he wasn't going to do that in front of his father.

"Listen, Stevie, there aren't enough bad things I can say

about those guys right now," his dad said. "You were great on TV and you don't deserve to be treated like this. You're right, we should have listened more seriously to Bobby Kelleher when he told us not to trust these TV people. And I know that if you call Susan Carol and tell her what happened, she will quit right away because she's your friend and she's going to be loyal to you."

"And you think that's a bad thing?"

He was shaking his head. "No, I think it's a very good thing. But think about this for a minute: if she quits, they don't have to pay her for the rest of the year. You they have to pay because they made the decision to get rid of you. If she walks away, she loses the money. This is just a guess, but I imagine that a minister in Goldsboro, North Carolina, doesn't make a fortune, and the money Susan Carol's earning right now probably means a lot for her family."

He had a point. Stevie remembered that Susan Carol had mentioned to him that she might be able to transfer to a private school in Charlotte that had a big-time swimming program. Susan Carol was a ranked age-group swimmer. And it wouldn't have been grades keeping her out of that school. . . .

"But, Dad, even if I tell her not to quit, she'll probably do it anyway."

"And if she does, she does, but I think if you encourage her *not* to, tell her you want her to stay on so that at least one of you will still have a say on the show, she might stay."

Stevie almost smiled. "Tell her to win one for the Gipper?"

"Something like that," his dad said. "Or at least stay on TV for him."

Stevie sat down on the couch across from his father to try to make sense of everything. His head hurt from how fast things seemed to be happening. He heard the phone ring.

"Probably your mother," his dad said, standing up to walk into the kitchen. A few seconds later, he was back, carrying the phone. "It's Susan Carol," he said. "She's crying."

Apparently the USTV boys had called her as soon as they got into their car, wanting to put their spin on things before she could talk to Stevie. He took the phone and stared at it for a moment, not sure what he was going to say. "Your call, Gipper," his father said, and left him alone in the room.

✦   ✦   ✦

For a few seconds, Stevie couldn't understand anything Susan Carol was saying. Between the rush of words and her Southern accent, most of what he heard was gibberish. He was picking up perhaps two words a sentence.

"Hate them. . . . Never, ever. . . . The nerve. . . . Can't be trusted. . . . Hate them."

The second time he heard "hate them," he broke in because he guessed she was repeating herself. "Calm down," he said.

Her next few sentences he understood quite clearly: "CALM DOWN! DON'T YOU DARE TELL ME TO CALM DOWN, STEVEN RICHMAN THOMAS. I WILL NOT CALM DOWN, NOT FOR ONE SECOND!"

He realized he was smiling. Her anger was one part

amusing and about five parts touching. She seemed to be more upset about what had happened than he was. And her tirade was making him feel much better.

"What did you tell them?" he said when she finally paused to take a breath.

"I told them they better find themselves another girl, that there was only *one* person I would work with and some eye-candy guy named Jamie Whitsitt, of all things, was *not* that person."

"Who is Jamie Whitsitt?"

He heard her sigh, the kind of sigh he usually heard when she seemed convinced he was too stupid to live.

"Jamie Whitsitt is the lead singer of the Best Boys. He *is* gorgeous, but I couldn't care less. I'm *not* working with him."

Remarkably, Stevie had heard of the Best Boys, if only because he had heard the girls in his class oohing and aahing about them at lunchtime. "Aren't those guys a lot older than us?" he asked.

"He's eighteen. They don't care. Shupe said we were a 'perfect match.' I told him I didn't care, that the show was supposed to be about two kid reporters—*reporters*—not some damn rock star."

Stevie almost choked. He had never heard Susan Carol say anything stronger than "gosh darn" up until now.

"So what did they say to all that?"

"They said they were going to talk to my dad—who's not home right now. They said they understood why I'd be upset about this and they thought loyalty was a great thing, but I'd breach my contract if I didn't keep doing the show;

and that not only would I not get paid, but they might take me to court."

"Whoa! They threatened to *sue you*? Unbelievable!"

"Remind me to listen to Bobby and Tamara when they say something from now on, will you?"

Tamara Mearns was Bobby Kelleher's wife. He was a sports columnist for the *Washington Herald*, she for the *Washington Post*. The two of them had become Stevie and Susan Carol's journalism mentors. Both had urged them strongly to resist the temptations of money and fame put on the table by USTV. They hadn't listened.

Stevie took a deep breath. "I want you to listen to *me* for a minute," he said.

"Okay. What?"

"I don't want you to quit."

"WHAT . . . ?"

"Hang on a minute. First, there *is* the money issue. They're probably bluffing about suing you. But *I* still get paid in this thing and you don't. Second, you're good at this and there's no reason for you to stop doing it on my account. I'll be fine. It isn't as if my career's over—I'm fourteen. Third, when the year is over, you can either walk away from doing this kind of stuff or, if you want, there will be ten other TV jobs at other places you could have."

There was a long silence on the other end of the phone.

"Did your dad tell you to say all this?"

Why was it, he thought, that she always knew everything. He considered lying for a second, but decided the heck with it. Lying was for TV guys.

"Yes, he did," Stevie said finally. "But I thought about it before I actually said it, and I think he's right. And if *you* think about it when you calm down a little, you'll probably decide he's right too."

"Stop telling me to calm down."

"Okay. But you'll think about it?"

She sighed again, this time not the "too stupid to live" sigh but one of sadness. "I'll think about it," she said.

"Good. Call me after you talk to your dad, okay?"

"I will."

He was about to say goodbye when he heard her say, "Stevie?"

"Yeah?"

"I really do love you, you know."

He wasn't sure how to answer that one. They were fourteen and had kissed once. Still, the answer that came out of his mouth felt right.

"I love you too."

◆　◆　◆

The phone calls went back and forth over the next two days: Stevie and Susan Carol talked. Their dads talked. Their moms talked. Around and around they went.

The major question for Stevie and Susan Carol was what Susan Carol was going to tell USTV on Monday when they needed an answer—and when she was scheduled to fly to Indianapolis. The fathers talked about legal matters: Could USTV actually take Susan Carol to court for quitting? Could the Andersons counter-sue by saying the show wasn't what they signed on for without Stevie? Don Anderson wondered if the Thomases could sue USTV on the grounds that the contract said Stevie was to be on-air for a year, not just get paid for a year. Bill Thomas's legal opinion was that USTV had the right to take Stevie off the air as long as he got paid, but Susan Carol had the right to walk away—as long as she did *not* get paid. Bill Thomas called some of the other lawyers in his office to see what they thought and they seemed to agree.

The mothers talked mostly about how awful it was that the children were seeing this side of the TV business—or any business—at such a young age. "I feel like I've failed you," Carole Thomas said to Stevie after one phone conversation.

The one phone call Stevie was truly dreading was the one he knew he had to make to Bobby Kelleher. He knew Kelleher would never *say* "I told you so," but he was bound to think it—*entitled* to think it. Stevie still had a copy of the e-mail Kelleher had sent him in October:

"I know why this is tempting," he'd written. "I've done enough TV to know how intoxicating it can be. People recognize you, they think you're more important. I call it being famous for being famous. And I know the money would probably help your family and Susan Carol's out a lot. Which is why I can't absolutely tell you to say no. But I have to warn you: *these are not good people*. I've dealt with them. They'll say whatever they need to to get what they want from you—and make it sound good. You just turned fourteen. You don't *need* to do this. Neither does Susan Carol. You'll both be big stars in journalism someday. Be patient."

They hadn't listened. The money *was* tempting. And the show and the fame *had* been fun—intoxicating, as Kelleher called it. But now Stevie was facing a serious hangover of embarrassment when USTV announced the change on Monday.

He finally made the call on Sunday morning. He knew Bobby and Tamara were home in Washington before they flew to Indianapolis on Monday night. It pained him to think of all the people who would be in Indianapolis while he sat at home. And he had to admit that a small jealous part of him wanted Susan Carol to say no to USTV, no matter what he had said before.

There was a long silence on the other end of the phone when he told Kelleher the story.

"Stevie, I'm really sorry," he said finally. "Even for a TV network, that's remarkably low-rent behavior."

"They're announcing it tomorrow," Stevie said.

"You want to let them make the announcement, or can I rip them in tomorrow's paper before they put their silly spin on it?"

Stevie hadn't even thought of his firing as a story. Maybe a sub-paragraph in the story about Jamie Whitsitt coming on board.

"A whole column?"

"Oh yeah. There's a column in this. Bad enough when they treat professionals this way—but teenagers? Unconscionable."

"Let me talk to my dad."

"That's fine. One more thing."

"What's that?"

"Do you still want to go to the Super Bowl?"

"How? The NFL isn't going to give out a credential this late—especially to someone who just got fired by a network that pays it a billion dollars a year in rights fees."

"You are a very smart kid—and you're a hundred percent right about that. But who's playing in the Super Bowl?"

"The Ravens and the Dreams."

"And where do the Ravens play?"

"Baltimore . . . Wait a minute. You mean . . . ?"

"I mean that the *Herald* covers the Ravens on a regular basis. We had a beat writer and a columnist at every game. I have no doubt I can get my boss to add you to our credential list. He liked the stuff you did at the Open for us, and he would *love* to tweak USTV and the league."

"And the league can't say no?"

"They can tell us how many reporters we can send but not *who* we can send."

"I don't know if my parents will go for it."

"I'll talk to them if need be. But my guess is they'll go for it. How mad did you say your dad was at USTV?"

He was right. And Stevie'd already been cleared by his teachers to go. "You sure about this?"

"Never been more sure. Pack your bags, Stevie. You're going to Indy and you're going as a real journalist."

Stevie wanted to scream "yippee!" but that wouldn't be a real journalist thing to do. He settled for "thanks."

"Don't mention it," Kelleher said. "Now, tell me exactly what happened."

3: PUNT RETURN

BY MONDAY MORNING, everything was set.

It took a phone call from Kelleher *promising* to keep an eye on Stevie and make sure he stayed out of trouble—"for once," his father had said—to convince Bill and Carole Thomas that it was okay for Stevie to make the trip to Indianapolis. He already had plane reservations, and Kelleher said the newspaper had booked extra hotel rooms in case the Ravens and the Redskins—who had lost to the California Dreams in the NFC final—made it to the Super Bowl. As soon as Susan Carol heard that Stevie was making the trip, she agreed to stay on the job for at least one more week—partly because she wanted to go to the Super Bowl and, she said, because getting paid to work that week would make quitting a lot less painful financially if that was what she ultimately decided to do.

"Plus, I can't let you be wandering around out there by yourself," she said. "I don't care what Bobby promised your parents, you *will* get into trouble."

"As if being with you at the Final Four and the Open kept me out of trouble?" he responded.

"Good point," she said, laughing. They had come a long way since Friday night.

The only thing Stevie hadn't thought about was what would happen once the news of his firing got out—which it did on Monday morning in Kelleher's column.

"So now USTV is firing fourteen-year-old kids," he began. It got worse for USTV after that. "Let's pretend for a minute that Steve Thomas did terrible work, just wasn't right for the job," Kelleher wrote. "This would still be a cruel move, three months after the show went on-air. Given that he happened to be very good at the job, this is completely inexcusable on every level. Bottom line: Steve Thomas got fired because he's not six feet tall and doesn't sing in a boy band. When did USTV decide to become MTV?"

Shupe was quoted in the story. "On a personal level, we liked Stevie very much," he said. "He just wasn't right for TV."

Kelleher's response to that quote was direct: "Shupe's right. Steve Thomas has far too much class and smarts to waste his life in front of a camera. He'll be at the Super Bowl as a working journalist. He should be proud of that. It is his former employer that should be ashamed."

Stevie loved reading the column. What he didn't love was that the phone started ringing at 6 a.m. with calls from TV and radio stations and from print reporters all wanting him to comment or go on their shows.

And then he had to go to school. When he got off the school bus, there were no fewer than six TV camera crews waiting for him. The school principal, Mr. Bates, was there too, telling the TV people they could not come onto the school grounds.

"You walk with me from here to the front door and they can't do anything but film you walking," Mr. Bates said.

Stevie wished he had consulted with his father or Kelleher, but he hadn't anticipated being stalked at school. He made a snap decision.

"Let me talk to them for a minute," he said. "Maybe that will get it over with."

"It might," Mr. Bates said. "Until you get to Indianapolis."

Stevie cringed. He didn't like *being* the story, but he didn't feel right ducking other reporters—whether they were TV or radio or print.

Mr. Bates found a spot a few yards away from the bus drop-off point and told the crews Stevie would talk for no more than five minutes. Stevie could see all the local stations were there, along with Comcast Sports and CN-8. There were a couple of other people with tape recorders he didn't recognize.

A blond woman wearing a good deal of makeup asked Stevie the first question as soon as everyone had trained their cameras on him.

"Steve, are you crushed by what USTV has done to you?"

Stevie shook his head. "You know, I was stunned on Friday night," he said. "And I'm hurt because I thought Susan Carol and I were good together. But I'm going to the Super Bowl to write for the *Washington Herald*, and I know I'll enjoy myself."

"Was it fair what they did?" asked someone else, whom Stevie couldn't see because of the lights now shining in his face.

"I don't think so," Stevie said. "But I'm a little bit biased."

That got a laugh from everyone.

"Any thoughts of suing?" someone else said.

"Not as long as they pay me what they owe me," Stevie said with a smile—bringing another laugh.

Mr. Bates, who had been standing off to the side, decided that was enough. "Stevie's got to get to class," he said. "His science teacher does not consider doing interviews an excuse for being late."

That reminded Stevie: he never *had* finished that chapter about rocks.

Even if Stevie had done the reading, he probably wouldn't have remembered a word of it. Fortunately, none of his teachers was in the mood to pick on him. Everyone in school appeared to be on his side. Andrea Fassler even stopped by his locker to tell him she would *never* watch that show again if he wasn't on it.

Stevie couldn't resist. "So you aren't a fan of Jamie Whitsitt?" he said.

She gave him a big smile—not a Susan Carol smile, but a pretty one nonetheless—and said, "I'm a fan of *yours*."

Whoo boy! Stevie was flattered—and a little scared.

The rest of the day whizzed by, and before he knew it, his dad was driving him to the airport.

"Call us as soon as you land," he said.

"Don't worry, Dad."

"I know, I know. I just hope you don't get jumped on by the media in the airport the way you did at school this morning."

"Dad, it's the Super Bowl. The media out there have better things to talk about than me."

"You would think so, but given the frenzy here today, I'm not so sure."

"Dad, this is my hometown. People in Chicago or Miami or Houston aren't going to care."

Bill Thomas was quiet for a minute. "Stevie, just promise me you won't get into any trouble this week."

"I'll do my best, Dad." He smiled in the darkness of the car. "I doubt there will be any blackmailings or fake kidnappings this week."

"We can only hope," his father said.

Stevie's flight was—thankfully—uneventful. His father's worry had made him a little paranoid, though. As the plane was landing, he had a sudden vision of walking off the Jetway into a barrage of TV lights.

There were no lights, but plenty of action with people

everywhere. As he walked through the concourse, he turned on his cell phone and called his parents. Then, as instructed, he called Kelleher, who had arrived earlier in the day.

"It'll take you a while to get out of the airport," Kelleher said. "Get a taxi and I'll meet you in the lobby of the Marriott in about an hour. There's a lounge right there in the lobby when you walk in. Tamara and I will be there waiting for you. We'll get you a hamburger before you go to bed."

That sounded good to Stevie. He had eaten dinner at five o'clock before leaving for the airport, and the bag of pretzels he'd had on the flight hadn't exactly filled him up.

It took him a solid forty-five minutes to make his way through the terminal to baggage claim and then to the taxi line. Standing in line, he heard someone calling his name— although it was obviously someone who didn't know him well, because he kept yelling, "Steve, Steve!" His friends called him Stevie, though he was thinking it was getting to be time to ask people to switch.

He scanned the crowd and finally saw someone waving at him. He had no idea who it was. The man walked over and put out his hand. "Sorry to startle you," he said. "I'm Sean McManus."

Stevie had no idea who Sean McManus was, although the name sounded vaguely familiar. The look on Stevie's face clearly told McManus just that. "We've never met," he continued. "But I'm a big fan of yours. I'm with CBS Sports. We're televising the game on Sunday."

Stevie knew it was CBS's turn to televise the Super

Bowl. And when he heard CBS, he knew exactly who McManus was from the sports pages. He wasn't just *with* CBS Sports, he was its president—and president of CBS News too, if Stevie was remembering correctly.

Stevie shook hands with McManus. "Of course. It's nice to meet you."

"Where are you staying?" McManus said.

"The Marriott," Stevie said.

"We're at the Canterbury," McManus said. "It's only a couple of blocks from the Marriott. Come on, I've got a car here. I'll give you a ride."

Stevie recognized the hotel name because that was where he *had* been staying when he was still working for USTV. He remembered Tal Vincent saying, "It costs about twice as much as the chains, is twice as nice, and best of all, the only people staying there are NFL hotshots and the important people from CBS, ESPN, and USTV. No media riffraff."

Now Stevie was back at a chain hotel with his fellow media riffraff and glad of it. Still, a ride from CBS sounded good, since Stevie was about twentieth in the cab line. "Are you sure?" he said.

"Absolutely," McManus said. "To be honest, you were high on my call list for tomorrow. This will save me some time."

He followed McManus and a young woman, whom McManus introduced as his assistant, to a waiting car. Once they were inside, Stevie's patience gave out. "Did you say you wanted to talk to *me*?" he asked.

"I did," McManus said. "I'd like you to work for us this week."

"Me, work for CBS?" Stevie said. "Doing what?"

"Doing what you do," McManus said. "I'd send you out with a crew each day and see what you come back with. You seem to have, as the old saying goes, a nose for news. We have a late-night show each night here starting Wednesday and we have a four-hour pregame show Sunday with lots of time to fill."

Stevie was staggered. He had just been fired by USTV—a major cable network, but still cable—and now the president of CBS Sports was recruiting him to work for him during Super Bowl week?

"Well, um, wow. I mean, I'm really, really flattered, but . . ."

"You're here to work for the *Washington Herald*," McManus said. "I know. I've read all the stories. I think we could work things out so you could do some work for us in the morning and then have time to write in the afternoons. I don't want to push you, but give it some thought."

"Well, I'd have to talk to my parents," Stevie said. "And to the *Herald*." He wasn't all that sure he wanted to jump back into any kind of TV work after what had just happened. But McManus was only talking one week, and he was already here. . . .

The car pulled into the circular driveway in front of the Marriott. Stevie got out and went around to the trunk to retrieve his bags, and McManus got out with him. Stevie spotted Bobby Kelleher walking out the front door. When he saw Stevie standing with McManus, a smile crossed his face.

"Stevie, what have I told you about accepting rides from strange men—especially strange men who work in TV," Kelleher said, walking over to shake hands, first with Stevie, then with McManus. "Hey, Sean, trying to steal my reporter?" Given the way Kelleher felt about people who worked in TV, Stevie was surprised that he seemed so friendly.

"I'm not stealing—just borrowing," McManus said. "You may be a hack, Bobby, but you are very good at spotting talent—look at who you married."

He was smiling at Tamara Mearns, who had walked up behind Kelleher. She gave McManus a hug, then gave Stevie a bigger hug. The collegiality of it all confused Stevie.

McManus took out a card and handed it to Stevie. "Talk to your parents," he said. "You should talk to Bobby too. Give me a call tomorrow. Or, if you prefer, have your dad call me."

Kelleher's smile faded a bit. "You're serious, aren't you, Sean? You *are* trying to recruit him."

McManus smiled. "Yes, Bobby, I really am."

He clapped Stevie on the back, and before Stevie could even thank him for the ride, he jumped back into the car.

Stevie looked at Kelleher for a reaction. "Come on," he said. "Let's get you checked in. Then we'll get you something to eat *and* we'll have a talk."

Stevie nodded. He was suddenly very tired. There had been an awful lot of talking going on the last few days.

✦ ✦ ✦

Once Stevie had checked in, Kelleher and Mearns told him to come to room 1748 after he had dropped his bags in his room. "I thought we were going to eat?" Stevie said.

"We are," Kelleher said. "Or, you are. Tell me what you want and I'll order room service. We have a surprise for you."

Stevie wasn't sure he could handle any more surprises. But he asked Kelleher to order him a hamburger, french fries, and a Coke and took the elevator to his room on the twelfth floor. He dropped his bags on the bed and noticed it was after eleven o'clock. No wonder he felt exhausted. He knew media day for the two teams began at nine the next morning. Just going to sleep was appealing, but he *was* hungry. "A quick hamburger, then right to bed," he told himself as he walked back down the hall to the elevator.

He took it up to seventeen, walked around two corners until he found 1748, and knocked on the door. Almost before he had finished knocking, the door swung open and Stevie's jaw just about hit the floor.

"Stevie!" Susan Carol Anderson said, pulling him into the room and throwing her arms around him. "I didn't think you were *ever* going to get here."

Stevie saw Kelleher and Mearns sitting in armchairs behind her. Susan Carol stood back from him. "Let me look at you," she said. "Tamara, you're right—he's at least five eight."

Height had been an issue from the first time they had met ten months earlier in New Orleans. Stevie had grown about three inches since then, but Susan Carol was still taller.

"Generous," he said, laughing. "And when are you going to stop growing?"

"Soon, I hope," she said. "You are catching up, though. I used to be five inches taller than you—"

"Four," he interrupted.

"Okay," she said, smiling. "Four. Now it's closer to two."

It looked more like three to Stevie, but why argue. She was as pretty as ever, even with her hair tied into a long ponytail. Stevie could see by the looks on Kelleher and Mearns's faces that the entire conversation amused them.

"I thought you were at the Canterbury?" he said, following her into the room.

"I am. Bobby and Tamara asked me over so I could surprise you. I was so glad to get out of there. When I checked in, there were a bunch of TV crews who wanted to talk about what happened."

"Did you talk to them?"

"No. There were like three USTV PR guys there and they kept saying there was nothing for me to say because I had nothing to do with the change. Which is true, of course. But what's more true is they know I'd blast them. They've told me if I say anything negative about the network, I'll have breached my contract."

"What are they going to do, fire you?" Kelleher said. "You're the big star, remember?"

"I guess you're right," Susan Carol said. "But if I'm going to have to live with these people all week, it's easier if I'm not fighting with them every second."

There was a knock on the door and Tamara stood up to

answer it. "Susan Carol's right," she said. "And she doesn't need to rip USTV. Everyone else is already doing it."

She opened the door for the room service waiter. As soon as he had put Stevie's food on the table and left, Kelleher switched topics.

"So how did you end up riding with Sean McManus?" he asked. "What kind of job is he recruiting you for?"

Stevie told them all the story as he ate, finishing with "I know what you're going to say, Bobby—and this time I'm going to listen. No more TV for me."

"Except this is different," Kelleher said.

"Why? Because it's CBS?" Stevie said.

"Because it's Sean," Kelleher answered. "He's not your typical TV exec. Maybe it's because of who his father is, I'm not sure, but he's never acted like being in TV makes him important. He's as nice as he seems, and, more important, he's honest."

"Who's his father?" Susan Carol asked.

Kelleher gave her a surprised look. "Susan Carol, as much as you know about sports history, I thought *you'd* know. His dad's Jim McKay."

"*The* Jim McKay?" Susan Carol asked, repeating a name Stevie didn't know.

"Uh-huh," Kelleher said. "You've never heard of him, have you, Stevie?"

"Um, no."

Susan Carol gave him the lack-of-sports-knowledge-sigh-and-eye-roll combination. "Jim McKay is only *the* most important sports broadcaster in history," she said, looking at

Kelleher, who nodded in affirmation. "He was the voice of ABC Sports for years and years. *Wide World of Sports,* the Olympics, golf. He was the one who said 'the thrill of victory, the agony of defeat.'"

"He was also the one who gave the world the news when the hostages were killed in Munich," Tamara added.

"That *was* twenty years before I was born," Stevie said—a weak defense, he knew, but the best he had.

"The point is," Kelleher said, "Sean grew up in a TV home, he grew up around famous people. He respects Jim Nantz and Dick Enberg, and he knows the importance of having stars working for the network, but he seems to take the glitz stuff in stride."

"So are you saying I should do it?" Stevie asked.

"I'm saying you should listen to what he has to say. It's only for the week, and if he promises not to tie you up all day, the *Herald* won't have a problem with it. Plus"—Kelleher paused as a grin crept onto his face—"it would be a great way to *really* stick it to USTV."

Stevie hadn't thought of it that way. But a little revenge did sound sweet. He looked at Susan Carol. "What do you think?" he said to her.

She gave him her smile, the one most people found irresistible. "I think you ought to go for it," she said. "Mostly because you'll be good. But I'd also like to see the look on Mike Shupe's face when he finds out."

"Maybe you can," Stevie said. "If it works out, you can give him the news yourself." He took a massive bite of his hamburger. It tasted very, very good.

4: TOP DRAFT PICK

WHEN STEVIE FINISHED EATING, they walked Susan Carol downstairs to put her in a cab.

"I thought the hotel was only a couple blocks away," Stevie said when Kelleher suggested it.

"Yeah, but they're long blocks, it's about twenty degrees out, and it's close to midnight," Kelleher said.

The mention of midnight reminded Stevie how tired he was, and Bobby had already suggested meeting for breakfast at 7:30 so they would have time to walk to the Dome—which was across the street from the Marriott—and deal with picking up credentials and getting through security before media day, as the Tuesday of Super Bowl week was called, began at 9 a.m.

"I have a breakfast too," Susan Carol said, rolling her

eyes. "They want me there when they brief my new partner."

Stevie liked her apparent disdain for Jamie Whitsitt, although he could still hear her saying on the phone, "He *is* gorgeous," a few nights earlier. That didn't thrill him.

It was snowing lightly when they said good night to Susan Carol. Mearns shook her head as they walked back inside the lobby. "Snow in Indianapolis in February," she said. "Who would have guessed?"

Stevie was probably asleep about five minutes after he put his key card into the door lock, which was a good thing since his wake-up call came soon after that—or so it seemed. Except it wasn't his wake-up call. It was Sean McManus.

"I know it's early," he said. "But I was hoping to catch you before you leave for the Dome. Have you had a chance to talk to your parents about what we discussed last night?"

He hadn't. He told McManus he was about to call his father and one of them would call him back shortly one way or the other.

"I'm curious," McManus said. "What'd Bobby think of the idea?"

"Surprisingly enough, he wasn't against it," Stevie said. "He's not usually very high on television."

"I know," McManus said. "But I think he knows me well enough to know I'm not like the guys you've been working for. I'll be straight with you one way or the other."

Stevie hung up with McManus and called his dad's cell phone—knowing he would be en route downtown to the office at that hour.

"Dad, I'm going to ask you something, and I know your first reaction is going to be *absolutely not*, but listen to the whole story first," he said.

"Given your history at big events, whatever it is you're up to, the answer is *no*," his father said. He was laughing when he said it, though, so Stevie plowed ahead and gave him chapter and verse on what had happened since his plane had arrived in Indianapolis.

"Never a dull moment in your life, is there?" Bill Thomas said. "Tell you what, give me McManus's phone number and I'll talk to him. I think I'll call Bobby first so I can hear firsthand what he thinks. If nothing else, we owe it to him to be sure he's okay with the idea since he's the reason you're there."

"I agree."

By the time Stevie reached the lobby restaurant, Kelleher had talked to Stevie's father. "As long as they offer you decent money—which I'm sure they will—there's no reason for you not to do it," Kelleher said. "The only day you're on a tight deadline for us is the night of the game, and you won't be doing anything for CBS then."

Tamara laughed. "The way things are going, Stevie might replace Jim Nantz by Sunday night."

"I see myself more in the Phil Simms role," Stevie said. "I'm more of an analyst than a play-by-play guy."

"Sure," Bobby said. "And just like Phil, you can talk about the Super Bowl in which you completed twenty-two of twenty-five passes and were the MVP."

"Who was that against?" Tamara said. "I'm blocked."

"Denver," Bobby said. "Twenty years ago. I was a senior in high school."

"I wasn't born," Stevie said.

"You're killing me, kid. Let's go. You know what security will be like."

Stevie remembered from the Final Four that it could take forever to pick up credentials and clear security on the first day. Even so, he wasn't prepared for the mob scene that greeted them once they had walked through the Indianapolis Convention Center, which was connected to the Dome, down a long hallway, following signs that said MEDIA and CREDENTIAL PICKUP. The good news was that the NFL public relations people clearly knew what they were doing. There were six lines for pickup arranged alphabetically. The only bad thing about that was that Stevie had to split from Mearns and Kelleher to get in the line marked T–Z.

While he was waiting, he heard someone behind him say, "So, even celebrities have to wait in line, eh?"

The voice was familiar. He turned and saw Joe Theismann standing behind him, a friendly smile on his face.

"Well, if you're on line, Mr. Theismann, then I guess celebrities *do* have to wait," Stevie answered.

Theismann laughed and put out a hand. "It's Joe," he said. "The only people not waiting in line this week work for CBS."

That reminded Stevie that he still hadn't heard back from his dad about Sean McManus. Maybe he should have waited, he thought. He might have avoided waiting on line.

"What are you doing this week since ESPN isn't airing the game?" he asked Theismann.

"Little of everything. With ESPN, there's always some kind of show—radio or TV—that they want you on just about twenty-four hours a day. Today I'm supposed to take a crew onto the field and ask the quarterbacks if any of them can remember watching me when I played in the Super Bowl. Given that Eddie Brennan was two years old the last time I played in one, I don't like my chances."

Stevie remembered that Theismann had quarterbacked the Washington Redskins into two straight Super Bowls—winning the first and losing the second.

"I think I've seen tapes of the second one," he said, then stopped, because what he remembered was an awful interception Theismann had thrown.

"Yeah, I know, the interception," Theismann said. "Every year about now people show that again and remind me. Twenty-four years ago and it might as well be yesterday."

They had reached the front of the line. Stevie had learned his lesson from the Final Four about needing ID to pick up a credential. He'd had to send a JPEG photo because all Super Bowl credentials had photos on them. Now he showed the young woman working behind the desk his passport—which he had gotten after being hassled in New Orleans—along with his school ID. He waited to be told he needed a driver's license.

"I've seen your show," the young woman said. "I'm sorry about what happened, but I'm glad you're here. Welcome."

While she talked, she was pulling out a large envelope and a handsome computer case that said SUPER BOWL XLII—which in English, Stevie knew, meant Super Bowl 42.

"Your credential is inside the envelope," she said. "Make sure you keep it around your neck at all times—the security folks are pretty strict about it. And if there's anything I can do to help you during the week, my name is Valery Levy."

She put out her hand and gave him a smile that left Stevie a bit dazzled. Behind him, Stevie heard Theismann say, "Steve, there's no one better in the league office than Valery. She can solve any problem there is."

"Oh, Joe," Valery Levy said with a laugh, "you say that to all the girls."

"Not anymore," Theismann said, also laughing.

Kelleher and Mearns were waiting when Stevie thanked Valery Levy and put his credential around his neck. None of them had carried their computers over from the hotel since there would be plenty of time to go back to their rooms and write.

"The best thing about having the Super Bowl in Indianapolis is the logistics," Kelleher said as they waited to go through the security checkpoint. "I was worried when they said they were building a new dome that it wouldn't be as convenient as the old one. But they just put a bigger, more modern building on essentially the same site."

Stevie was about to walk through the metal detector when his cell phone rang.

"Sir, you need to turn the cell phone off to come through here," a security guard said.

"Sorry," Stevie said. He stepped out of line and answered the phone. It was Sean McManus.

"Can I call you right back? I'm going through security," he said.

"Actually, our office is about fifty yards from where you are," McManus said. "Why don't you just drop by here for a minute. I talked to your dad."

"Okay," Stevie said. He hung up, turned off the phone, and put it into the tray with his room key and some change. The security man was eyeing him skeptically, the way he was frequently eyed in these situations because of his age.

"Ever done this before?" he asked as Stevie stepped through the detector.

"Not at the Super Bowl," Stevie answered.

That seemed to work. Stevie picked up his things and told Bobby and Tamara that he had just talked to Sean McManus.

"There's their office," Kelleher said, pointing at a sign on the right side of the curving hallway they were now in. "The players will be on the field in about ten minutes. Don't take too long in there. You need to wander around, get a feel for all this."

Stevie nodded. He and Bobby had discussed his role for the week. In part, Kelleher wanted Stevie to look for the offbeat story—players, or others, who weren't getting that much attention, the classic sidebar sort of story. But he had also told him to keep his eyes and ears open for anyone or anything that looked odd or different or out of place. "Generally speaking, there aren't many real stories here during the week," Kelleher said. "These teams have been covered to death during the season. That's why anything—including Stevie Thomas being fired by USTV—can be a story."

As he walked through the doors marked CBS COMPOUND, Stevie glanced at his watch. It was 8:53. The Ravens were due to arrive at nine. They would be available for ninety minutes, and then the Dreams would follow them onto the field for their ninety minutes. The teams would also be available on Wednesday and Thursday mornings, but only for sixty minutes. The extra thirty minutes, Stevie guessed, was why this was called "media day."

Stevie knew from his football fanatic research that each team would go straight from their meetings with the media to practice and then head off for afternoon film sessions with their coaches after lunch. The coaches liked to say that they wanted Super Bowl week to be like any other week of practice prior to a game. Only there was no way that could be the case. For one thing, there was no other week in which the players were required to meet with 2,000 media members on Tuesday, Wednesday, and Thursday; and no other week when they were locked into hotels for seven straight nights instead of just the night before the game.

In past years, Stevie remembered, there had occasionally been problems with restless players showing up at night on Bourbon Street in New Orleans or South Beach in Miami. He guessed that wouldn't be a problem in Indianapolis.

Sean McManus was waiting for him just inside the doorway. The CBS compound was actually part of a dimly lit backstage area of the Dome. It looked to Stevie as if a bunch of plywood walls had been thrown up for the week to create temporary office space.

"Home sweet home, huh?" McManus said, noticing Stevie looking around. "The glamorous world of TV. Come on back. Let's talk for a couple minutes. I know you need to get onto the field."

He led Stevie through a maze of desks. All around, people were shouting at one another about which camera crew was where. He heard someone yelling, "Where is all the talent? We need them outside now for publicity shots!"

Stevie's brief TV experience had taught him that "talent" was a term for the people who worked on camera. In CBS's case that would include Jim Nantz, Phil Simms, Dick Enberg, Lesley Visser, and Greg Gumbel—among others. At USTV, he and Susan Carol had been talent. Now she was still talent, and he was, in the words of his old boss Tal Vincent, "print riffraff."

McManus led him into a small room that had a desk, several chairs, and a large-screen TV—which at that moment was showing what Stevie guessed was a closed-circuit picture of the playing field. He could see hundreds—maybe thousands—of media people milling around awaiting the Ravens' arrival. McManus offered him a chair and sat behind the desk.

"I think your dad and I have reached an agreement," he said. "He's understandably leery of you jumping right back into TV. So I suggested that you do some work for us on

Wednesday and Thursday and, if it goes okay, maybe do a piece for the pregame show. If it's too much, I'll back off. I told your dad I'd pay you the same if you're on one piece or on three—so there's no pressure and you can still primarily focus on working for the *Herald*."

Stevie thought that was fair, especially since it meant he had today to get acclimated before he had to do anything for CBS.

"What do you want me to do exactly?" he asked.

"I'm not a hundred percent sure," McManus said. "I'd like to have a crew with you during the time players and coaches are available. See what you find. If nothing else, we could have Dick interview you about what it's like to be a fourteen-year-old reporter at the Super Bowl."

He knew Dick was Dick Enberg, the longtime play-by-play man who would be hosting the late-night show for CBS this week.

"Well," Stevie said, "if my dad's okay with it, I'm willing to give it a try. I'd rather find the stories than be the story, but I hope you aren't expecting too much. There's a lot of media out there."

"I have no expectations," McManus said. "But I know your work pretty well. I have very high hopes." He reached into his desk, pulled out a credential, and slid it across to him. Stevie picked it up and did a double take. It had his name and picture on it, but instead of having the word MEDIA across the top in black letters, it had CBS in the network's trademark blue and gold.

"I wanted to be prepared if things worked out," he said.

"The NFL PR office had your photo already, so it was pretty easy to get it done quickly."

He pointed at the credential around Stevie's neck. "That will get you a lot of places," he said. "Ours will get you almost anyplace—including being able to come and go back here without checking in at reception or anything like that."

Stevie was putting the new credential around his neck when McManus stood up and put his hand out. "I'm looking forward to this, Steve," he said. "I have two goals: one, for people to say I'm a genius for signing you up for the week, and two—more important—for you to tell me when the week's over that you're glad you did it."

Stevie stood and shook his hand. "I'll try to make you happy you did it too, Mr. McManus," he said.

"Everyone who works for me calls me Sean," McManus said. "Go on and get out there. You are about to witness the greatest media circus of your young life."

As soon as he walked through the revolving doors that led to the field area, Stevie knew McManus wasn't exaggerating. He had been in the Superdome in New Orleans, but the new Hoosier Dome—negotiations to stick a corporate name on the building were apparently still ongoing—made the Superdome look like a high school gym.

Stevie had read that it seated 82,000 people, but there were so many corporate boxes about a third of the way up in the stands that the upper deck appeared to be above several clouds. There was a wide expanse of turf between the first row of seats and the field. They were cleverly raised high enough so that spectators could see over the heads of the players on the sidelines. But even in the front row, fans were pretty far from the action. And in the upper deck? Stevie wasn't sure if they could even see one of the JumboTron screens. The place was *massive*.

It was also, he noticed, kind of cold out on the field. He knew the game-day temperature would be seventy-two degrees inside, but that would be with 82,000 people in the place. Now, with a couple thousand people milling around on the field and no one in the stands, it was considerably cooler. Since only a few of the lights were turned on, the floor of the Dome felt almost bleak. It was chilly and overcast—not much different from the weather outside.

Everywhere Stevie looked there were people with microphones, tape recorders, and TV cameras. He had done some research when he thought he was going to be doing a daily TV show from the Super Bowl, and he knew that the NFL credentialed more than 2,000 media members for the game. Doing the math, Stevie realized that meant there were about forty media members for each of the fifty-three players from each team. The numbers got a little worse when you figured that only forty-five of the fifty-three players on the roster would actually be in uniform for the game.

Platforms had been set up for some of the Ravens' bigger names—Coach Brian Billick; Ray Lewis, the star linebacker; Steve McNair, the starting quarterback; and Todd Heap, the tight end. Other players were in roped-off areas while some others—the nonstars—were seated at tables with name cards in front of them. Stevie was trying to figure out exactly where he should start when he heard a familiar voice behind him.

"Why, Stevie Thomas, look at you with not one but *two* credentials. You *really* are a star!"

It was, predictably, Susan Carol. Only she wasn't alone. In fact, she had what amounted to an entourage. There was a cameraman, a guy carrying sound equipment, someone he didn't recognize in a suit, a makeup woman, a couple of large men he guessed were bodyguards of some sort, and, walking with a young woman he guessed was *another* PR person, someone who could only be Jamie Whitsitt. He was about six feet tall, and had sandy blond hair, blue eyes that Stevie figured most girls would consider dreamy, and a bored look on his face.

Turning to face Susan Carol and company, Stevie smiled. "At least I work alone," he said.

She twirled his CBS credential to get a better look and laughed. "Not if you're working for these guys, you won't be," she said. "I guess you said yes."

"They made me an offer I couldn't refuse," he said. "I don't start till tomorrow, though."

"Susan Carol, I'm sorry, but we need to get you guys to work here," the suit said.

"Right," Susan Carol said. She turned toward Whitsitt and said, "Jamie, I want to introduce you to my friend Steve Thomas."

Whitsitt didn't look all that eager to meet Stevie, but he

walked over, hand extended. "Hey, dude, no hard feelings, I hope," he said.

At least, Stevie thought, he knows who he replaced. "None where you're concerned," Stevie said, accepting the handshake. "Just make sure you're nice to Susan Carol."

Whitsitt grinned. "I don't think that will be too painful, huh, dude?"

Stevie wondered if Whitsitt could complete a sentence without the word *dude*. He was tempted to keep the conversation going to find out, but the suit was frowning and the PR person was waving at someone upfield to get their attention.

"Gotta go, kids," the PR guy said, unwilling or unable to look at or acknowledge Stevie.

"Hey, nice talking to you too," Stevie said to the PR guy and the suit, who looked at him blankly and started walking.

"I'll talk to you later," Susan Carol said quietly.

"Oh yeah, absolutely, dude," Stevie said.

She half made a face at him. "He's not a bad guy."

That surprised—and disappointed—Stevie. "Yeah, he's great. But, dude, are you sure English is his native language?"

"Don't be mean, Stevie," she said. "This isn't his fault and he really *is* nice."

Stevie watched her jogging to catch up with her posse. All of a sudden, surrounded by several thousand people, he felt entirely alone.

5: FIRST AND TEN

"STEVIE! HEY, STEVIE! Earth to Stevie!"

The third time Bobby Kelleher called his name, Stevie caught on that someone was trying to get his attention. He had been staring down the field where Susan Carol and Whitsitt were being set up next to one another, each holding a microphone with two cameras trained on them. He was thinking that they looked like the perfect teenage couple: she with long brown hair and a dazzling smile, he an inch or two taller with wavy hair, bright blue eyes, and a charming crooked grin.

"You still with us?" Kelleher asked as Stevie turned around when he approached from behind.

"Huh? Oh yeah, I'm fine. Just trying to, you know, figure out what I want to do."

Kelleher looked down the field in the direction Stevie had been staring and smiled.

"Kinda sucks seeing her with the rock star, doesn't it?"

Stevie shook his head. "I can handle that. It's just that . . ."

"What?" Kelleher asked.

"I think she likes him. How in the world can she like him? The guy calls everyone dude!"

Kelleher gave him a sympathetic smile and put his arm around his shoulder. "Listen to me, Stevie," he said. "Susan Carol is about as smart and mature as any fourteen-year-old girl you're going to meet, but she's still a fourteen-year-old girl. You can't blame her for being a little bit starry-eyed around a teen idol."

"She's smarter than that," Stevie said.

"Of course she is. And she'll come to her senses very soon. Try to be patient with her."

Stevie smiled. "Easy for you to say."

"True," Kelleher said.

Stevie took a deep breath and gathered himself. "Okay, I'm just not going to think about it for now. I'm ready to get to work."

"Good," Kelleher said. "Follow me."

Kelleher led Stevie across the field, zigzagging through various clusters of media members and around roped-off areas and platforms with stars on them. When they reached the far sideline, he pointed at a guy wearing a purple Ravens sweatshirt who was opening a large box that appeared to have footballs inside.

"There's your guy for today," Kelleher said.

"An equipment guy?" Stevie said. He had expected to do a story on an obscure player—maybe the long-kick snapper from one of the teams—but not on someone who dealt with uniforms and footballs.

"That's Darin Kerns," Kelleher said. "He's from Summit, New Jersey. Played high school football there. Wide receiver."

"And this is a story because?"

"Oh, come on, Stevie, think for a minute. I know you're up on stuff like this."

Stevie was stumped. Even worse, he knew that if Susan Carol had been there, she would have picked up on why Darin Kerns's being from Summit, New Jersey, was significant.

"I give up," he said, shaking his head in frustration.

"Who is going to be the most watched player in this game?" Kelleher said.

"That's easy," Stevie said. "Eddie Brennan." Brennan was the quarterback for the Dreams, who had emerged during the season as the league's MVP and—as Susan Carol had once called him on the show—MEB: Most Eligible Bachelor. He was on the cover of glamour magazines, sports magazines, and newsmagazines, and was featured as frequently on *Access Hollywood* as on *SportsCenter*.

"And Eddie Brennan went to college where?"

"Harvard," Stevie said, knowing that was partly why

Brennan was such a media darling. He had been drafted by the Dreams in the seventh round prior to their first season—presumably to hold a clipboard and upgrade the team's IQ. But he had become a starter in his second season and a true star in this, his third season, leading the Dreams on their unlikely Super Bowl run.

"And he went to high school where?" Kelleher said.

Finally it hit Stevie. "Summit High School in Summit, New Jersey. Let me guess—this guy played with him."

"Didn't just play with him. Was his number one receiver and, apparently, one of the main reasons Harvard recruited him."

"And no one else knows this story?"

"I think some of the Baltimore guys probably do. Brian Billick mentioned it to me when I was talking to the Ravens during the off-week, but I haven't seen anyone write about it yet. Coach Billick introduced me to him, and Darin said he'd be happy to talk this week. I'll introduce you."

They walked over to Kerns, who was now opening another box. "Darin, how are you?" Kelleher said.

Kerns looked confused for a moment, then recognition flickered in his eyes. "Hey, how are you?" he said, shaking hands with Kelleher. "Bobby Kelleher, right?"

He turned quickly to Stevie. "And I know who you are," he said. "I watched your show. It was entertaining. Smart stuff. I'm really sorry. . . ."

"It's okay," Stevie said, accepting his handshake. "I'm here, and I've got plenty to do."

"Including, I hope," Kelleher said, "interviewing you."

Kerns smiled. "I think that can be arranged," he said. "I just have to get some of my guys to store this stuff in the locker room and check on a couple other things. Can you wait about ten minutes?"

"Of course," Stevie said. "Should I wait for you here?"

Kerns glanced around. "Nah, why don't you walk back to the locker room with me. It'll be quieter there."

That was fine with Stevie. He and Kelleher agreed to meet near the goalpost closer to the locker room at 10:30, which was when the Ravens were scheduled to leave and the Dreams were supposed to arrive. That gave Stevie almost an hour to interview Darin Kerns, learn his way around "backstage," and then see if he could think of a way to get close enough to Eddie Brennan to get a quote from him on his old high school buddy. That, Stevie realized, would be the hard part, since Brennan would be in high demand from the media while he was on the field.

For now, though, he'd concentrate on the interview at hand. He followed Kerns up the tunnel leading to the locker rooms. When they reached the hallway, a yellow-jacketed security guard put a hand up to stop Stevie.

"No media back here today," he said. "Field only."

Kerns was about to say something when the guard put his hand down. "Oh, wait, you've got a CBS credential. You're fine."

Stevie almost wanted to tell the guard that CBS was media just like everyone else, but he knew that wasn't the case. For one thing, CBS was *paying* to televise the game as part of its multibillion-dollar deal with the NFL. For another, he knew from his own brief experiences that *TV* was a magic word in the English language.

"Where *did* you get the CBS badge?" Kerns asked as they walked down a long hallway filled with signs directing people to locker rooms and holding areas and elevators and the field.

"They want me to do some work for them this week," he said. "Right now, I'm working for the *Washington Herald*, but I'm going to do some CBS stuff too."

"Good for you," Kerns said. "Sure made our lives easier just now."

They finally reached a door that had a huge sign on it that said BALTIMORE RAVENS—AFC CHAMPIONS. Stevie followed Kerns inside and was stunned by the size of the locker room. It fanned out in both directions from the doorway. There were at least a dozen men wearing Ravens purple working in different parts of the massive room.

"Biggest locker rooms in the world," Kerns said, seeing the look on Stevie's face. "You could comfortably get a hundred lockers in here with lots of open space. We only need forty-five. There's a separate room in the back for the coaches that's almost as big as our *player* locker room back in Baltimore."

He led Stevie to an office that was clearly his headquarters for the week. "We'll practice over at IUPUI this week, but I'll be back and forth setting things up here," he said, plopping down and offering Stevie a seat.

"What's IUPUI?"

Kerns laughed. "Sorry. It's Indiana University/Purdue

University–Indianapolis. It's a huge commuter school run by Indiana and Purdue together and it has fantastic athletic facilities. We got lucky they put us there because it's right downtown. The Dreams have to schlep to some high school in the suburbs and they're not happy. Meeker is already screaming to the commissioner's office that the league wants us to win."

Stevie smiled. Don Meeker—better known in NFL circles as Little Donny—was the Dreams' owner. He had a reputation for being short, insecure, and a bully—but he was very rich. He was the first owner in history to pay a billion dollars for a sports team—that had been the Dreams' expansion fee when they joined the league. But even that was a small percentage of the wealth Don Meeker had amassed by buying and selling telemarketing firms. Stevie remembered Tamara had once written: "Don Meeker is the most successful cold caller in history."

"So why *did* you guys get IUPUI?" Stevie said, slowing down to make sure he got all the letters right.

"That's what's so funny about it," Kerns said. "It was a blind draw they held last summer at the owners meetings. Li'l Donny himself pulled 'Watsonville'—that's the name of the high school—out of a hat for the NFC long before anyone thought the Dreams had a chance of being here. Actually, I know the Dreams' equipment guy, and he says it's a great facility. It's just a little out of the way. The players and coaches don't really care, but Li'l Donny does like to be angry about things."

Stevie was soaking in all the background information

but figured it was time to get started on Kerns's relationship with Eddie Brennan. Kerns reached behind him into a refrigerator and offered Stevie a bottle of water, which he accepted. Then, for most of thirty minutes, he talked about Brennan—giving Stevie anecdotes that would easily have filled three stories.

"He's smart, he's a great athlete, and most women get weak-kneed when he walks into a room. You want to hate him but you can't. He's been the captain of every team he's ever played on, and he's a real team player. Plus, he's got a great sense of humor."

Stevie asked Kerns about his playing days with Brennan. Kerns leaned back in his chair and smiled.

"What you have to understand is that Eddie really was the star," Kerns said. "I was okay, a decent enough receiver, but I was never fast enough that anyone in Division One was going to recruit me seriously."

"Not even Harvard?"

Kerns laughed. "Harvard? You need grades to get into Harvard even if you're a football player. I got lucky and got a scholarship to Fordham—which plays okay football and is a good school but a far cry from Harvard. But when I was with Eddie, I was a star—he was so good at finding receivers and putting the ball right on the money that all you had to do was be okay and people thought you were Terrell Owens." He paused. "That's on the field, not off it," he added.

Stevie asked if he had a favorite memory. "Oh yeah, that's easy," Kerns said. "It was in the state championship game against Newark Catholic. We were down 10–6 in a pouring rain with four seconds left, and Eddie threw me a perfect ball in the corner of the end zone—to this day I swear I don't know how he gripped it to throw it that well— and I couldn't hold on. It was like trying to catch a seal. So we had time for one last play from the four-yard line. Everyone knew we would throw, we had no running game, but how was anyone going to catch the ball?

"We called time-out, and our coach was talking about running some kind of double reverse. He thought we'd surprise them, but I'm thinking there's no way we're going to be able to make two handoffs *and* get our footing *and* get around the corner. So, going back to the huddle, I said to Eddie, 'Let's run E-D Special.' He looked at me like I was nuts."

"What was 'E-D Special'?" Stevie asked.

Kerns smiled. "Eddie-Darin Special," he said, grinning. "It was a play he and I first came up with in peewee football when we were ten. Absolute trick play. You don't even tell the other nine guys! You call a pass play in the huddle. Everyone—I mean everyone—thinks it's a pass. Quarterback goes back and everyone is blocking to keep the pass rushers to the outside. One receiver—me—takes a step as if to go out in the pattern, then turns and goes straight to the middle of the field because *you know* there's going to be one blitzer coming straight up the middle to try to get to the quarterback. He blocks the blitzer just as the quarterback fakes a pass, pulls the ball down, and runs straight up the middle with the ball. Quarterback-draw play."

"Did it work?"

"Yup. I got the blitzer, and Eddie walked into the end zone completely untouched. We're all jumping up and down and celebrating, and our coach is out there screaming, 'What the hell was that? What are you guys doing running some school-yard play with the state championship at stake?!' And Eddie just said, 'Yup—and that school-yard play just won you the state championship, Coach.'"

Stevie could see that the memory was still pretty vivid for Kerns—even eight years later. "One thing you have to understand about Eddie," he added. "He's never afraid on a football field. People miss that sometimes because he went to Harvard and uses SAT words when he talks. But there's no one more fearless than Eddie Brennan."

That quote, Stevie realized, would need to go very high in his story.

Kerns was telling Stevie that he and Brennan had bet dinner on the outcome of the game, when his phone rang. "Gotcha," Kerns said to whoever was on the other end.

"They're wrapping up out there," he said. "Have you got enough?"

"To start a book," Stevie said, thanking him.

Kerns laughed and gave Stevie his cell phone number. "Anything I can help you with during the week, give me a call. I'd give you some Ravens gear, but I doubt you want to be seen with it around here."

Stevie laughed. "Imagine what Li'l Donny would say. He'd think there was a media conspiracy to get the Dreams."

Kerns nodded. "You really are sharp for fourteen," he said. "USTV will be sorry they went for the pretty boy over the smart kid."

They were walking out of the locker room at that point. "Thanks," Stevie said. "But the pretty girl is very, *very* smart. She can probably cover for the pretty boy."

"Won't be the same," Kerns said, shaking hands as he prepared to duck into another room. "She'll miss you. The show will miss you."

Stevie could only hope he was right. Especially about Susan Carol missing him.

6: FLAG ON THE PLAY

THE RAVENS were starting to make their way up the tunnel as Stevie was heading back to the field, and Stevie was struck by just how huge they were. He walked past Jonathan Ogden, the team's six-foot-nine-inch, 345-pound All-Pro left tackle, and felt as if he had stepped into a hole. He must have been staring, because Ogden smiled at him and said, "I'm only this tall on Tuesdays."

Reaching the field, Stevie could see Ravens quarterback Steve McNair still surrounded by a number of reporters. Some of the Dreams were starting to drift onto the field to start their session. He spotted Bobby and Tamara talking to a slender man with straight black hair who was wearing a shirt that said "Dream the Dreams" on it.

"Stevie, this is someone you not only want to meet but you *need* to meet," Kelleher said.

"Dewey Blanton," the man said, giving him a smile and a warm handshake. "I do PR—at least I try to—for the Dreams."

He had an easygoing manner that made Stevie feel comfortable right away.

"I told Dewey about your interview with Darin Kerns," Kelleher said. "He's going to try to grab you a minute with Brennan toward the end of the session."

Blanton was nodding. "He finishes on the podium about eleven-forty-five, and then we're going to take him to a taping room under the stands. He's got to do some pieces with CBS and then ESPN and, finally, a couple minutes with USTV."

"Who from USTV?" Stevie asked, realizing he sounded semi-panicked when he asked.

"Easy, Stevie," Kelleher said. "It's them, but it'll be brief."

"If you just walk with me back to the room, when he finishes all that, I'll get you a minute with him," Blanton said.

Stevie really didn't want to see Susan Carol and her new favorite dude in action. "Maybe I can just get a question in while he's on the podium?" he said.

Kelleher was shaking his head emphatically. "First of all, you won't get a good answer up there," he said. "Second of all, you'll be sharing the story with five hundred other people. Out of the question. This way, you'll get a couple quotes on a story no one else will have at the Super Bowl. That's pretty rare."

"Okay then," Stevie said, squaring his shoulders, ready to do what he had to do for his story. "Thank you, Mr. Blanton. Where should I meet you?"

"I'll be standing right behind the podium when Eddie comes off," Blanton said. "You meet me there and just walk with us. I'll get you through all the security so you can walk up the players' ramp with us. Gotta run—see you later."

Stevie turned to Bobby. "What are you writing today?"

Kelleher grinned. "Are you kidding? Li'l Donny. He's already thrown one tantrum over where his team is practicing, and now I hear he's threatening to boycott the NFL dinner on Friday night. Bisciotti told me the rest of the owners are hoping he *does* boycott."

Steve Bisciotti was the Ravens' owner. Stevie had read a couple of stories the previous week about how he was the anti-Meeker—equally rich but without the attitude. Meeker was known for demanding that everyone who worked for him call him Mr. Meeker. Bisciotti was Steve to everyone. The contrast made for a great story.

Stevie spent most of the next hour wandering around, listening to various members of the Dreams talking about how much respect they had for the Ravens. He listened to Coach Skyler Kaplow for a minute but gave up when Kaplow said his team would win the game on Sunday "if it's the Lord's will." Kaplow was extremely religious and was frequently seen crossing himself on the sidelines before big plays. He was a great coach, but the gesture really bugged Stevie's dad. Every time he saw it, Bill Thomas would say, "For crying out loud, Kaplow, if God is watching this game he should be fired!"

Shortly before 11:45, he wandered toward the back of Eddie Brennan's podium, only to find the inevitable security guard blocking the entrance to the roped-off area behind the podium. Just as inevitably, the guard stepped aside when he saw the CBS credential dangling from his neck. Stevie still didn't like it that TV had such power, but he had to concede that he could get used to wielding that power pretty quickly.

Dewey Blanton was waiting at the podium stairs with several more security guards and a gaggle of people wearing various TV credentials. Susan Carol and Whitsitt were nowhere in sight.

"Where are, you know . . ."

Blanton, reading his mind and his discomfort, answered before he finished. "All the TV talent are waiting in the back," he said. "Lesley Visser's doing CBS, Berman's doing ESPN, and, well, you know who's doing USTV."

One of the men waiting with Blanton came over with a hand extended. "I'm Andy Kaplan from CBS," he said. "I'm one of the segment producers this week. I think we're going to work together starting tomorrow. Looking forward to it."

"Me too," Stevie said, comforted that he would have at least one ally inside the room. He heard a commotion behind him and looked up to see Eddie Brennan coming down the stairs with security front and back and a couple of suits walking next to him.

"NFL PR guys," Blanton said, again showing a remarkable ability to read Stevie's mind. "The league keeps an eye on everything this week."

As soon as Brennan hit the bottom step, everyone started walking across the field toward a tunnel in the corner, but not one of the tunnels Stevie had seen the teams using to come and go. Blanton fell into step with Eddie to go over the plan with him for the next few minutes.

"Is there anything to drink in the room?" was Brennan's only response.

"What do you want, Eddie?" one of the NFL PR people said. "We'll get it for you."

"A cup of coffee would be great," Brennan said. "That was a long seventy-five minutes. Some guy asked me if Harvard was still in the Ivy League."

Everyone laughed—a little too hard, Stevie thought. He had read a story in the paper once about the stupidest questions asked on media day. His favorite was someone asking Dexter Manley of the Redskins, "If you could be a tree, what kind of a tree would you be?"

This wasn't quite up there with that. "Did you see the guy's credential?" someone asked Brennan.

They were now nearing the end of the tunnel, and one of the PR guys had run ahead to open the door to the room. "Yeah," Brennan said. "I think he was from the *Yale Daily News*."

Now *that*, Stevie thought, was funny.

Brennan and entourage made their way into the room. Stevie could see that three camera crews were set up in front of three separate mini-stages. Lesley Visser was sitting on a set with the CBS logo in the backdrop. Next to her was a similar set for ESPN and Chris Berman, and next to

Berman he could see Susan Carol and Whitsitt sitting not in comfortable armchairs like the others but on tall stools. There was a third stool between them that was obviously for Brennan when it was their turn.

Stevie found a spot in the back of the room so he could stay out of sight and out of everyone's way. Eddie Brennan, having been given his marching orders already, headed straight for the empty chair on the CBS set. There were several calls for quiet, the CBS technicians turned on the shooting lights, and Visser spent the next ten minutes asking about, as she called it, "the remarkable journey" that had brought him to the Super Bowl. Brennan's answers were, Stevie thought, warm and genuine. He had done this before; he was a pro—and yet he managed not to fall into jock clichés.

As soon as they were finished, the CBS lights went out and Brennan moved over to the ESPN set, pausing to take the coffee someone had brought him. "I need a towel," he said. "Hot under these lights." A towel was magically produced.

Visser was walking toward the door when she veered off and walked directly over to Stevie.

"Lesley Visser," she said, putting her hand out. "Sean tells me you're going to be working with us this week. I think it's great."

Visser was tall—though not as tall as Susan Carol—and had huge brown eyes and brown hair.

"Thanks," he said. "I hope I'll do okay."

"You'll be fantastic," she said, lowering her voice because quiet was now being called for again. "I'll see you soon."

She slipped out the door as Chris Berman began his intro.

"You realize, don't you, that the Schwam picked you guys to be here," he said, turning to Brennan.

The Schwam was a swami-like character Berman had created to predict the winners each week during the NFL season. Stevie could almost hear Kelleher's voice in his head as he listened: "Typical TV guy—it's always about *him*."

Brennan was clearly unbothered by the answer posed as a question. "You picked us to beat the Redskins two weeks ago, I know that," he said. "But where'd you have us when you made your preseason picks?"

Berman got a little huffy. "Well, I thought you'd be better than 'ast season, but I guess not this much better. Who could have seen this coming?!"

"Peter King had us in the Super Bowl," Brennan said with a smile, referring to *Sports Illustrated*'s football expert. "So did Tony Kornheiser. Now that was visionary!"

"Yes, well, now that you're here, let's move on to the important stuff." He launched into a number of technical questions about how the Dreams would attack the Ravens' defense, which led to an interview that wasn't nearly as interesting, at least to Stevie, as the one Visser had conducted. The strengths and weaknesses of each team were well known already, and Brennan surely wasn't going to give away his team's strategy six days before the big game. When they were finished, Berman barely managed a handshake before being whisked off the set by several ESPN producers and suits.

"Lot to do today," he said, as if explaining his hasty exit. "They never let me rest during Super Bowl week."

Brennan wasn't even listening. He had his ESPN mic off and was walking to the USTV set. He was shaking hands with Susan Carol and Jamie Whitsitt when Stevie heard a voice from just off the set say, "Hey, what's he doing in here?"

Tal Vincent, who had been his producer until four days ago, was standing directly behind one of the cameras pointing a finger at Stevie.

"I invited him," Dewey Blanton said before Stevie could find his tongue to try to respond. "He's on Eddie's schedule once you're finished."

"Fine, then," Vincent said. "He can wait outside in the hallway. This is my room right now and I don't need some former employee lurking around."

Stevie could feel steam coming from his ears. He had never liked Vincent very much when he was working for him, and he liked him even less now.

"Tal, ease up," Blanton said. "He's not lurking. He's doing what I told him to do."

Vincent walked over to Blanton. "Well, now you can do what *I'm* telling you to do and get him the hell out of here."

Part of Stevie wanted to just leave. No sense making Dewey Blanton's life any more difficult. Part of him wanted to slug Tal Vincent. And part of him was waiting for Susan Carol to say something in his defense.

It wasn't Susan Carol who spoke up, though; it was Eddie Brennan.

"Hey, pal, tell you what—if the kid goes, I'll go too," he

said, setting the USTV microphone down on his stool. "The league asked us to cooperate with all of the media and I'm willing to do it. But I know what you guys did to him last weekend, and I'm not going to stand here and watch you bully a fourteen-year-old kid."

"Look, Eddie, we're all just trying to do our jobs here and—"

Brennan cut him off. "Your choice. You want me to do this interview, then the kid stays. I'm fine either way."

There was complete silence for several seconds that felt to Stevie like several minutes. Finally Tal Vincent nodded in the direction of the set and said, "Jamie, Susan Carol— whenever you're ready, let's roll this."

There was no further discussion of Stevie's presence. As the interview proceeded, he could still feel himself shaking with tension and anger. He wasn't really listening to Susan Carol as she introduced Brennan, but he almost laughed out loud when it was Whitsitt's turn. His opening question was "Dude— Harvard? What's that about?" He looked closely to see if Susan Carol had an off-camera reaction, but her expression didn't change. Though she did laugh when Eddie answered, "Dude! A mind is a terrible thing to waste!" As soon as Susan Carol had thanked him and closed the segment, Brennan was on his feet. He shook hands with Susan Carol and Whitsitt and bounded off the set past Vincent without saying a word.

He walked directly back to where Stevie was standing and put out his hand. "Eddie Brennan," he said. "Walk with me down the hall and I'll talk to you about Darin."

"Thanks," Stevie said, falling into step as Dewey Blanton

and the security people took up their positions around Brennan. "But thanks even more for what you just did for me."

Brennan looked down at Stevie, his face quite serious. "I don't like bullies," he said. "I'm surprised your friend is still doing the show without you...."

"I told her to keep doing it," Stevie said, breaking in. "There's no reason for her not to."

Brennan put a hand on his back. "Well, you're a good guy for saying that, but that show's going down in flames with Mr. Boy Band. Dude doesn't know a thing about sports."

Stevie remembered throwing something at his television set earlier in the fall when Brennan had dominated the Philadelphia Eagles. Now Brennan was rapidly becoming Stevie's favorite football player. Seeing that they were approaching the locker room, Brennan braked to a halt, nearly causing a ten-person pileup in the hallway. "So, tell me what Darin told you," he said, changing the subject.

"He told me about E-D Special," Stevie said, figuring that would be a good starting point.

Brennan laughed. "Giving away old secrets, huh? And I'll bet he told you the key to the play in the state championship game was his block."

"He did say he knocked the guy down."

Brennan nodded. "It's true, he did. We've always argued about whether I'd have been able to get around him if Darin hadn't blocked him. Mobility has never been my strength. The best part about it is that I don't think our coach has ever completely forgiven us for running the play without telling him."

For the next ten minutes, he talked about his high school friend, a warm smile on his face throughout.

"So, here's your big scoop for the day," he said, seeing Dewey Blanton not-so-subtly pointing to his watch. "Darin and I have violated league rules this week."

Blanton appeared to turn a bit pale. Eddie plowed on. "We bet on the game," he said. "Gambling is, of course, strictly forbidden in the NFL."

"What'd you bet?" Stevie asked.

"Dinner at the Summit Inn," Brennan said. "Best restaurant in our hometown. If the commissioner wants to suspend me from the game for that, he knows where to find me."

Stevie saw Blanton sigh in relief. "Give me your notebook," Eddie said as Stevie was about to shut it. "And your pen."

Stevie handed them over. Brennan wrote something on the back cover. "That's my cell," he said. "You need anything during the week, you call me."

Stevie thanked him, then thanked Blanton. He could see another gaggle waiting for Brennan just outside the locker room door. Brennan rolled his eyes as he said goodbye to Stevie. "Talking-to-playing ratio is way too high this week," he said, and was gone, the security wave following behind.

Stevie watched for a minute and then headed down the hall in the opposite direction. He had a story to write. A story no one else would be writing that day. He didn't miss TV at all. But he did miss Susan Carol.

7: UNSPORTSMANLIKE CONDUCT

THE FIELD WAS ALMOST EMPTY when Stevie walked back down the tunnel. A number of TV crews were still doing stand-ups, but all the players and team and league officials were long gone. Stevie noticed that Susan Carol and Whitsitt were doing a stand-up in front of one of the goalposts, the one right in front of the tunnel he had to walk through to get back to the media area. Tal Vincent was standing a few feet behind the two cameras and, for an instant, Stevie thought about walking over to say something to him. He decided against it, though. He'd already won the battle; no need to start a war.

He walked to his right as he passed the area where USTV was set up and noticed that a makeup woman was redoing Jamie Whitsitt's forehead while Susan Carol waited.

She didn't even glance in his direction as he walked by. Unfortunately, Vincent did.

"Hey, Thomas!" he yelled. Apparently he was taking the approach that if you lose one battle, you start another one. Stevie stopped and waited until he walked up to him.

"I don't care if some PR guy invited you or not, I don't want to see you around any of our shoots the rest of the week," Vincent said.

"What makes you think I have any interest in your shoots?" Stevie said. "Do you think I'm going to steal questions like 'Dude—Harvard, what's that about?'"

Vincent reddened slightly. "Look, I know you're jealous of Jamie. He's got your job and your girlfriend. Deal with it."

Stevie had an urge to tackle Vincent—who wasn't that much bigger than he was—but resisted. Instead, he changed the subject. "Look, Tal, Eddie Brennan made a fool of you in there," he said. "Deal with it."

He started to turn away, but Vincent grabbed his arm. Stevie stiffened and pulled away. "Don't you touch me," he said, his voice now raised, turning back to face Vincent, who was completely red-faced. "I'm going now. I can't wait to give Bobby Kelleher a note about what Brennan did to you."

"You put that in the paper and . . ."

"And *what*? You'll fire me?"

"And I'll never speak to you again." The speaker was Susan Carol. She had dropped her mic and left her stand-up position to walk over to the argument. Her arms were folded and she was glaring at Stevie. Her drop-dead smile was nowhere in sight.

"*What?*" Stevie said. "Are you defending him?"

"He was doing what the network people wanted him to do," she said. "He told me that a few minutes ago. Mike Shupe doesn't want you around this week and Tal was just following orders. You don't humiliate someone for that."

Stevie could feel his heart racing. He couldn't believe this was happening. "Oh—but it's okay for him to humiliate me because the network told him to? Because it's his *job* to be an arrogant—"

"Stop it, Stevie. It's not the same."

"You really have lost it," he said. "Do you hear yourself defending this suck-up, two-bit TV producer who has now twice tried to pick a fight with me?"

He realized his voice was shaking with anger and emotion. Susan Carol looked like she might cry. "I have work to do," she said.

"Yeah, work," Stevie said. "That's some great journalism you've got going on the Pretty Dude and Dudette show. Very impressive."

Susan Carol stared at him for a long second as if measuring a response. "Go to hell, Stevie," she said finally and turned to walk away.

"Got a minister's daughter to tell you to go to hell," Tal Vincent said, the sneer returning to his face. "Impressive."

Stevie knew Vincent had a point—which made it even worse. Chances were good that Susan Carol had never told anyone to go to hell in her life. He didn't respond to Vincent's final gibe. It was time to leave the building.

✦　✦　✦

As soon as he turned his cell phone on, it started to ring. "Did you get Brennan?" Bobby asked. "Everything okay?"

"Yeah, fine," Stevie said, trying not to sound glum. He must have failed.

"What's wrong?" Kelleher asked.

"Nothing important," Stevie said, not wanting to get into it. "I'll fill you in later. I'm going back to my room to write."

"You want to eat first?"

Stevie glanced at his watch. It was 12:30 and he hadn't eaten anything since breakfast. But he didn't feel like talking to anyone at the moment. "I think I'll just order some room service. I'm a little tired from staying up late last night."

"That's fine. Call me in a few hours and I'll take a look at your story before you send it."

Stevie agreed and hung up. He was tempted to call Susan Carol's cell to try to talk, but he knew it was a bad idea. He walked back across the street and into the lobby of the Marriott, which was packed, wall to wall. He put his head down and was trying to maneuver his way through the crowd when he heard someone calling his name.

"Steve, hey, Steve! Steve Thomas!"

He turned and saw a short, middle-aged man with wavy brown hair and glasses approaching. "Randy Merkin," he said, working his way through a couple of men in Dreams jerseys. "I work for Sporting News Radio. I'm glad I spotted you. We'd love to get you on the air."

A lot of radio stations sent people to events to broadcast live. Most of them set up shop at one of the downtown hotels and sent producers—like Merkin, Stevie presumed—in search of celebrities they could grab and put on their shows. He was mildly flattered to be asked, but at that moment Stevie wanted three things: to be alone, to order something to eat, and to write his story.

"I'm really busy right now, to tell you the truth," he said. "I have to write a story, and then I've got some stuff to do for CBS. . . ."

"You're working for CBS now?" Merkin said. "Wow. I didn't know about that. Actually, I wasn't thinking about now. I was thinking about four o'clock this afternoon. Your old pal Chip Graber is supposed to come on with us then and I thought it might be fun for you."

"Chip's *here*?" Stevie said. "What's he doing here?"

"He's promoting a new video game. The Timberwolves play tomorrow night in Chicago, so the team gave him a day off to come here to do promo stuff. Everyone in the world comes to the Super Bowl to pitch products."

Stevie had read about that but didn't quite get it. He and Susan Carol had kept close tabs on Graber's career since the Final Four. After hitting the shot to win the championship in dramatic fashion, Graber had been taken with the twelfth pick in the draft by the Minnesota Timberwolves, his hometown team. A lot of people had been surprised that he wasn't picked sooner, but some teams had been scared off by his size—he was five foot eleven standing up very straight. The Timberwolves, a team struggling to draw fans, had happily taken a local hero, and the pick had proven to be golden. Graber was averaging fifteen points and seven assists in his rookie year as the starting point guard and, as might be expected when a good-looking white kid makes it in the NBA, he had become a marketing star. With all that had gone on in recent days, Stevie had lost track of where and when the Timberwolves were playing. Now he knew.

"Well, I'd love to see Chip," he said.

"Just come to the second floor at four o'clock then," Merkin said. "You'll see radio stations up and down the hallway. We're at the far end once you turn the corner, just beyond the escalator." He handed him a card. "Any problems, just call my cell."

"So radio row is here?" Stevie asked.

Merkin laughed. "*One* of the radio rows is. There's another one at the Hyatt and another one at the convention center. There are probably close to two hundred stations here."

"Wow," Stevie said, not even caring that he was using that word again. "That's a lot more than at the Final Four, isn't it?"

"Probably double—at least," Merkin said. "So, four o'clock okay?"

Stevie thought for a second. If there was anyone in the world he would feel comfortable talking to about what was going on with Susan Carol, it was Chip Graber. The three of them would always be bonded by what they had gone through in New Orleans. He knew Chip e-mailed regularly with Susan Carol, just as he did with Stevie.

"I'll be there."

He worked his way to the elevator, aware that he was actually smiling. The thought of seeing Graber had certainly picked up his spirits.

Once he was settled in his room and had ordered some food, it didn't take him long to write the story. Darin and Eddie's stories of high school glory and friendship were so great he could easily have written 2,000 words. Kelleher had told him anything beyond 1,000 words would get cut no matter how good it was, so he tried to be disciplined and pick only the best material. It wasn't easy. His first version was about 1,400 words. It took him almost as long to get the story down to 1,033 words as it had taken him to write 1,400. It was nearly three o'clock by the time he called Bobby to tell him he was finished.

"I'll be right down," Kelleher said.

He was at the door a minute later and sat in front of Stevie's computer reading the story—occasionally pausing to laugh or nod. "It's good," he said. "Very good. Now you need to cut another two hundred words out of it."

"Whaa?" Stevie said. "You said I had a thousand words."

"I know. The desk called before and said they could only take eight hundred from you today because a feature on the home life of the Ravens' cheerleaders came in long."

"Come on."

"True story. Look, Stevie, the newspaper business isn't perfect either. We screw up just like TV people do. I'll call them back and tell them you got Brennan and no one else did on this topic. It may help, but you have to be prepared for the answer to be no." He was half right. The desk offered an extra hundred words.

"Now," he said, plopping down in the armchair next to the bed, "tell me what you were so upset about when I called before."

Stevie filled him in on both run-ins with Tal Vincent and Susan Carol's reaction. "Let it go," Kelleher said. "She's got a lot of TV people spinning her head around, clearly. But she's very smart and all her instincts as a human are outstanding. She'll come around. I know that's easy for me to say, but it wasn't *that* long ago that I was fourteen. I *do* remember what it was like."

Stevie decided not to argue. He didn't doubt that Bobby remembered what it was like, but he was sure that Kelleher would have been just as depressed if the first girl he'd ever really cared about had told him to go to hell. So instead, he told Kelleher he had to go downstairs to do Sporting News Radio with Chip Graber and asked if he wanted to come along. Kelleher said he'd love to see Graber but needed to finish writing his column on Little Donny.

They walked to the elevator bank together, Kelleher going up, Stevie going down. When Stevie got to the second floor, he was confronted with a mob unlike any he had ever seen. It wasn't as if he hadn't been in big crowds at major events before. But this was a new level. People were crowding around the desks and small podiums where each radio station had set up headquarters as if the stations were handing out money. He picked his way through the alleyway that had been created between the desks and podiums, pausing every few steps as another famous face went past. As he rounded the corner near the escalator that Merkin had described, he heard someone yelling, "Coming through, clear the way, please!" Bearing down on him were several very large men. Behind them was Michael Jordan. The burly men veered to the right, where Stevie saw a banner that said ESPN RADIO. Behind a glass partition he could see Dan Patrick, the *SportsCenter* anchor, talking into a microphone and waving at Jordan, who was apparently going to make Patrick's show his next stop. People were shouting Jordan's name, sticking pieces of paper as close as they could get to him given that there were bodyguards in front of him and behind him. Jordan just kept walking.

"Wonder what he's selling," Stevie said aloud, forgetting that he was surrounded by people.

"A motocross team," someone right behind him said. He turned and, much to his surprise, saw Michael Wilbon, cohost of *Pardon the Interruption* and a longtime Jordan friend.

"A what?" Stevie said.

"Michael bought a motocross team last year," Wilbon said. "He's trying to drum up interest in the sport. He just did Jim Rome, now he's doing Patrick, and then he's going to WFAN."

"What are you doing here?" Stevie asked.

"Need a column," Wilbon said. "Michael Jordan selling motocross is definitely a column."

He wasn't wrong about that.

"You're Steve, right?" Wilbon said. "Steve Thomas. We met in New Orleans. You were with your friend who is thirteen but looks eighteen—Susan, right?"

"Susan Carol," Stevie said. "She's fourteen now and a TV star."

"Yeah, I know," Wilbon said. "But being a TV star is vastly overrated."

He turned toward Patrick's interview area. Stevie waved goodbye and walked a few steps down the hall until he reached another large banner with the Sporting News Radio logo. Merkin was standing there next to Chip Graber. When Graber saw Stevie approaching, he raced up to him and wrapped him up in a hug. "Look at you!" he said. "You look like you've grown six inches since New Orleans!"

Then Graber grinned. "So how tall is Susan Carol these days?"

"Eight foot six," Stevie answered.

Graber laughed. "Don't worry, you'll catch up."

At that moment, Susan Carol's height was the least of Stevie's worries.

Merkin introduced Stevie to Tim Brando, the network's midday host. The interview was, for the most part, routine. Chip talked about the video game and adapting to life in the NBA. Brando asked Stevie about being "let go" by USTV. Stevie was happy to be able to report that even though USTV didn't think he was pretty enough to share a set with Susan Carol, CBS thought enough of him to hire him for the week.

"That's a nice comeback," Brando said.

"Well," Stevie said, "I may not be able to sing like Jamie Whitsitt, but I can complete a whole sentence without using the word *dude*."

That got a big laugh from Brando and Chip. When they were finished and Merkin had thanked them, Chip walked him back down the hallway. There were so many celebrities walking around that Chip, dressed in one of his "disguises"—droopy sweatshirt and baseball cap—went completely unnoticed.

"Look over there," Chip said, pointing to a corner where a gaggle of reporters, Minicam operators, and photographers was trying to get close to someone who looked familiar although, right at that moment, Stevie couldn't place him.

"Tom Cruise," Chip said, seeing the puzzled look on Stevie's face. "He's got that movie deal with the owner of the Redskins."

They paused at the escalator. "So, are you really okay?" Chip asked.

"Oh yeah," Stevie said.

Chip looked at him closely. "I'm not so sure. How has Susan Carol been with all this?"

"Oh, she's fine with it," Stevie said before he realized how sarcastic his tone was.

Chip smiled. "Let me guess, she likes Whatsitt or Whitsitt."

"Uh-huh. She thinks I'm being mean because I made fun of the fact that he's a dope."

Chip was smiling now. "Uh-huh. And you're not being extra hard on him because you're jealous?"

"Well . . ."

"You two will work it out," Chip said. "You're good together."

He looked at his watch. "Damn," he said. "I've got to get to some store to sign autographs. This is more work than playing." He gave Stevie a hug. "Hang in there, kiddo," he said.

With that, he was gone, heading down the escalator. Stevie hoped he wouldn't have to hang in for too long.

✦　✦　✦

Dinner wasn't all that different from Stevie's walk through radio row. Bobby and Tamara took him to a place called St. Elmo Steak House, which Kelleher explained was *the* place to eat in Indianapolis and one of the best steak houses in the country. The minute they walked in the door, it was clear Kelleher was right.

Wayne Gretzky, arguably the greatest hockey player in history, was sitting at the bar with Mario Lemieux, who had to be in the top five himself.

"What are *they* selling here?" Tamara asked when she spotted them.

"Hockey fantasy camps," Bobby said.

As they were led back to their table, Stevie's head was on a swivel. He spotted Jim Nantz and Phil Simms (his new colleagues) sitting at a large table, and Fred Couples and Davis Love—the golfers—seated right behind them.

"Okay," Tamara said after Bobby stopped to say hello to Couples and Love. "What are *they* selling?"

"Nothing," Kelleher said. "They like football and they're buddies with Nantz."

As they followed the hostess, they came to a door being guarded by several large men. "Who's in there?" Stevie asked the woman as they turned the corner and went into another room that was much larger than the one they had just been in.

"Michael Jordan and Tiger Woods," she said in a hushed voice.

"Did you know Jordan was into motocross?" said Stevie.

"No—really?"

On instructions from Kelleher, Stevie ordered a shrimp cocktail. When he tasted the sauce, his eyes began to water and he thought he might faint. "Oh my God!" he gasped. Bobby and Tamara laughed. They had seen this before.

"Want to stop?" Tamara asked.

"God, no," Stevie said, recovering. "I might want seconds."

"You wouldn't live through seconds," Kelleher said.

The porterhouse steak Stevie ordered was equally good. Throughout dinner, more celebrities passed by, some of them stopping to say hello to Kelleher and Mearns. A few recognized Stevie.

"Don't let the TV people get you down," counseled

David Wright, the New York Mets' star third baseman. "Good things happen to good people. You'll be fine."

Stevie realized it would now be tough for him to root for Wright to strike out when the Phillies played the Mets once the season began.

"You're good on the air," Bob Costas said, pumping his hand after chatting with Kelleher and Mearns. "But I'm not sure you won't find writing more gratifying." That was interesting coming from someone who had made millions on TV.

By the time dinner was over, Stevie's spirits had lifted considerably. He was about as full as he could ever remember being, and he was amazed at all the famous people they had encountered. As they were leaving, Tamara, who seemed less impressed with all the stars than anyone, stopped dead in her tracks. "Bobby, look," she hissed, pointing at a small man with curly, graying hair sitting in the corner. Kelleher's eyes went wide too. "Jeez, I never thought I'd see him here," he said.

"Big sports fan," Tamara said.

"Who?" Stevie demanded as they walked out the door. "Who is that?"

"You don't know?" Tamara said. "That's Billy Joel."

"Billy who?" Stevie said. "Who does he play—"

"Not who—what. Piano."

Then it came to him. He'd heard one of his songs when his father categorically refused to change the station in the car.

"You guys like him?"

"Like him?" Kelleher said. "The man's a genius."

Time to go home, Stevie thought. Kelleher and Mearns were morphing into his parents.

✦　✦　✦

The long day had worn him out and he went right to bed once he got back to his room. He set his alarm for seven o'clock because there was a message from someone at CBS asking that he report to the CBS work area at eight to discuss his assignment for the day. Kelleher had already suggested they meet for breakfast at 7:45. Stevie decided he'd go down a few minutes earlier than that and tell them he had to leave ahead of them to walk to the Dome.

He fell asleep quickly, and when the alarm went off, he was still in a deep sleep. He couldn't believe it was already morning. He forced his eyes open, stunned that it was already seven o'clock. He was reaching out to turn off the alarm when he noticed the time: 1:42. He half sat up, trying to shake the cobwebs from his head. That was when he realized the alarm wasn't going off. It was the phone that was ringing, not the clock.

He fumbled for the phone in the dark, suddenly fearful that maybe something bad had happened at home.

"Hello?" he said, finally getting the receiver to his ear.

"Stevie, we need to talk."

"Huh? Whaa?" He was about to say "Who is this?" when his ears made the connection to his brain. It was Susan Carol, sounding both breathless and a little bit hysterical.

"Need to talk? When? Isn't it the middle of the night?"

"Yes, it is. And we need to talk *now*. What room are you in?"

Now Stevie was awake. "Room? Me?"

"Yes, Steven, you. What room are you in? I'm on my way over there now."

"*Now?*" he said, awake but still somewhat stunned by the call and the conversation. He was trying very hard to remember his room number. Finally he got it. "I'm in twelve-forty-eight," he said, actually proud of himself for remembering.

"I'll be there in ten minutes."

The line went dead. Stevie sat there looking at the phone. He rubbed his eyes, wondering if he had been dreaming. Apparently not. It was 1:45 in the morning and Susan Carol Anderson was on her way to his room. He had to be dreaming. Except he was now wide awake.

8: PASS DEFLECTION

STEVIE PULLED ON SOME SWEATS, walked into the bathroom, and decided that brushing his teeth and combing his hair was a good idea. He was nervous—although he wasn't sure why. He couldn't imagine why Susan Carol would call him in the middle of the night and insist she had to see him right away. Guilt? Anger? Either one could wait until morning.

He checked himself in the mirror. "You're no Jamie Whitsitt," he murmured, just as he heard an urgent knock. He took a deep breath and, without checking to see who it was, opened the door.

Susan Carol was standing there, bundled in a coat that went to her knees. He stared at her until she said, "Are you going to let me in?"

"Oh yeah, sorry," he said. "Come on in."

As she walked past him into the room, Stevie felt as if she had grown a couple of inches since that morning. Maybe he was so sleepy that he was slumping. But as she took off her coat, he glanced down and saw the reason for her growth spurt: she was wearing high heels. Forgetting that she was clearly in a state of high anxiety, he pointed at them and said, "What's the deal with the shoes?"

She gave him an annoyed look and then looked down at her feet. "Tal Vincent," she said. "We had to go to this big muckety-muck party tonight with a bunch of NFL corporate contributors and some people from the league and some players."

"Players? Don't the players have curfews and—"

"Not players from the Dreams or Ravens," she said. "Other teams. Peyton and Eli Manning were there; Terrell Owens was there—"

"Terrell Owens, I thought everyone hated him—"

"Will you stop interrupting?! Vincent told me to wear the damn shoes, okay? He's a jerk. You've got him pegged right. Now, can I sit down somewhere and tell you what's going on?"

"Please do," he said, pointing to a chair next to the bed. The idea of getting her to sit was appealing. He was getting a little bit dizzy trying to look up at her.

She sat down, her body sagging into the chair. "Do you want something to drink?" he asked. He had not seen her look this upset since she had learned her uncle had been part of the kidnapping plot at the U.S. Open tennis tournament in September.

"Yes," she said. "Thank you. Is there a Coke in your minibar?"

He handed her one, and after she had taken a long sip, he sat down across from her and said, "Okay, start at the beginning and tell me what in the world happened."

She nodded and took a deep breath. "We went to this party," she said. "I felt completely out of place as soon as we got there. It was in some private club—a really big place—and it seemed like half the men were smoking cigars and everyone was drinking. I was getting a lot of the 'aren't you pretty' and 'you can't possibly be fourteen' lines you've heard me get before. And all I could think was, 'If my dad knew I was here right now, he'd kill me and he'd kill Tal Vincent.'"

"Did you think about just leaving?" he said.

She half smiled. "Yes. But I figured I'd just get through the night and then tell Tal I wasn't going to any more parties, that there was no way my parents would have let me come out here if they'd known this was part of the deal."

"So what happened next?" he said.

She took another sip of her Coke. "I'm standing as far into a corner as I possibly can when this guy comes up. It's obvious he has no idea who I am. He just sees a tall girl in a dress. He says he's doctor somebody and he works with the Dreams. I tell him who I am, thinking maybe he'll make a connection and realize I'm fourteen and get that look off his face.

"Well, he's very impressed that I'm on TV. In fact, he says, 'I should have known when I first saw you that you were on TV.'"

"But he's still not realizing you're fourteen."

"No. I probably should have said something about the original concept being to put two *teenagers* on the air together. But by this time he's going on about *his* job and how close he is to all the Dreams' players, how most of them would never get on the field without his help. At one point he says, 'I'm kind of a magician. I wave my magic needle on Sundays and everyone plays. Eddie Brennan wouldn't have seen the field the last two months without me.'

"So now he's got my attention. I ask him what he's talking about, and he tells me about all the players who need painkilling shots to play, that Brennan's had a bad knee since November, and that if not for painkillers, half the league wouldn't play in December and January."

Stevie knew players got cortisone shots and other painkillers to play, so this was no shock, although he hadn't thought that *many* players did it. He let Susan Carol continue, though, falling back on his reporting experience, which told him to shut up and let someone tell a story when they were willing to do so.

She sighed. "I'm getting to the important part."

He hoped so.

"I asked him a few questions about the shots, if they were legal, if the league knew how often the players got them—that sort of thing. He gives me this look and says, 'I've never given a player an illegal shot of any kind. A player gets suspended, it isn't because of anything that comes out of my needle.'

"Something in the way he said it made me think there

was something else he wanted to tell me but, even drunk, he knew he shouldn't."

"And?"

She put up a hand to indicate Stevie should be patient, which wasn't easy for him at that moment. "So I said to him, 'What gets a player suspended these days?'

"He laughs and says, 'Oh, come on, sweetheart, you read the papers—HGH, the preferred drug of champions. Champion football players anyway.'"

Stevie had read about players getting suspended during the season for testing positive for HGH—human growth hormone. He wasn't all that familiar with it except to know that it was a steroid that helped players become bigger and stronger. If his memory was right, most of the players suspended had been linemen—the biggest men in the game trying to get even bigger. Or so it seemed.

Susan Carol had paused for a moment as if catching her breath. Now she plowed on. "I didn't want to act too interested, so when he brought up HGH, I just said, 'What's the big deal? A few guys got suspended for it this season—so what?'

"He leaned in very close to me, too close, and said, 'What if I told you not everyone who tested positive has been suspended?'

"My eyes must have gone wide because he kind of leaned back with a smirk on his face and said, 'That got your attention, huh, gorgeous?'"

"This guy is really a sicko," Stevie said, even though he knew the lecherous nature of the doctor wasn't the issue.

"Forget that," Susan Carol said. "I told him I couldn't believe someone had tested positive and not been suspended, and even if they had, what did it matter now—in the middle of Super Bowl week. He laughed again and said, 'Would it matter if a couple players—let's, for the sake of argument, say five players, maybe even five offensive linemen—were getting away with a positive test right now?'"

"WHAT?!!" Stevie interrupted. "He said that?"

"Yeah, he did. Obviously, he must be talking about five of the Dreams, otherwise how would he know? I tried to bluff him. I told him I didn't believe him, that he was making it up, that there was no way something like that could stay secret during Super Bowl week."

"What'd he say?"

"He said I would be right—unless someone was covering up test results."

Stevie gasped. "Oh my God! Is he saying that five Dreams tested positive for HGH and the league is covering it up?"

She shook her head. "He never said *who* was covering up—I tried to get it out of him, but I think I came on a little too strong at that point, because he started backpedaling, claiming he was just trying to get my attention with a wild story."

"You don't believe that, do you?"

"Not for a second. I could see in his eyes that he knew he'd said too much and was trying to get out of it."

"Okay," Stevie said, still trying to make sense of what he had just heard, "what do we do now?"

She pointed at his computer. "We need to get online and find out more about HGH and, if we can, about how testing for it works."

She was—as usual—right. Even if it was almost three o'clock in the morning.

The next thirty minutes were spent online. Stevie knew how important drug testing had become in all sports. He vividly remembered how crushed he had been in the summer of 2006 when it had come out that Floyd Landis, after winning the Tour de France as an unknown, had tested positive for steroids. He'd heard all the rumors about Lance Armstrong, not to mention all the stories about Mark McGwire, Barry Bonds, and Sammy Sosa in baseball. According to what they read, HGH was the latest in a long line of steroids—one that could only be detected through blood testing, and even then some doctors believed the testing wasn't one hundred percent accurate. According to the NFL Players Association Web site, the players had agreed to include HGH as a tested drug only after the owners had agreed that a player could only be tested once during the regular season and that no test results would be revealed until a second, confirming blood sample had turned up positive.

"Here's the crucial part," Susan Carol said, reading through the information. "It says here that once the play-offs begin, players on play-off teams can be tested at any time because the league *and* the union agree that any kind of drug use on a play-off team would be very bad for the league's image."

"Didn't a Super Bowl team have a drug issue a few years ago?" Stevie asked.

"*Yes*," she said, sounding exasperated. "The Carolina Panthers."

"Oh right, your hometown team."

"The team my dad worked with, remember? I guess this part of the deal could be called the Panthers Rule."

"Sounds like, if this doctor—what's his name anyway?—is telling the truth, it may become known as the Dreams Rule."

"*If* they get caught," she said. "His name's Snow, by the way."

Stevie didn't hear the name. He was deep in thought. "You know what?" he said. "It may be up to us to catch these guys."

"Whoever *these guys* are," she said. "Or is it whomever?"

Stevie blinked at her for a moment and then laughed.

"What?" Susan Carol asked.

"Only you would care if it was 'who' or 'whom' at three-thirty in the morning."

"Shut up," said Susan Carol, though she was starting to blush.

"No, I love that about you."

"You know, it's funny, but when I finally got away from this Snow guy, all I could think was, I have to talk to Stevie. As mad as I was at you today, I knew you were the only one I could talk to about this."

"You didn't want to talk to Jamie the dude?" Stevie was immediately sorry he hadn't kept his big mouth shut.

"Okay, I deserved that," she said. "I wasn't very nice today."

"That's not important right now," he said. "The question is, what do we do with this? We can't just go on the word of a drunken doctor."

"You think he was lying?"

"No. But he *was* drunk and he was trying to impress you, and you know as well as I do that no one—not the *Washington Herald*, USTV, or CBS—is going to run a story like this based on so little."

"Nor should they," she said. "Okay. I could call Dr. Snow in the morning and ask him to go on the record."

"You have his number?"

She smiled. "Oh yeah, he gave me his card. Said if I needed *anything* to call him."

"My guess is 'anything' doesn't include repeating his story for the record."

"No kidding. Plus, we'll have tipped our hand. If we stay away from him, he'll figure I was just a silly girl who didn't really understand what he told me. If he even remembers that he told me."

"We can only hope. By the way, how'd you get rid of him?"

"You won't like it," she said.

"Go ahead."

"I told him I had to leave with Jamie and that he was *very* jealous."

Stevie shrugged. "As long as it worked."

"Yeah," she said. "But back to the big question: Where do we go with this? Should we tell Bobby and Tamara? I don't think this is one we can tackle by ourselves."

"You're right," he said. "But I *do* have an idea."

"What?"

"Eddie Brennan. He might talk to me, at least on background."

"Rat out his teammates? We don't even know if he knows."

"Well, it's worth asking. He strikes me as the kind of guy who wouldn't be happy with this sort of cover-up."

She stood up and stretched. "It's nearly four o'clock," she said. "We both have to get some sleep. And I need to soak my feet or something. The person who invented high heels should be killed."

She looked very tired, very stressed, and *very* tall standing there. But still beautiful. He could see why dirty old men would want to hit on her. Being tall and pretty, he decided, wasn't all good.

"We'll talk more in the morning," he said. "I have to be at the CBS compound at eight to find out my assignment for the day."

"Let's meet when the media sessions are over," she said. "I'll call you on your cell and we'll figure out when and where."

"Okay," he said. "I'll know my schedule better when the sessions are over. I think they end by eleven."

"They do," she said. "We're interviewing Ray Lewis at the end of the Ravens' session. The Dreams go first tomorrow." She paused. "I mean today."

Susan Carol had her hand on the doorknob when, much to Stevie's surprise, she started to laugh.

"What's so funny?" he said.

"How is it," she said, "that this *always* happens to us?"

He laughed too. "Just lucky, I guess."

She turned to face him. He wished he had a box to stand on. But Susan Carol stepped out of her shoes and leaned in to hug him. So Stevie took his chance and kissed her—a really *good* kiss.

"Don't give another thought to Jamie Whitsitt," she said.

He smiled. Actually, he probably grinned goofily. "Don't worry," he said. "He's the last thing on my mind right now."

She kissed him again quickly, then stepped back into her shoes. "Here we go again," she said.

"Yeah," he said. "Here we go again."

9: READING THE DEFENSE

STEVIE RARELY HAD TROUBLE SLEEPING, especially when he was exhausted—which he certainly was after Susan Carol left the room. But he tossed and turned for a while, trying to figure out what had just happened and, most important, what should happen next.

Part of him was still reveling in his encounter with Susan Carol, not just the kiss but her comment about him being the only one she could come to with this story. But every time he caught himself smiling about it, he flashed back to how serious this was. He was pretty much convinced Dr. Snow had been telling the truth. His father always said that drinking too much alcohol was almost like taking truth serum: somehow you ended up revealing things you really shouldn't. And in his obvious desire to impress

Susan Carol, Dr. Snow had revealed a piece of information he would never have shared had he been sober.

The last time Stevie looked at the clock, it read 4:12. He finally dropped off to sleep, but was awakened just before seven by a dream in which Susan Carol was telling him she had decided Dr. Snow was her one true love. Tired as he felt, he knew he wasn't going back to sleep, so he got up and took a long shower. He decided a cup of coffee would give him an extra jolt, so he went downstairs to the coffee shop and was finishing his first cup when Bobby and Tamara walked in to join him.

"Long night, Stevie?" Kelleher said, pointing at the coffee mug in his hands.

"Didn't sleep very well," Stevie said.

Tamara gave him a smile, the one that showed her dimples, and put an arm around him as she sat down. "You'll work it out with Susan Carol. Just give it a little time."

Stevie was tempted to tell them what he and Susan Carol really needed to work out, but resisted. They had agreed to sleep on it and talk more before bringing in Kelleher and Mearns. Though Stevie wasn't doubting the story even in the cold morning light. He almost wished he did.

Once Stevie had bolted down some French toast and had half of a second cup of coffee, he had to leave to get to the CBS compound by eight. He was tingling slightly from the coffee as he crossed the street in front of the hotel. It was snowing again, and traffic around the Dome was moving very slowly. When he walked into the compound, a man whom he guessed to be in his early thirties was hovering near the doorway.

"Steve Thomas?" he asked. When Stevie nodded, he put out a hand and said, "Andy Kaplan. We met yesterday for a second. I'm going to be producing you today. In fact, if I don't screw up, I'll probably be producing you all week."

Stevie laughed and shook hands with Kaplan, who was soft-spoken and had an easy smile. Stevie liked him right away.

"You want some coffee?" Kaplan asked as they walked back through the maze of desks and temporary cubicles. "Wait, I forgot. You're fourteen. We've got juice around here somewhere."

"Had some coffee already," Stevie said, feeling quite adult. "I probably better not have any more."

Kaplan smiled as they reached a cubicle that had a desk with a computer on it and a chair on either side of the desk. "Look, I think today will be easy," he said. "I read your story on Darin Kerns and Eddie Brennan in the *Herald* this morning. You did the impossible: you wrote a story on media day at the Super Bowl no one else had."

"I can't take credit," Stevie said. "Bobby Kelleher fed me the idea. I just talked to the two guys and the story wrote itself."

Kaplan nodded. "Well, then Kelleher is good *and* nice. You did a good job writing it too. So I'm thinking we should do almost the same story: get Kerns and Brennan on camera. I've already got a guy in New York tracking down some video and still shots from Summit High we can use with the piece."

"The only problem might be getting Brennan alone for a couple minutes," Stevie said.

Kaplan shook his head. "Remember who you're working for. Dewey Blanton will make it happen for CBS."

Stevie leaned back and felt himself relax. He was relieved that Kaplan was doing all the thinking for him because he was in no condition to think about anything except what he and Susan Carol would do next. What's more, seeing Brennan again might give Stevie a chance to talk to him about the Dreams' offensive line.

"Steve?"

"Oh, sorry, I was just trying to think about getting my work done for you and finding something to write for the *Herald*."

"Well, I wouldn't presume to tell you what to write, but the Dreams show up first today. We can knock out these interviews, and then you would have time to find a Ravens story when they show up."

That made sense. Since the two teams would only be on the field for an hour this morning, there was a thirty-minute break between sessions. That would give him a chance to consult with Kelleher in case there was something he needed Stevie to write that day.

Kaplan said he'd gather a camera crew and talk to Dewey Blanton about getting time with Eddie. He asked if Stevie could track down Darin Kerns. So Stevie left Kaplan and walked through the tunnel onto the field. It was still a few minutes before nine and TV crews were setting up equipment in various places in anticipation of the Dreams' arrival. He spotted Dewey Blanton talking to a couple of cameramen and walked over to say hello.

Blanton saw him coming and, without saying hello, said, "Hey, Steve, great piece this morning."

Stevie often forgot that in the age of the Internet, there was really no such thing as a local newspaper anymore. His story in the *Herald* was as available in Indianapolis as in Washington.

"I couldn't have done it without you," he said. "Which makes me feel bad asking you another favor."

Blanton laughed. "I just hung up with Andy," he said. "We'll go back in the same room we were in yesterday as soon as Eddie finishes on the platform. Andy's going to set his crew up there so you guys can get right at it when Eddie walks in."

"He doesn't have any other one-on-ones today?"

Blanton shook his head. "No. We got 'em all done yesterday. That was our deal. He'll be happy to talk to you for this story, though; I'm sure he saw the newspaper piece."

He thanked Blanton and told him he was going back to the locker rooms to see if Kerns had arrived yet.

"If he's anything like our equipment guy, he's been here since six," Blanton said. "If you have any trouble getting back there, let me know."

"I should be okay, thanks," Stevie said. He walked up the tunnel and, sure enough, the CBS pass caused the security men to part like a yellow curtain at each checkpoint.

Kerns was in his office on the phone. He waved Stevie in and held up a finger to indicate he was almost finished.

"Well, thanks for having me on, Mike," he said. "In fact, the guy who wrote the story just walked in here." He nodded and said, "Will do. Take care."

"Who was that?" Stevie asked.

"ESPN Radio," he said. "The phone's been ringing off the hook all morning. I've got to stop answering." He pointed a finger at Stevie. "And it's all *your* fault."

He was smiling, clearly enjoying the attention.

"Well, I've got one more thing I need you to do even if you hate me," he said.

"What's that?"

"My other bosses this week—CBS—want me to do basically the same piece for their late-night show. Have you got time to tape an interview before your guys get here?"

Kerns nodded. "Hey, anything for you—not to mention for CBS."

Stevie nodded. He was beginning to not hate TV nearly as much as he had a few days earlier.

The Darin Kerns interview went quickly and smoothly. Andy Kaplan had his crew ready to go by 9:30, and Kerns was just as good a storyteller on camera as off, a relief to Stevie because he knew some people got nervous with a camera rolling. Once Kerns left, Stevie wondered if he should go on the field to make sure Brennan was coming. Kaplan advised against it: "Dewey's reliable," he said. "Plus, it's better if you're here, miked up and ready to go when he gets here."

He was right. Blanton was as good as his word. At 10:10, he and Brennan and four security people appeared in the doorway. Blanton told the security people to wait outside. Brennan walked over with a big smile on his face. "You and I are going to have to stop meeting like this," he said, hand extended. "Great piece this morning. I'm sure Darin really enjoyed it."

Stevie loved the compliments, but he was struggling to focus on the interview at hand. The real work would begin once that was over. As with Kerns, the interview was easy. Brennan was a pro: he knew just what was needed to make the story work on television.

"Perfect," Kaplan said when they were finished. "Steve, we'll need to tape an open and a close on the field once the Ravens finish their session. So we'll meet you on the fifty-yard line at eleven-thirty, okay?"

Stevie nodded and began unhooking his microphone, helped by one of the crew. Brennan was doing the same thing. He put out his hand to Stevie, who took it but said quietly, "I know this is a lot to ask, but can I talk to you for one more minute—alone?"

Brennan looked surprised, but shrugged and said, "Sure, I guess. Right now?"

Stevie nodded. "Maybe we can just walk down the hallway for a minute in whatever direction you need to go."

Brennan looked at Blanton. "Dewey, we're done, right?"

"Uh-huh," said Blanton, who had his cell phone out.

"There's a car waiting for you at the exit down the hall past our locker room."

"Like yesterday? Okay, fine. I'm just going to talk to Steve for a minute while we're walking. I'll see you later at the hotel."

Blanton told whomever he was talking to on the phone to hang on for a minute and then said, "Perfect. Steve, he's got a meeting in thirty minutes, so don't hold on to him for too long, okay?"

"Not a problem, I promise," Stevie answered.

Freed from their microphones, he and Brennan headed to the door. As soon as they were in the hallway, two of the security guards started walking ahead of them while the other two fell into step just behind.

"So what's up?" Brennan asked as they started walking.

Stevie glanced uneasily at the yellow jackets surrounding them. "I need to be sure no one else hears this," he said.

Brennan gave him a quizzical look, but braked to a halt. "Fellas, give me a minute alone with my friend," he said. The four men, who Stevie guessed had an average weight of about 250 pounds—which would have made them small for offensive linemen—peeled away, giving Brennan and Stevie some space. Brennan appeared to be looking straight down at Stevie, which reminded him that even though Eddie didn't look all that big when he was in the huddle, he *was* six foot five.

"Okay, we've got privacy," he said, for the first time appearing just a tad impatient. "What's the big scoop?"

That was an interesting choice of words under the

circumstances. Stevie took a deep breath. "Do you know Dr. Snow?" he asked.

"Tom Snow?" Brennan said. "He's one of our doctors. Sure, I know him."

"Good guy?" Stevie didn't want to rush into this.

Brennan smiled. "He's okay. Why?"

Stevie looked around to make sure the security guys hadn't crept any closer. They hadn't. One of them was lighting a cigarette.

"He was at a party last night. He was talking to my friend, you know, Susan Carol?"

"The pretty girl from USTV. Your ex-partner. Oh God, don't tell me he got out of line with her?"

"Well, not exactly. But apparently he *had* been drinking."

Brennan shook his head in disgust. "No surprise there. Jeez, how bad was he?"

Stevie took another deep breath. "Well, this bad: he told Susan Carol that your entire offensive line tested positive for HGH after the NFC Championship game."

Stevie could see all the color drain from Brennan's face. For a moment, he said nothing. Then he said, "Snow told Susan Carol that? He actually said that?"

Stevie was almost hoping Brennan was going to say that Snow was nothing but a drunk and a show-off. But he didn't. Instead, he balled his right hand into a fist and punched his left hand with it, saying through gritted teeth, "That dumb, drunken SOB."

"So it's true?" Stevie said.

Brennan looked at him almost as if he'd forgotten Stevie

was standing there. "I don't know," he said. But his eyes were now darting around the hallway. Stevie's gut told him Eddie was lying. He took a chance.

"Yes, you do," he said. "I can tell by the look on your face." He decided to throw out one more idea: "And you know there's some kind of cover-up going on."

Brennan gasped. "Oh jeez, he told her *that* too?"

Stevie almost said, "No, you just did," but he kept up the act.

"So it's all true then," he said.

"You aren't going to write it, are you?" Brennan said, looking panicked.

"I can't write something that a drunken letch said to impress a girl," he said. "But if it's true, you shouldn't be part of the cover-up. You need to tell the truth."

Dewey Blanton was walking down the hall, a smile on his face. "Hey, Steve, my guy needs to get going."

"We're done, Dewey," Brennan said. "Don't worry." He lowered his voice again. "You still have my cell number from yesterday?"

Stevie nodded.

"Call me later. We'll talk more."

"You won't try to duck me?" Stevie said, worried he might not get another chance to talk to Brennan if he let him go now.

"I promise," he said. He turned and began walking quickly down the hall, the security guards chugging to try to catch up with him.

Blanton walked up to Stevie just as Brennan turned a

corner that Stevie knew led to a loading dock, where the car was no doubt waiting for him.

"Gee, I didn't mean he had to run," Blanton said. "Did you get what you needed?"

"I think so," Stevie said. "Thanks for everything."

"Anything I can do to help," Blanton said. "You're a talented guy, Steve. I wish you the best."

Blanton headed off down the hall. Stevie watched him go, wondering if he would wish him the best if he knew what Stevie had been talking to Brennan about. He hoped Dewey Blanton wasn't part of the cover-up. He wondered how many people *would* know something like this. The doctor, Eddie . . . the whole team? Their "God's been good to me" coach? What about their smug little owner?

It was time to find Kelleher. Stevie needed to talk to him about a story for the day. And a lot more.

10: GAME PLANNING

THE RAVENS WERE JUST COMING ONTO THE FIELD, each of them wearing game jerseys with their names and numbers on them, just as they had done the day before. Bobby had explained to Stevie that this was another example of the NFL understanding the public relations game: "They know that most people can't recognize anyone except the stars unless they're wearing a uniform. So they put them all in uniform tops to make it easy to identify them."

Stevie worked his way across the field and found Kelleher talking to a short, dark-haired man wearing a black golf shirt with the Ravens' logo on it. "Stevie, this is Kevin Byrne," Kelleher said. "He's the Dewey Blanton of the Ravens."

"Wrong," Byrne said with a friendly smile. "Dewey is the

Kevin Byrne of the Dreams. Nice piece this morning, Steve."

"Thanks," Stevie said, wondering how everyone seemed to manage to read everything.

"So, Stevie, I'm leaving you with Kevin, who will take you to Pam Lund, who is going to take you to your story today," Kelleher said. "I have to chase Jonathan Ogden because he grew up in D.C. and he's still one of the best left tackles in football."

"What am I doing?"

"Steve Bisciotti," Kelleher said, starting to walk away. "Kevin will explain."

Byrne laughed. "Pam will be here in a second. She's Steve's assistant and she's going to take you to him. He hates doing interviews, because he thinks the focus should be on the team, not the owner. He'd be perfectly happy if Donny Meeker was the headline maker all week, not him. But he and Bobby are pals, so he's agreed to talk to you."

Stevie was amazed by Kelleher's connections. A fashionably dressed woman with an easy smile approached them.

"Is this our guy, Kevin?" she asked.

"Steve Thomas, this is Pam Lund," Byrne said. "She's the person who actually runs the Ravens. But we humor Steve."

Pam Lund laughed. "Especially when he's writing the checks," she said. "Steve, are you ready to go meet Steve? He's upstairs in one of the luxury boxes."

"I guess so," Stevie said. Things seemed to be moving

awfully fast this morning. It was only 10:35 and he had done two TV interviews, terrified the starting quarterback for the Dreams, and was now about to meet the owner of the Ravens. He followed Pam Lund off the field, down another hallway to an elevator. It was, naturally, manned by a security guard, but it wasn't one of the yellow jackets; it was a man in a suit.

"Good morning, Vernon," Pam Lund said as they approached the elevator.

"Hiya, Pam," Vernon answered.

"Stevie, this is Vernon Holley. He's part of our security group."

Stevie shook hands with Holley. "You mean teams have their own security people?"

Lund nodded. "Absolutely. They work at our practice facility, they're on the field during games, and they deal with any kind of strange mail or phone calls we might get. You'd be amazed. Vernon's a retired homicide detective. He knows what he's doing. All our guys do."

The elevator arrived and Stevie and Lund got on. There were no floor buttons, just a keypad. Lund pressed several numbers and the elevator rocketed upward.

"This elevator goes right to the owner's box," she said. "Since the Colts are an AFC team and we're the AFC representative, Steve gets to use it on game day. Apparently Mr. Meeker is furious because he's in a regular luxury box, which 'only' seats twenty-five people."

"Poor guy," Stevie said.

Pam Lund smiled. The elevator door opened and they

walked directly into a room about the size of the gym at Stevie's school. That was where the similarities ended. The owner's box had thick carpeting with a giant Colts logo in the middle of it. There was a long bar on one side of the room and couches and armchairs scattered around. Steve Bisciotti was sitting at the bar with a bottle of water in his hands, staring at a television set that hung from the ceiling behind the bar. He was dressed casually in a long-sleeved blue work shirt and khaki pants. When he saw Stevie and Lund, he turned off the TV and walked over to greet them, hand outstretched.

"Steve Bisciotti," he said, a wide smile creasing his face. He didn't look to be fifty yet.

"Steve Thomas," Stevie said. "It's nice to meet you, Mr. Bisciotti."

"Call me Steve," Bisciotti said.

Bisciotti offered him something to drink and they sat in comfortable armchairs overlooking the field, where they could see the Ravens and the media going through a second day of parrying with one another. "Look at Billick," Bisciotti said, gesturing down at the podium where the Ravens' coach was standing. "I don't think I've ever met anyone more comfortable on stage than Brian."

That was a perfect setup for Stevie to ask Bisciotti about his desire to *not* be on stage. "The only reason I hesitated when I had the chance to buy this team was that I didn't want to give up my family's privacy," he said. "But I understand that owning a football team makes you a public figure. I try to walk that line of living up to the responsibility I have to the public, but not jeopardizing my family's privacy."

He talked easily and comfortably. Bisciotti's theory on how to be an owner was clearly quite different from Don Meeker's. "I look at it the way I look at my business," he said. "Just because I've made money doesn't mean I'm an expert on football. So I try to hire people who I think know football and know how to deal with people—because coaching is as much about communicating with people as it is about knowing football. I think we've got a great general manager in Ozzie Newsome and a great coach in Billick, and I leave it to them to hire the best possible people to work for them. I run the business side of the team—I let them take care of the football side."

He smiled. "I always tell Ozzie if he's making a big deal to please just let me know about it in advance so I don't get a call from one of my buddies telling me my team has just traded its first-round draft pick. *That* would make me unhappy."

Stevie realized as Bisciotti talked that Kelleher had again handed him a good story that would be easy to write. Tomorrow, he decided, he would come up with his own idea.

Bisciotti glanced at his watch. "Have you got enough?" he said. "I told Brian I'd come down and see him before they leave for practice."

"Plenty," Stevie said. "But if I have a follow-up question, is there some way for me to reach you today?"

Bisciotti smiled. "Spoken like a veteran reporter." He took out a piece of paper and scribbled something. "That's my cell. If you don't get me, it's because I'm on it. Leave a message and I'll get right back to you."

Stevie thanked him and they rode back down the elevator together. "Do you ever look around and think, 'Wow, this is amazing that I'm here'?" Stevie asked—mostly because it was how *he* felt at the moment.

Bisciotti nodded. "Every day," he said.

✦ ✦ ✦

The Ravens were heading out when Stevie got back to the field. He spotted Andy Kaplan and his two cameramen standing on the 50-yard line. As he walked over, he noticed Susan Carol and her crew set up a few yards away. When Susan Carol saw him, she put down her microphone, unhooked herself from her earpiece, and jogged over to Stevie. As soon as she did, Tal Vincent followed her. Stevie sensed more trouble coming.

"Hey," she said, a tad breathless. "I've been looking for you all morning."

"I've been flat-out—but I talked to Eddie."

"Really?"

"We should talk as soon as we're done here."

She was about to respond when Tal Vincent put a hand, not so gently, on her shoulder. "We've got work to do."

"You just said we were five minutes away from being ready, Tal," she said. "I'll be back before you're ready."

His hand was still on her shoulder. "You were told yesterday not to talk to him," he said, acting as if Stevie were invisible.

"Yes, I heard you. But USTV doesn't get to tell me who I can or can't talk to," she said. "Now take your hand off my shoulder."

He glared at her and she glared right back. Stevie was about a split second from pushing him away from her when he removed his hand and turned away. "Two minutes," he said. "You better be ready in two minutes."

She ignored him. "What a jerk," she said. "I may have to quit before the end of the week, money or no money."

"I may have to kill that guy before the end of the week if he touches you again."

"I'll take care of that," she said. "Where should we meet later?"

"How about the coffee shop at the Marriott?" he said. "I'll catch you up and then we can decide what to do next."

She nodded. "Good idea."

Andy Kaplan was now starting to look just a little impatient—which was understandable. "Let's get this TV stuff done and then get to work," Stevie said.

They walked over to their respective crews. Stevie wondered how in ten short months they'd gone from a couple of kids who were amazed to be at the Final Four to practically being bored at the thought of appearing on national TV. He thought again about what Kelleher had said about TV: "If you feel like you're floating when you're on camera, it's because most of what you're doing is lighter than air."

Stevie taped his introduction to the piece and then the close. "You make it look easy," Andy Kaplan said when he was finished. "Nicely done."

"You've got all the real work to do," Stevie said, being honest. "You've got to piece the whole thing together and make sense of it."

"It's not hard when you've got good tape," Kaplan said.

Stevie decided that not everything about TV was lightweight. Andy Kaplan was clearly a man of substance.

Now, though, it was time to get to work.

He could see that Susan Carol and Jamie Whitsitt still hadn't finished what they were doing. So he decided he'd head back to his room and start writing his Bisciotti story. Susan Carol would know where to find him.

He put his coat on to head outside. He'd thought it was chilly in the Dome, but outside the wind had picked up and it was snowing, and Stevie was shivering after even the short walk to the hotel.

The message light was blinking on his phone when he got to his room. He wondered who it was, since almost everyone who might call him would call his cell and he had just checked it for messages.

He hit the message button on the phone and listened. The message was brief and to the point: "Steve, it's Eddie. We need to talk. Call me on my cell after four o'clock."

Stevie stared at the phone for a second. At the very least, Brennan was keeping his word about not ducking him.

He needed to get his Bisciotti story written for the *Herald* before the drug-testing story took over his day, so he set up his computer and dove in. He was so engrossed in what he was doing that the ringing phone caused him to jump in surprise. He looked at his watch. It was after two o'clock. He had been writing for close to two hours.

"Stevie, I'm sorry. It took us forever to get that done."

It was Susan Carol. "Where are you?"

"In the lobby. You want to come down? I'm starving."

"Be right there," he said.

He hit the count button on his computer and gasped when he saw he had written more than 1,300 words. That was about thirty-two inches—ten more than Kelleher had told him he could write. Well, he would worry about cutting it later.

He found Susan Carol pacing up and down in the crowded lobby, looking exasperated. "I'm not sure I'm going to survive the week," she said. "It's bad enough that Tal has turned into such a jerk, but poor Jamie can't do *anything* unless it's put on a cue card for him. That's why it took me so long to get here."

"*Poor* Jamie?"

She gave him the smile. "Stevie," she said, "Jamie is quite handsome, quite sweet, and quite dim. You should know me well enough by now to know that I may *notice* handsome but I *like* smart. There is no need to be jealous."

"What makes you think I'm jealous?"

She gave him a "who do you think you're kidding?" look.

"Okay, maybe I'm a little jealous."

"Uh-huh. Well, you've got nothing to worry about with Jamie. Now, if we were talking about Eddie Brennan . . ."

"*What?!* He's twenty-five years old. . . ."

He stopped, realizing belatedly that she was teasing him.

She winked and walked in the direction of the hotel coffee shop with Stevie, red-faced, two paces behind.

◆　◆　◆

The problem with eating in the hotel coffee shop was that they kept getting interrupted every couple of minutes by people who recognized Susan Carol—or, in a few cases, recognized both of them.

"Let's eat and then go for a walk," she said. "We can't really talk here."

"It's snowing outside," Stevie said. "Why don't we just go up to my room?"

"Why, Steven Richman Thomas, what exactly are your intentions?"

He managed a laugh. "My intention, Scarlett, is for us to figure out what to do next."

They managed to get through lunch with only a couple more interruptions—Stevie found it a bit unnerving when people asked Susan Carol for autographs—and headed back up to Stevie's room.

Susan Carol tossed her coat on one of the beds and sat down in the same chair she'd sat in at two o'clock that morning. She looked tired. That is, until Stevie filled her in on his conversation with Brennan—then they were wired again. This was real—and huge. But all they could do was speculate before they talked to Eddie at four, so they killed the remaining time reading through Stevie's story so she could help him cut it.

"I like it," she said. "You don't think there's any way they would run it the way you wrote it?"

"The *Herald* has eight people here," he said. "They're all writing. I'm last in line, don't you think, to get extra space?"

"Probably right," she said. "Too bad, though. This is good stuff."

"Yeah, but tomorrow I've got to find my own story. Bobby's set me up two days in a row."

She laughed. "You may be the single most competitive person I've ever met," she said. "You can't just be happy you did a good job. You have to do a good job with *no help*."

But he did let her help him cut the story down to size, and they were just finishing when the phone rang. Stevie glanced at his watch. It was a couple of minutes before four.

"Stevie, it's Eddie," Brennan said.

"We were just about to call you."

"*We?*"

"Susan Carol and I . . ."

"Oh yeah, I forgot. Sorry. Look, I can't meet with you tonight, we've got meetings and a team dinner. I can't get away. It will have to be tomorrow morning."

"Don't you guys have to be at the Dome by nine o'clock?"

"Yeah. I was thinking we could meet at about seven-thirty. We just need to find a place where no one will see us. I don't need anyone asking me questions about why I'm hanging around with the world's most famous kid reporters so much."

Stevie sort of liked that description. But he understood.

He turned to Susan Carol and told her what Brennan was suggesting.

"I've got an idea," she said. "Give me the phone."

He handed it to her. "Hi, Eddie, it's Susan Carol," she said. "Do you think you can find the IUPUI Natatorium? It's not far from the Dome at all, but if we meet there at seven-thirty in the morning there's almost no one around."

She waited for a moment while he answered. "Just tell the cabdriver you need to go to the IUPUI Natatorium. Everyone in town knows it. Stevie and I will meet you in the hallway right outside the entrance to the gym at seven-thirty."

She paused again. "I was there yesterday. Trust me, there won't be anyone in the hallway. I walked down it by accident because I went the wrong way on the way out. Everyone goes in and out by the pool in the morning. Wear a cap or a hood or something just in case you see someone, but I'm pretty sure you won't."

She listened for another minute, then gave him her cell phone number and Stevie's. "Okay, see you then."

She hung up.

"IUPUI—that's where the Ravens are practicing, right?" Stevie said.

"Yes, but not that early and not that close by—the campus is huge," she said. "It also happens to have one of the great swimming facilities in the country. They hold national championships and Olympic trials there all the time."

Now he was beginning to understand. Susan Carol was ranked seventh in the country in the 100-yard butterfly and fifth in the 200-yard butterfly in the thirteen-to-fourteen-year-old age group. He had looked it up on the Internet—she never would have told him. "Let me guess," he said. "You went there yesterday to work out."

She nodded. "I promised my coach I would swim at least every other morning while I was here," she said. "We're only a month away from the state championships, and AAU nationals are two weeks after that. He wasn't happy I'd be gone for a week, but I promised him I'd get my workouts in."

"So what time do you go over there?" he said.

"They don't open until five-thirty—"

"What do you mean, 'don't open until five-thirty'?"

"At home, we're in the water at five. I'll have to cut my workout a little short tomorrow, but that's okay." She smiled. "You want to go over there with me at six? You could get in the water a little bit. Wake you right up."

"*No way*," he said. "First of all, I can swim the four strokes—barely—and that's it. Second, there's no way I'm getting up that early. Third, I have no interest in being humiliated by you."

She was laughing. "Okay then, meet me on the deck at seven-fifteen. I'll get out and we can walk upstairs together after I get dressed. Just tell them you're meeting someone on the deck and they'll let you in."

"You're sure?"

"Oh yeah. They let Jamie in."

"Jamie?!"

"He said he wanted to see me swim."

"I'll bet he did."

She stood up and put her coat on, pushing her long brown hair back over her shoulders. "I have to go get changed for this NFL party tonight," she said. "I assume you're going too?"

He had completely forgotten about the party. Bobby had told him it was *the* bash of the week, that everyone in football would show up for it. It was in some gigantic ballroom in the Westin Hotel, which fortunately was right next door to the Marriott.

"I guess I'll be there," he said, standing up. "I'll walk you downstairs."

She held a hand up. "No need. I'll just get a cab outside."

She took a step toward him, put an arm around his back, and kissed him, almost casually—as if they did this all the time.

She didn't wait for a response, which was good since at that moment about all Stevie could think to say was "whaa?" Either that or "Can we try that one more time?"

"See you at the party," she said, and she was gone.

Stevie sat on the bed, a bit dazed. The thought of Jamie Whitsitt going to watch her swim *still* upset him. He decided he would get there in enough time the next day to see her swim himself. He had a feeling he would be impressed.

11: INTO THE RED ZONE

STEVIE WALKED TO THE PARTY with Bobby and Tamara. He and Susan Carol had decided not to say anything to them about the drug tests until after they had heard what Brennan had to say in the morning. "It might help if we can say that we haven't talked to anyone about this yet," she said. "It might make him more comfortable."

Stevie agreed. What's more, there wasn't anything Kelleher or Mearns could do before morning anyway. Letting it ride until then couldn't hurt and it might help. Plus, they wanted to hear from Eddie how many people were in the know on this. They didn't want to start asking too many questions and tip their hand to the wrong people.

The Marriott was only about a five-minute walk from the Westin, but the walk felt like five miles to Stevie. The wind was swirling and, with the sun down, the temperature had dropped well below freezing.

"They couldn't hold this thing at the Marriott?" Kelleher said, his teeth chattering a bit as they walked up the drive to the Westin.

"The NFL people are staying here," Mearns said. "If someone's going out on a night like this, it isn't going to be them."

"I suspect the commissioner's staying at the Canterbury," Kelleher said.

"Probably," Mearns said. "But he isn't walking over."

The ballroom of the Westin was the single largest room Stevie had ever seen. Once they had checked in and been given name tags, they found themselves practically tripping over celebrities everywhere they turned. Within five minutes, Stevie had spotted—among others—Phil Mickelson, Derek Jeter, Albert Pujols, Wayne Gretzky (yet again), Peyton and Eli Manning, David Letterman, Bob Costas, Ben Affleck, and Matt Damon.

"I think Susan Carol will faint if she gets anywhere near Matt Damon," Stevie said.

"*I* might faint if I get anywhere near him," Tamara said, smiling.

They had made their way into the middle of the room, where Stevie could see a massive buffet with enough food to feed the entire population of Indiana. He was about to tell Mearns and Kelleher that he was going to get something to eat when he heard a voice behind them say, "Well, well, what a surprise. Free food and Bobby Kelleher in the same place."

Stevie turned and saw a short man with dark hair and thick glasses standing a few feet away from them. Two very large men Stevie took to be bodyguards stood a couple of feet behind him. Kelleher looked at the man with barely concealed contempt. "Don, just seeing you makes this anything but a free meal," Kelleher said.

As soon as he heard the name, Stevie figured out that the sneering little man was Don Meeker, the owner of the California Dreams. Kelleher's column on him had run that morning. He said that the Dreams were exactly the kind of team he liked to pull for—the underdog, lots of young players, a rising-star quarterback. Unfortunately, their owner was just the kind of guy you had to root *against*—an obnoxious bully who thought that being rich gave him the right to treat people like dirt. He had cited several examples of Meeker's boorish behavior to back up his premise. Stevie thought the column was a riot, but seeing Meeker and Kelleher face to face wasn't so funny.

"What gives you the right to libel me the way you do?" Meeker said. "You don't know me well enough to rip me."

"I know you plenty well enough, Don," Kelleher said, his voice a lot softer and calmer than Meeker's. "I know that you fired a secretary in your public relations department who was twenty years older than you because she called you Don instead of Mr. Meeker. I know you screamed at an elevator operator in your stadium because she let someone get on the elevator with you. I know you fired your defensive coordinator because you told him to bench a cornerback and he didn't do it. You want me to go on? There's plenty more I didn't print."

Meeker was red-faced. "Why don't you write about the money I give to charity? What about that?"

"Your motives aren't so charitable if you're only doing it to balance out your bad press. I'm willing to bet that Steve Bisciotti gives more money to charity than you do and he would *never* bring it up to anyone."

"You better not ever try to cover a game in my stadium," Meeker said. "You'll never get inside."

Kelleher laughed. "Oh, please, go ahead and deny me a credential. You'll make me famous—not to mention a hero. Judge a man by his enemies, Donny. I'm happy to count you as one."

"You call yourself an objective reporter?"

"Absolutely not. I'm a columnist. They pay me for my opinions. While you have to pay people pretty well to listen to yours."

Meeker's response was a profanity, one Stevie frequently heard in school but which was strictly verboten around his parents.

"Clever," Kelleher said.

He was about to go on when a man with well-coiffed blond hair walked up and put an arm around Meeker. "Now, Don, we're not quarreling with the media tonight, right?" he said. "We're all here to celebrate a great season and to have a good time."

Stevie recognized the man right away as Roger Goodell, the commissioner of the NFL. Clearly, he didn't want one of his owners yelling profanities at a reporter in front of a room full of media. A small crowd had gathered around as Meeker and Kelleher went at it.

"Guy shouldn't even be in here," Meeker said. He tossed Goodell's arm off his shoulder, pointed at Kelleher, and said, "Either he goes or I go."

Goodell's smile disappeared. "Come on, Don, lighten up. Your team's in the Super Bowl. It's all good," he said.

"Don't tell me to lighten up," Meeker said. "And don't call me Don. Remember who you work for."

He turned and stalked away, followed closely by the bodyguards. Goodell looked exasperated. "Bobby, you don't have to print this, do you?" he said.

Kelleher looked at him. "All due respect, Commissioner, but are you kidding me?"

Goodell put a hand up. "I understand. I think I'll go buy myself a drink."

Kelleher was swarmed by other reporters, who had only seen part of the confrontation. Stevie decided it was time to find Susan Carol, who had to be around somewhere. He pushed his way out of the circle that had formed around Kelleher and began wandering around the room. He was about to take a respite from his search and get some food when he saw her—talking to Matt Damon.

"Figures," he said to himself.

She was wearing the high heels again, and she looked pretty spectacular in a dark-colored dress. It was a conservative dress, the kind you would expect a minister's daughter to wear to a party, but on her it looked great. Feeling a bit nervous, he walked over to where she and Damon were standing.

"Stevie!" Susan Carol said. "I've been looking for you all night. Have you met Matt Damon?"

Sure, Stevie thought, Matt and I go way back. "No, I haven't," he said, shaking hands with Damon. "Nice to meet you, Mr. Damon."

"It's Matt," he said with a friendly smile. "I'm not *that* old. I read the story you wrote on Ed Brennan and his high school buddy, the equipment guy. It was really good."

"It'll be on CBS later tonight," Susan Carol said.

"I'll have to watch," Damon said.

"Matt's in town doing research on a movie," Susan Carol said. "He's thinking of doing something based on Ed Brennan's story."

"That could make a great movie," Stevie said.

Damon nodded. "I think so—plus, you've gotta love research that brings you to the Super Bowl."

Someone was calling his name. Damon shook his head. "Gotta go," he said. "My agent wants me to meet some of the money people here. Believe me, I'd rather chat with you two."

He shook hands with both of them. "Enjoy the week," he said. "I'll be watching for your stuff. Susan Carol, if you ever want to get into acting, give me a call."

She laughed. "I like journalism," she said. "But thanks."

Damon walked off, heads turning to follow him, Stevie noticed, as he crossed the room. "If you want to sigh about him, I won't mind," he said. "He seems extremely nice."

"I thought so too," she said. "What was that commotion I saw a little while ago over near the buffet?"

"Let's walk outside and I'll tell you about it," he said.

They headed out of the ballroom into the lobby, where it was ten degrees cooler and ten decibels quieter. Stevie had just given Susan Carol the blow by blow when he noticed that Don Meeker had not yet left the building. He and his bodyguards were standing with another short man who also appeared to be accompanied by bodyguards.

"Hey, look at that," Susan Carol said. "It's Little Donny and Little Danny."

Sure enough, Meeker was talking to Dan Snyder, the owner of the Washington Redskins. Meeker appeared to be doing most of the talking, waving his arms angrily.

"He's probably telling him about what happened with Kelleher," Stevie said.

"He's got a good audience then—Snyder hates Bobby," Susan Carol said. "I think Bobby's the one who first started calling him 'Little Danny.'"

Stevie giggled. "Can't imagine why that would upset him. Look at the two of them. They look like a couple of windup toys."

Meeker and Snyder shook hands, and Meeker started to walk away. "Come on," Susan Carol said. "I've got an idea."

Without waiting for him to respond, she started walking as fast as she could in heels, reminding Stevie that he needed to ask her why she was wearing them again. He followed her as she followed Meeker and his bodyguards, who were headed for an escalator.

"Mr. Meeker," she called. "Excuse me, Mr. Meeker?"

She had put on her full Southern accent, the one that had caused Stevie to start calling her Scarlett. Hearing a female voice, Meeker stopped a few yards short of the escalator and turned around. Seeing Susan Carol walking in his direction, Meeker smiled.

"Yes?" he said. "What can I do for you, young lady?"

Susan Carol gave him the smile. "My name is Susan Carol Anderson. I just wanted to meet you because I have *so* admired the way you've built the Dreams."

Meeker's smile was now a smirk. "Why, thank you, young lady. What brings you here tonight?"

"Oh, well, I do this little show on USTV? *Kid-Sports?* Not anything you would watch with your schedule, I'm sure."

Meeker grunted. "I don't watch much TV. Most of it's crap. Your network is better than the others, I'll say that much."

Susan Carol looked sympathetic. "Oh, I know," she said. "I don't think the media have gotten your story right at all. It must be so hard to own a team. And you've come so far so quickly."

Stevie was tempted to slap a hand across his mouth to keep from laughing. He had seen this act before and could see it was working again, just as it always did.

"*No* one knows how hard it is to own a team," Meeker said, completely charmed. "For someone so young, you are very wise. And very pretty."

Susan Carol appeared to blush. "Do you think there is *any* way we could get you to appear on our show?"

Stevie wondered where she was going with this. Meeker was well known for not talking to the media at all—at least not publicly. He was famous for calling a small handful of reporters he liked and leaking dirt about other people—sometimes his own players and coaches—that was always attributed to "a source close to Dreams owner Donald M. Meeker."

Meeker was shaking his head. "I'm afraid I have a strict policy against TV interviews. And if I appeared with you, I would be bombarded by everyone else wanting me too."

He snapped his fingers at one of the bodyguards. "Notebook," he said.

The bodyguard reached into his coat pocket and produced a small notebook. "Pen, you idiot!" Meeker roared, making Stevie wish the bodyguard, who was almost a foot taller than Meeker, would simply crush him like a grape. Instead, he produced a pen. Meeker opened the notebook and wrote something inside it. He ripped the page out and handed it to Susan Carol. "If you have any questions about our team, or if you want to know what's *really* going on with the league, you call me," he said. "That's my cell phone number. There aren't a dozen people who have it, so *please* don't share it with anyone. But I will gladly talk to you—strictly background, of course."

Susan Carol took the piece of paper and turned the wattage up on her smile. "Oh, that is so nice of you," she said. "I know how busy you must be. But I will call because I know I can learn so much from you."

Stevie felt just a little bit nauseated. He noticed that

one of the bodyguards was eyeing him. Maybe he should tell him that he was Susan Carol's bodyguard.

Meeker had moved a step closer to Susan Carol—in her heels she towered over him—and had taken her hand. "People don't understand me," he said. "I enjoy helping people. That's why I do so much for charity."

She smiled down at him. "I've heard that. Well, it was a *thrill* to meet you, sir."

"The pleasure was mine," Meeker said, still smirking with self-congratulations.

He turned toward the escalator, snapping once more at the bodyguards, who fell into place—one in front, one behind. Stevie and Susan Carol watched as they disappeared at the bottom of the escalator.

"What was that all about?" Stevie said.

"This," Susan Carol said, holding up the piece of paper on which Meeker had written his cell phone number. "At some point, we're going to want to talk to him—either for a comment or maybe to try to bluff some information out of him. I couldn't imagine any other time we'd get that close to him."

"I thought being close to him was a pretty disgusting experience myself."

She nodded. "Completely gross. What a jerk. I feel like I should take a shower. But it worked."

"What would you have done if he had said yes to going on the show?"

She shrugged. "I was pretty sure he'd say no. But if he had said yes, the USTV people would have been thrilled. They'd have run around screaming, 'exclusive, exclusive!' even if he didn't say anything worth hearing—which he wouldn't."

"So what do we do now?"

She shrugged. "We wait to hear what Eddie Brennan tells us tomorrow."

That sounded about right to Stevie. And so did going back inside to finally get something to eat.

12: QUARTERBACK SNEAK

NOT SURPRISINGLY, Stevie ate far more than he should have, unable to resist going back for second and third helpings of shrimp and roast beef and ice cream. He and Susan Carol were sitting at a corner table watching the stars go by when someone Stevie didn't recognize came up and began nervously telling Susan Carol she was needed for some kind of photo shoot with the rest of the USTV talent.

Stevie wondered yet again how other people who worked in TV—producers, directors, camerapeople—felt about the on-air people being called talent, as if they were the only ones who had any. The man never even looked at Stevie.

"Josh, I'm sure you talked to Steve Thomas at some point on the phone," Susan Carol said. "Wouldn't you like to say hello to him?"

The man reddened slightly, then turned to Stevie and said, "Josh Krulander," offering Stevie a quick, limp handshake. Stevie recognized the name. He was a USTV public relations type whom Stevie had spoken to on the phone on several occasions when USTV had wanted him to do interviews about the show. Before Stevie could respond at all, Krulander turned to Susan Carol and said for a third time, "We really need you right now."

"Okay, okay, I'm coming," Susan Carol said, standing up. She pushed past Krulander, bent over, and kissed Stevie on the lips. The look on Krulander's face was almost as good as the kiss. She walked off with Krulander trailing her.

Stevie knew he had a huge grin on his face. If he had been old enough, he would have sat back in his chair and lit up a cigar. Instead, he spooned up the last of his ice cream.

It was still pitch-dark outside when the alarm went off at 6:15, and Stevie was tempted to hit the snooze button. But knowing that Jamie Whitsitt had made it to the pool early enough to see Susan Carol swim was enough to get him out of bed and into the shower. He dressed in what he had come to think of as his "TV clothes"—dress shirt, clean pants, tie, and sports coat—and was out the door within twenty-five minutes of the alarm's going off.

The lobby was almost empty at 6:40. The doorman got him a cab and Stevie told the cab driver he needed to go to the IUPUI Natatorium, as Susan Carol had instructed. He was convinced the cabdriver would look at him blankly, but he simply flipped on the meter. It took less than ten minutes to get to the pool.

Following Susan Carol's instructions, he found the check-in desk. He was explaining to the woman at the desk that he was meeting a friend who was inside swimming when she stopped him. "Your friend is the tall girl with the dark hair, right? From the South? She told us you were coming. You can get to the pool deck through the men's locker room. Just take your shoes off before you go on the deck."

She pointed him down the hall to the locker room, where he stopped to take off his shoes and socks and put them in an empty locker. Since it was steamy warm inside the locker room, he took off his jacket too, hanging it on a hook inside the locker. He walked out onto the deck and knew immediately that Susan Carol hadn't been joking about this being one of the best pools in the country.

There were actually, by Stevie's count, three pools. One 50-meter pool and two 25-yard pools with eight wide lanes and the kind of thick lane dividers Stevie had seen when watching the Olympics on TV. Hanging over each lane was a banner with the name and a photo of a great American swimmer: Michael Phelps, Natalie Coughlin, Tom Dolan, Clay F. Britt, and Wally Dicks. Stevie recognized most of them.

There was a swimmer in almost every lane of the pool at the end where Stevie had entered, but no one who looked like Susan Carol. He walked gingerly to the second 25-yard pool, which was separated from the one nearer the locker room by a bulkhead. Stevie guessed it was the movable kind that could be manipulated to make the pool any length people wanted it to be. Then behind the second pool was a completely separate diving well.

Walking past the bulkhead, Stevie spotted Susan Carol. She was at the far end, wearing a blue-and-white bathing cap, hanging on to the edge of the pool. He started to wave at her, but just as he did, she and the man in the lane next to her pushed off and began swimming butterfly—fast. They both reached the wall near where Stevie was standing, turned, and pushed off. They were stroke for stroke with one another until the last five yards, when Susan Carol seemed to find an extra burst of energy and got to the wall about a half-stroke ahead of her competition.

Stevie was amazed. Even though he knew she was ranked in the top ten in the country, he hadn't really thought about what that would look like in the water. He began walking toward the end of the pool where Susan Carol and the man had stopped when, to his surprise, they pushed off again. Again, they went down and back—fifty yards, Stevie figured—and again Susan Carol got to the wall just barely in front.

"How many?" Stevie heard the man say as he reached the end of the pool.

"That was eight," she said. "Two more. Let's push."

An instant later, they were off again. Stevie watched, deciphering the brief conversation. His guess was that they were swimming the 50 butterfly ten times. Butterfly was by far the most difficult stroke in swimming. The thought of trying to swim one 50 made him tired. Ten? No way. And yet Susan Carol was plowing through them as if she could keep going all morning.

She finished the ninth one, looked up, and saw Stevie staring at her.

"Hey," she said, breathing hard. "One more, okay?"

Stevie barely had time to say "Okay" before she and her companion pushed off again. This time Susan Carol pulled away the last few yards, winning by several strokes.

"Susan Carol, you're just too young and too good for me," the man said, panting as they hung on the wall.

Susan Carol shook her head. "You stuck right with me until the very end, Jason. I thought you told me you were out of shape."

"Compared to you, I *am* out of shape," Jason said.

Susan Carol looked up at Stevie. She was still breathing hard but appeared perfectly capable of ripping off ten more 50 butterflies if asked.

"Stevie, this is Jason Crist. He's in town for the Super Bowl and he's a Masters swimmer. He offered to swim a couple of sets with me."

"Which was my mistake," Crist said. He looked to be in his mid-forties, with dark hair that was tinged with gray. He had an easy, friendly smile.

"What is a Masters swimmer?" Stevie said.

"Someone who is old," Crist said, climbing slowly out of the pool. "It's just a term used for people over twenty-five who are still silly enough to try to compete. I'm well over twenty-five and quite silly." He looked at Susan Carol. "We on for tomorrow?"

"Same time, same place," she said.

He gave them both a wave and headed in the direction of the locker room. "I need a shower too," Susan Carol said. "Why don't I meet you by the check-in desk in fifteen minutes."

"Susan Carol, I can't believe how good a swimmer you are," he said.

"We were only doing fifties," Susan Carol said. "If it had been hundreds, I might not have looked so good."

"Yeah, right," he said. "I'm going to read the paper while you change. Don't take too long. We don't want to be late."

She looked at the swim watch she was wearing. "Oh—it's seven-ten," she said. "You're right. I'd better hurry. I have to get my hair dry so I can look good on TV in a few hours."

"You'll look good," he said. "You always do."

"Why, Stevie," she said, going into full Scarlett mode. "You are just all flattery this morning."

She left him standing there, still feeling a bit overwhelmed by what he had just seen.

At 7:28, she walked out of the locker room, her hair tied back but dry, her swim bag hanging from her shoulder.

"You know where we're going?" he asked.

"Yup. Follow me."

He did—up the steps and down a long hallway. It was dark, with no signs of life anywhere until they rounded a corner and saw someone sitting on a bench wearing a hooded gray sweatshirt. Hearing the footsteps, Eddie Brennan looked up.

"Right on time," he said.

Stevie almost laughed out loud when he saw the sweatshirt. It said "Baltimore Ravens."

"You going over to the enemy?" he said, pointing at the shirt.

Brennan laughed. "Darin gave it to me," he said. "I figured between the hood and the logo no one would look twice."

"Good thinking," Susan Carol said. She pointed down the hall to an open door. "That's the gym down there. No one will be inside. Why don't we go sit in there?"

The gym was completely dark except for a spotlight in the rafters that was shining on a banner. The banner said NCAA TOURNAMENT 2005, which reminded Stevie that he *had* heard of IUPUI. The school had made it into the NCAA basketball tournament a couple of years earlier, causing all sorts of jokes about how you correctly pronounce I-U-P-U-I as a word. The gym was set up for a game: bleachers rolled down, chairs in place for team benches. They sat down on chairs marked IUPUI on the backs.

"So," Brennan said, "where should we begin?"

As usual, Susan Carol took the lead. "Probably at the beginning. When did you find out about the positive tests?"

Brennan put a hand up. "Hang on, hang on," he said. "We need some ground rules here. I'll talk to you guys, but at least for right now, we have to agree we're off the record."

"Why?" Stevie asked.

"When I tell you, you'll understand. But you have to trust me. I'm trusting you just by being here."

"That's fair," Susan Carol said. Stevie was thinking the same thing. "Okay, at least for now, we'll be off the record. But please—this is too big a story for us to drop, and we need to know what's really going on here."

Brennan sighed. "I understand." He sighed again. He had pushed the hood back off his head and he ran a hand through his hair as if thinking about what he was going to say next.

Finally, with one more deep breath, he began talking. "Unfortunately, Susan Carol, the story that idiot Snow told you the other night is essentially true. How much do you guys know about the new collective bargaining agreement?"

"We looked on the Internet to find out about drug testing and HGH," Susan Carol said.

Brennan nodded. "HGH was the diciest part of the new contract," he said. "No one is sure yet that even blood testing is a hundred percent accurate, although the doctors I've talked to say they're pretty close—especially if the HGH level is so high that there's no doubt."

"Why has HGH become such a big deal all of a sudden?" Stevie asked.

"Yeah, it's the drug of choice right now. Mostly because it can't be detected in a urine test, and that was all they used to do under the old CBA, and also because it helps you get big very fast. Look at the size of all the linemen in the league these days. You think that's all from some workout regimen?"

Neither of them answered, so he plowed on. "We all knew once we made the play-offs that we'd get tested again—at least once. The coaches warned everyone that if anyone *was* doing something, they should stop."

"How many guys on your team are users?" Susan Carol asked.

Brennan shrugged. "I honestly don't know. It probably wouldn't be that hard to figure out. You could just look at a guy's weight—everyone weighs in every single day. So if a guy comes out of college at two-sixty-five and then jumps to three-fifteen, odds are he's doing something.

"Every team has guys who are using something. But it just isn't talked about—even inside the locker room. It's part of the code. If you don't talk about guys doing steroids, then it means guys aren't doing steroids—even if they are."

Stevie wasn't sure if he understood that, but then he thought he sort of did. "Why do you think so many guys do it?" he asked. "Putting aside the fact that you get in trouble if you get caught, there are all sorts of stories about the health risks."

Brennan laughed. "Did you see that survey of high school football players a couple years ago? They asked, 'If you knew that by taking steroids you would guarantee yourself a ten-year career in the NFL *but* you would also guarantee losing ten years of your life, would you take them?' *Seventy-five* percent said yes. Because there's a lot of money and glamour in the NFL, and high school kids don't think they're ever going to die anyway.

"And you have to understand—the margin for error in

this league is tiny. You lose a half step of speed or a tiny bit of strength and you can be gone for someone younger, cheaper, stronger, healthier. Contracts aren't guaranteed. Everyone wants to keep playing—making the big money, hearing all the cheers, being a hero. Most guys will tell you they'd take the risk in an instant to extend their careers."

"Or to win a Super Bowl?" Susan Carol asked.

Brennan simply nodded. "Exactly. Obviously, these guys thought they needed that extra edge as we went deeper into the play-offs."

"So you guys didn't get tested until after you won the conference championship?" Stevie asked.

Brennan shook his head. "No, that's the thing, we got fooled. This is all new, remember? We were actually tested before we played the wild-card game against the Giants. I was one of the guys tested that time too—it's all random. They can test up to half the team at any given time. Everyone was clean. I think the guys just figured we were in the clear."

"Only they tested again after you beat the Redskins," Susan Carol said.

"Right. I remember some of the o-line guys looking nervous when they posted the list of who would be tested. Three of them had already been tested the first time like me and they were grumbling about it."

"So when did you hear about the positives?" Stevie asked.

"Friday," Brennan said. "Omar Nelson, our fullback, told me. He rooms with Pete Akombe on the road. I guess Pete told him that he and the other four o-linemen had come back positive. I said to Omar, 'My God, with the week off, they'll all be suspended once the B sample comes back. We're done.'"

"What's the B sample again?" Stevie said, remembering something about a two-test system from their late-night Internet scrolling.

"They take a second blood sample if the first one comes up positive, just to be absolutely sure," Brennan said. "It's the same kind of testing they do in the Olympics and the Tour de France—that's how Floyd Landis got nailed, remember? When I said that to Omar, he shook his head and said, 'Pete says there won't be a second sample. He says Meeker is taking care of it.'"

"Meeker?!!!" Stevie and Susan Carol both screamed at once, causing Eddie to look around the dark gym as if someone could hear them.

"Shhhh," Brennan said, putting a finger to his lips. "Yes, Meeker. He's at the center of this whole thing. When the tests came back, he told Coach Kaplow that he would take care of everything."

"But how?" Susan Carol asked.

"That I'm not sure of," Brennan said. "But with his money, he could maybe pay off someone at the lab to keep quiet for a while. It's up to the team to report test results. And if Meeker can say the results came back too late . . ."

"But sooner or later the test results will come out, right?" Stevie said.

"Yeah, I guess," Brennan said. "But if they come after the game, what's the league going to do? Declare the Super

Bowl a forfeit? No way. They'll just say it's regrettable, that we need to revisit the system and probably fine the team for being sloppy in dealing with the test results. Then Meeker will scream and yell and say we were the only team tested twice, which I know from Darin isn't true. The Ravens were tested twice too."

"And no positives?" Susan Carol asked.

"None."

They sat in silence for a while. "I assume," Susan Carol finally said, "that most if not all of the team knows about this." Brennan just nodded in response. "Won't someone go public with it? Are you all just going to sit back and let this happen?"

Brennan laughed—not a funny laugh, an angry one. "Go public?" he said. "If you go public, two things could happen: the first is, the entire o-line is suspended for the Super Bowl and we have no chance to win the game. Ray Lewis would sack me twelve times by halftime. Most likely they'd carry me out on a stretcher."

"What's the second thing?" Susan Carol asked.

"Oh yeah, even better than that, you become a pariah— not just on your team but in the entire league. You're the guy who ratted out his teammates. Not only that, you're the guy who cost your teammates the chance to get a Super Bowl ring."

"What about doing the right thing?" Stevie asked. "What about the fact that these guys cheated and your owner is cheating, lying, and buying people off? Should that be allowed to happen?"

"No," Brennan said. "No, it shouldn't. But that's another code among athletes—you don't turn another guy in."

"Even if he's guilty?" Susan Carol asked.

"Even if he's guilty," Brennan said. "Look at Jose Canseco. When he said that steroid use was rampant in the major leagues, he became the most hated player in baseball—even though he was telling the truth."

"He did that to make money," Susan Carol said. "He was selling a book."

"Yes." Brennan nodded. "But the book was true. Who do you think people hate more—Canseco or the other guys who were doping? And this would be worse because it would cost a team the chance to win the Super Bowl. That's all you'd be remembered for."

"You mean that's all *you'd* be remembered for, don't you?" Susan Carol said. "That's what has you spooked."

"Well, of course," Brennan said. "I don't want to go down in history as the quarterback who turned his teammates in. And remember, there are forty-eight guys on the roster who haven't done anything wrong. This might be the one chance any of us has to win the Super Bowl."

They sat in silence for a while. Stevie could understand Brennan's dilemma.

"Let me ask you a question," Susan Carol finally said. "Let's say you keep quiet. You guys win the Super Bowl. How will you feel when it's over? Will you feel like a real champion? Or will you feel like you let people cheat your sport and get away with it?"

Stevie added a thought: "How will you feel," he said,

"seeing Little Donnie Meeker holding the Lombardi Trophy?"

Brennan stared at the two of them. "Are you trying to make me completely lose my mind?" he said.

"No," Susan Carol said. "We're trying to make you understand why you should tell the truth."

"And what about after the game?" Stevie said. "When the story breaks—as you say it will—do you want to be the quarterback of the team that cheated their way to a Super Bowl title?"

"Aaaaaah! I need time to think," Brennan said.

"Okay," Stevie said. "But you have to decide what to do soon."

"I know," Brennan said. He stood up. "I'll be in touch."

He pulled the hood over his head and walked out of the gym.

13: THIRD AND LONG

STEVIE AND SUSAN CAROL sat and watched Eddie leave the gym, his sneakers squeaking quietly against the floor.

"I feel bad for him," Stevie said. "This isn't his fault, but he's going to have to pay the price anyway."

Susan Carol stood up. "You're right. He's trapped in a way, a little bit like Chip Graber was trapped back at the Final Four. He's not being blackmailed, but no matter what he does, it's going to be wrong. He can become a pariah and guarantee his team won't win the Super Bowl, or he can help his team win a tainted victory and live with the guilt."

"What do you think *we* should do?"

"I think we need to find a way to report the story without making Eddie the fall guy."

"How?"

"I haven't a clue, Stevie. I haven't a clue. Come on, I have to go change before the interview sessions."

✦　✦　✦

They found a cab and Stevie dropped Susan Carol at the Canterbury and then went straight on to the Dome. It was 8:30 when he walked into the CBS compound, which was already humming with life. He found Andy Kaplan reading the *Indianapolis Star*.

"Hey! Your piece got rave reviews last night."

"Our piece," Stevie corrected. "I didn't stay up to watch it, to tell you the truth."

"I can get you a tape," Kaplan said. "I hope your parents saw it."

Stevie had called his parents to tell them he was going to have a story on the CBS late-night show. They had planned to tape it since the show didn't come on until after Letterman.

"I saw your Bisciotti story online this morning," Kaplan continued. "Good stuff. I already made a call to see if he'd come on camera and got a flat no. He doesn't like to do TV apparently."

"Yeah, he told me that. He's very friendly, but he hates the spotlight."

"Unlike Don Meeker, who can't seem to stay out of it."

Stevie nodded. "What if we did something on Kyle Boller today?"

Kaplan looked baffled. "The Ravens' backup quarterback— why?"

"For one thing, he's a good talker. I've seen him. For another, he's had to come in a couple times this year when McNair's been hurt, and he's played well. Who knows, it could happen again on Sunday. Plus, how many guys who were starting quarterbacks as rookies in the NFL have had to deal with becoming a backup? It's a good story, I think."

"Sold," Kaplan said. "I'll call Kevin Byrne and set it up."

Stevie was proud of himself. He had come up with an idea—a good one, he thought—without Bobby Kelleher. Plus, he could probably write Kyle Boller for the *Herald* too. The old kill-two-birds-with-one-stone trick.

While Kaplan went off to make arrangements for the morning, Stevie went through the buffet line, grabbing some French toast and bacon. He was tired, he realized, so he poured himself a cup of coffee. He sat down at an empty table and thought about what Susan Carol had said back in the IUPUI gym. How could they possibly find a way to break the story without forcing Brennan to out his teammates?

The lab people would know the results—but what lab was it? Had Meeker really paid them off? Even if they found the lab, could he and Susan Carol really persuade someone to talk to them? No—they had the whole team here. . . .

"The doctor!" he said aloud. They certainly couldn't use the information he had given Susan Carol as source material, but what was to stop them from making him *think* they could?

He pulled out his cell phone and called Susan Carol. "Where are you?" he asked.

"In the car, on the way over to the Dome."

"We need to talk as soon as the morning session is over. I have an idea."

She sighed. "Why don't we meet in your room again. Who knows how long it will take for Jamie to read his lines right."

"Okay. I'll finish my CBS stuff, then go back to my room and write while I'm waiting for you."

"Deal." She paused. "Stevie?"

"Yes?"

"Am I going to like this idea?"

He smiled. "Probably not. But it might work."

The morning went quickly. Three days in, and Stevie felt like an old hand at pre–Super Bowl coverage. Of course, his job was a lot easier than most since people were hand-delivered to him to talk because of either Kelleher or CBS. There wasn't a lot of demand for Kyle Boller during the Ravens' session on the field, so they were able to get him one-on-one before the end of the time period. Boller was everything Stevie had hoped he would be: friendly and honest. He said if he were running the Ravens, he would have traded to get Steve McNair too. He had learned a lot of football from McNair. But yes, he hated watching from the sidelines.

"I'm a football player," he said. "Not a football watcher."

Stevie got all he needed for both CBS and the *Herald* from Kyle Boller, then he and the crew went off to pick up a couple of quotes from Steve McNair and Coach Brian Billick.

Kelleher was pleased that Stevie had come up with his own idea. "Better than what I had in mind for you. . . . Pretty soon, you aren't going to need me for anything," he said. "Which is a good thing, because Tamara and I will be tied up in writers' meetings and doing radio all day."

"That's fine," Stevie said. "Susan Carol is free, so we'll hang out."

"So you two are okay again?"

"Oh yeah—just like old times."

✦   ✦   ✦

It was one o'clock by the time Susan Carol knocked on Stevie's door. Since the Ravens had gone first, he had been back in the room by eleven and was winding up his *Herald* story when she arrived.

"Perfect timing," he said. "I'm starved. Let's order room service."

She agreed, flopping down in a chair and looking frazzled and tired. "Man, this is hard," she said. "I'm working with a producer I can't stand and a partner who has no clue." She looked at him. "I can't tell you how much I miss you on that show."

"Thanks," he said. "But we've got more important things to worry about."

"True," she said. "Call in the food order, then tell me your plan."

When he had, she said, "So you want me to call Dr. Snow and tell him I want to meet with him."

"Right. Tell him you need to discuss what he told you

the other night. If he claims not to remember, remind him."

"What if he just says no, he won't talk to me anymore?"

"You tell him you're prepared to go on air with the story and name him as the source."

"But I can't possibly do that."

"I know that. But *he* might not know that. At the very least, he won't be able to take the risk. He'll agree to meet with you, I guarantee it."

"I don't want to spend *any* time alone with that guy."

"You won't. I'll go with you. Not only will you not be alone, but we can tell him there are two of us prepared to go with the story."

"Bluff him? Okay, but what then? What are we really hoping for?"

"We tell him if he puts us in touch with the right people—the lab guys, other people in the organization who *must* know—we'll protect him as a source. If not . . ."

She nodded. "It might work," she said. "Move over so I can use the phone."

✦　✦　✦

Stevie was quite proud of the fact that, for once, he was the one who had come up with an idea. Susan Carol had kept the card that Dr. Snow had given her at the party, which had his cell number on it. Snow must have picked up on the first ring because an instant after she had finished dialing, Stevie heard her say, "Dr. Snow? Hi. It's Susan Carol Anderson."

She paused, clearly waiting to see if he remembered her.

"Right, at the party on Tuesday."

She rolled her eyes as he responded. "No, not quite six feet tall.

"The reason I'm calling is that I think you and I should talk."

Her face turned red at his next response. "No, not over drinks. I'm fourteen years old. I can't drink for seven more years.

"I understand. People get confused because I'm tall. We do need to talk, though, about what you told me the other night."

She listened for a moment. "If you'd like, I'll refresh your memory. It was about drug testing and the Dreams' offensive line. . . ."

Stevie thought he heard shouting coming from the other end of the phone.

"No, actually, you never said anything about off the record," Susan Carol finally said. "In fact, what you said was, 'I'll give you a scoop, gorgeous.'"

More shouting.

"No, I haven't spoken to anyone about it, except my friend Steve Thomas—who is here working for the *Washington Herald* and CBS. . . ."

Now Stevie could actually hear Snow's words: "CBS?! CBS knows about this! Are you out of your mind? Look, I was drunk, I didn't know what I was talking about—"

Susan Carol broke in. "I know you were drunk, doctor, but I'm pretty sure you knew exactly what you were talking about. I don't want to embarrass you. That's why we need to talk."

Susan Carol waited. Stevie heard nothing coming from the other end of the phone. "Well, then, let's find some sort of neutral spot where no one will see us."

She listened for a minute. "Okay, then, seven o'clock. Spell that for me." She began writing on a phone notepad that was sitting on the night table. "All right, Steve and I will meet you there at seven."

She hung up.

"And?"

"The team is staying at a hotel out in the suburbs. Apparently there's a YMCA just across the street where some of the players have been going to work in the weight room in the mornings. He wants to meet us there at seven tonight."

"Where is it?"

She looked at the notepad. "Greenbriar. Wherever that is. Look, I have access to a car with a driver. He'll know the area. Why don't you meet me at the Canterbury at six-thirty so we can go from there. I'm taping the rest of the show at four o'clock. Even with Jamie's screwups, we'll be done in plenty of time."

"The driver won't ask questions?"

"No. What does he care if I want to go to some YMCA?"

He nodded. "So, you don't want me to come over at six so we can have a drink first?"

For a split second she didn't get it. Then she started laughing. "He said he thought I was at least twenty-two. Even if I *was* twenty-two, he's like fifty or sixty or something. What is he thinking?"

"I don't even want to know," Stevie said.

Stevie walked into the Canterbury lobby just before 6:30. It was small but had plush carpeting and leather chairs and a long couch in front of a fireplace. The walls were lined with bookshelves.

A bellman standing just inside the door said, "Good evening, sir. Are you a guest in the hotel?"

"No," Stevie said. "But I'm meeting a guest here in a few minutes." He wondered if the bellman would give him a hard time.

"Welcome," he said. "There are hot drinks over next to the fireplace if you'd like to help yourself while you're waiting."

"Oh, thank you," he said. A hot chocolate sounded good. He was just about to sit on the couch with his hand wrapped around a mug when Susan Carol came off the elevator. She had shed her TV clothes and was wearing jeans, sneakers, and a dark blue sweater. Her overcoat was on her arm.

"Ready?" she said.

Stevie took a sip of the hot chocolate. It was very good. "Can I maybe sit here a minute and drink this?" he said. "The fire feels great."

She shook her head. "No time. Maybe when we come back. The car should be outside."

So Stevie set down his mug and followed her outside, where it had started to snow again. Several black sedans were waiting and Susan Carol walked to the first one in line. As she did, a man jumped out of the driver's seat and came around to open the door.

"Good evening, Ms. Anderson," he said. "I've got directions to the YMCA where you need to go."

"Thanks, Dave," she said. "This is my friend Steve Thomas."

Dave nodded at Stevie and put out a hand. "Nice to meet you," he said. "Ms. Anderson, it will take us about twenty, twenty-five minutes in traffic to get there."

"Great," she said.

They piled into the backseat. "Have you thought of a strategy when we get there?" Stevie asked.

"Yes," she said quietly, nodding in Dave's direction in the front seat. "I think I know what to do."

They rode in silence through the streets of Indianapolis. It was snowing harder and traffic was crawling. Stevie didn't mind. He wasn't exactly looking forward to meeting Dr. Snow—aptly named, he thought, given the weather.

They pulled up in front of a modern-looking low-slung building at a few minutes after seven.

"How long do you think you'll be, Ms. Anderson?" Dave asked as he opened the door for them, holding an umbrella over Susan Carol.

"I'm not exactly sure," she said. "But probably not more than half an hour."

"I'll just wait here then," he said. "Why don't you take my umbrella?"

"That's okay," she said. "We only have to walk a few feet to get inside."

Dave walked her those few feet to the front door, holding the umbrella over her head. Stevie trailed, saying nothing. When they were inside, he couldn't resist. "Nice to be a big TV star, I guess," he said.

"Shut up, Stevie," she said firmly and, he had to admit, not without justification.

There was no sign of anyone in the lobby except for a smiling woman with gray hair at the check-in desk.

"May I help you?" she asked when Stevie and Susan Carol approached.

"We're supposed to meet someone here," Susan Carol said. "He's about—"

"Dr. Snow?" she said, breaking in. "Are you the teenagers meeting Dr. Snow?"

"Why, yes, we are," Susan Carol said, surprised.

"He told me to look for you," she said. "If you walk down this hall to the right, the third door on your right is the conference room. He's waiting for you there."

"Thanks," Susan Carol said.

They found the conference room and Susan Carol knocked softly, then pushed the door open. A man with graying hair and a mustache was standing across the room looking out the window when they walked in.

"You're late," he said in a tone that made it clear there would be no small talk during this meeting.

"Sorry," Susan Carol said. "Traffic from downtown in the snow was slow."

Snow didn't seem to care one way or the other about why they were late.

"Let's get this over with," he said. "I've got a lot to do."

Susan Carol nodded at Stevie. "This is Steve Thomas."

"Yeah," Snow said. "The kid from CBS."

"And the *Washington Herald*," Stevie said, knowing Snow couldn't care less.

Snow sat down at a conference table in the middle of the room. Stevie and Susan Carol sat across from him.

"Tell me what exactly you expect to get from me here so we can move this along," Snow said.

"You know, it's funny, Dr. Snow, the other night you weren't in nearly so much of a rush to get away from me," Susan Carol said, flashing her smile for just a moment.

"The other night I thought you were in your twenties, and I'd been drinking," he said. "Now I know you're fourteen, I'm cold sober, and you're trying to blackmail me. What would you like me to do, offer you some candy?"

Before Susan Carol could say anything, Stevie jumped in. "Look, buddy, don't turn all sanctimonious," he said, surprising himself with his use of a big word under pressure. "You got drunk and ran your mouth trying to impress someone who, even if she *was* in her twenties, would still have been young enough to be your daughter. You are part of a big-time cover-up right now, and the only way you can get out of it is to go on the record and tell the truth."

Snow stared at him for a moment. "Just who do you think you are, kid? Edward R. Murrow?"

Stevie knew who Edward R. Murrow was from the movie *Good Night and Good Luck*. He was the CBS news anchor in the 1950s who had taken on the Communist-hunting senator Joe McCarthy and exposed him as a fraud.

"Actually, he's Woodward and I'm Bernstein," Susan Carol said. "But it doesn't really matter who we are. What matters is that we know what's going on and we want your cooperation."

"So what are you proposing I do?" Snow said. "Go on the record, get myself fired, and turn myself into a pariah throughout the entire NFL?"

"Or a hero," Susan Carol said.

He shook his head. "It won't work that way. Whistle-blowers don't become heroes until they're dead and some-one makes a movie about them."

"You don't have to go on the record," Susan Carol said. "Get us documentation of the drug tests. It must exist, right? We'll never say where we got it."

Snow looked at her for a moment, then shook his head. "I'd be breaking the law, giving you medical records."

"Aren't you breaking the law knowing evidence of ille-gal drug use is being covered up?"

"No," Snow said. "Just NFL rules." He smiled weakly.

"Get us the documents," Susan Carol said. "You aren't the only one with access to them. People can guess all they want where we got them, but we won't tell. Plus, we already have another source. You won't be our only source."

That seemed to surprise Snow. "Another source?" he said. "Who?"

Susan Carol gave him the real version of the smile. "You wouldn't want us to tell you that, would you? If we did, how could you believe we're going to protect you?"

He leaned back in his chair. "I don't think you're capable of pulling this story off without me, and if you want to scream and yell when the game's over, feel free." He paused as if thinking over his decision.

Susan Carol leaned forward. "You know what, doctor, you're right," she said. "We can probably never prove the cover-up. But the drug tests *will* come out after the game. You know that. And when I go on TV and tell people *exactly* how I knew about them before the game . . . how will that look for you? I checked the media guide. You're married with three children, aren't you?"

The snarl that Snow had worn throughout most of the meeting faded. "You would do that?"

"Not if you help us."

"I need time to think about this," he said.

"Take all the time you want," Susan Carol said. "But we tape our show tomorrow at noon. If you get me the documentation, I'll run with that and there will be no need to name you at all. If not . . ."

"Oh . . . damn," he stalled. "Give me your cell number. I will call you in the morning."

Susan Carol wrote her cell number down and passed it to him.

"You better call early," she said.

"Okay, okay," he said. "I get your message. I would have to get someone in my office in Los Angeles up early to fax them to me. . . ."

"Do what you have to do, doctor," Stevie said, his job as

tough guy made easy now by Susan Carol's complete cornering of Snow.

"Yeah, yeah," he said, standing up and walking to the door. He turned to Susan Carol. "Fourteen?" he said. "You're really fourteen?"

"Would you like to see my library card?" Susan Carol asked.

Snow didn't answer. He yanked the door open and walked out.

Susan Carol looked at Stevie. "I thought that went well, didn't you?" she said.

He shook his head and laughed. "You know what?" he said. "You're amazing. Maybe you should show *me* your library card."

"Fine," she said. "But it doesn't have my birthday on it."

14: TURNOVER!

THE TRIP BACK TO THE HOTEL didn't take very long—at least it didn't feel long to Stevie. They had decided that they really needed to track down Bobby and Tamara and let them know what was going on.

They held off on further discussions until Dave dropped them off in front of the Canterbury. It occurred to Stevie as they climbed out of the car and walked into the lobby that it was after eight o'clock and they hadn't had any dinner. "I'm starving," Stevie said.

"You want to walk over to St. Elmo's?" she said. "It's right next door."

He shook his head. "We'll never get a table."

"Yes, we will," she said. "Follow me."

They walked back outside, turned right, and walked to

the front door of St. Elmo. The entrance was packed with people, but Susan Carol was undeterred. They got to the maître d' station and were greeted by a tall man in a tuxedo.

"Welcome back!" he said to Susan Carol, leaning down to kiss her on the cheek.

Susan Carol turned to Stevie and said, "Mike D'Angelo, this is Steve Thomas. You may have seen Steve on CBS last night."

Whether D'Angelo had seen Stevie or not seemed irrelevant. He gave him a warm handshake and a smile.

"Lot of your colleagues in here," he said to both of them. "Steve, I just sat Mr. McManus's party a few minutes ago. Your crowd is downstairs, Susan Carol. Are you joining one of them, or would you like your own table?"

"If it's okay, we'd like our own table," Susan Carol said. "Is there anyplace that's a little bit quiet?"

He nodded. "Got just the spot for you. Follow me."

Mike D'Angelo delivered them to a booth in the back corner of the room farthest from the door of the restaurant. "Not exactly quiet," he said. "But as close as I can get you to it."

"It's perfect," Susan Carol said. "Thank you so much, Mike."

"Anytime," he said. "You know that."

He walked away. "So what's the deal with that?" Stevie said. "When did you charm him?"

She shook her head. "Not me," she said. "My dad. Remember I told you about the Bible study group he formed to help people addicted to sports? Mike was addicted to fantasy football—almost ruined his marriage. He heard about what Dad was doing, found some people to form a group here, and he's completely out of all fantasy sports. My dad called him and let him know I'd be in town. I met him when I came in for dinner on Monday, and he told me I could have a table anytime I wanted all week."

"Who'd you have dinner with on Monday night?" he asked.

She paused for just a moment. "Jamie," she said. "We'd just met. The network wanted us to spend some time together."

"Uh-huh."

"I told you. . . ."

"I know, I know," he said.

The waiter came and they ordered right away since it was late and they were hungry. Stevie got a laugh when he asked Susan Carol if she wanted to see a wine list.

"Okay," she said. "Let's say we get these test results tomorrow. How are we going to do this?"

"Well, I came here for the *Herald*, so I owe them first crack over CBS. But what about you? Will USTV be furious?"

"First, I don't care," she said. "Second, I'm not sure this is a story that anyone who has to negotiate TV rights with the NFL wants to touch."

Stevie hadn't thought about that. She was probably right. He couldn't imagine CBS being thrilled about a story that might blow up the Super Bowl—especially if the linemen were forced to sit out the game. In fact, there was a good chance they wouldn't be thrilled to see his name on the story if and when it broke. Oh well. Everyone had been nice to him at CBS, but he was still a writer, first and foremost.

"What do you think the chances are that Snow will actually come through?" he asked.

She shrugged. "I don't think he has much choice. He would be completely humiliated if I went on the air and repeated what happened the other night."

"Yes, but we both know you can't really do that. It all depends on whether *he* believes you can, and will."

Snow struck him as the kind of guy who would protect himself before he worried about protecting anyone else. Giving them the information was his only way out—*if* he fell for their bluff.

Their food arrived. Stevie was wolfing down a massive porterhouse steak when he heard Susan Carol's cell phone ring. He knew it was hers because it played the Duke fight song when it rang.

"Sorry," she said, putting her silverware down and reaching into her pocket. She rolled her eyes when she saw the number on her screen.

"I shouldn't answer this," she said, shaking her head. "Hi, Tal, what is it?"

She listened for a moment. "I'm at St. Elmo's, why?" More listening. "Right now?" And then: "I'm sitting upstairs with Stevie in the back room in the corner booth." She listened a moment longer, then said, "Okay, fine," and closed the phone.

"What was that?" Stevie asked.

"He's downstairs like Mike told us, with all the other guys from our crew. He said he has to talk to me right away."

"Oh God," Stevie said. "He's probably going to give you a hard time again about being with me."

"He didn't say anything when I said I was with you. He sounded strange—almost, I don't know, scared."

Stevie was about to ask her what she meant when he saw Tal Vincent approaching the table. Without so much as a hello, he slid into the booth next to Susan Carol.

"Nice to see you too, Tal," Susan Carol said, her voice dripping with sarcasm.

"Don't start," he responded. "What the hell do you think you two are up to? Have you lost what's left of your minds, trying to blackmail a team doctor?"

Stevie and Susan Carol looked at each other. Clearly, Snow had made a move they hadn't expected. Susan Carol gave Stevie a "stay calm" look.

"What are you talking about, Tal?" she said.

"You know what I'm talking about. Tom Snow called Mike Shupe about twenty minutes ago. He said you two were trying to blackmail him with a wild story about him coming on to you the other night."

"He *did* come on to me!"

"Be quiet. He said that he was trying to be nice to you and you asked him a bunch of questions about drug testing. He said he was explaining to you what happens when someone tests positive and you somehow got the idea that he was telling you someone on the team *had* actually tested positive."

"WHAT?!!" Susan Carol screamed.

Now Stevie was shooting her "calm down" looks. The one thing he knew they *didn't* want to do was tip their hand on the story to Vincent.

"Tal, he's a complete liar," Susan Carol said. "That isn't close to what happened—"

"What happened was that he tried to pick her up," Stevie said. "He's a dirtbag. We just told him that if he didn't leave her alone, we'd go public. He wouldn't stop calling her. We had to do something."

Vincent glared. "Then why's he claiming blackmail?"

"I guess we scared him too much."

"When did this become we? What have you got to do with this anyway?"

"Stevie's my friend," Susan Carol said. "I went to him for help because the guy wouldn't stop calling me. He said he didn't know I was fourteen."

"Did you tell him you were going to go on air and accuse him of coming on to you?"

She cast her eyes downward for a moment as if embarrassed. Clearly, she had picked up the idea that letting Vincent in on the whole truth was not a good idea. "I guess I did. I couldn't think of anything else to do to get him to go away."

Vincent's look softened a bit. "What's he talking about with all this drug-testing stuff?"

"I don't know," Susan Carol said. "He was bragging that half the team wouldn't be able to play without his painkillers. . . . Maybe that's his way of distracting you from the fact that he's a letch."

Vincent leaned back into the booth's seat cushion. "Okay, I'll take you at your word on that. Either way, just stay away from the guy. And whatever he said to you, there's no way it's coming up on the air—you got that?"

Stevie could see that Susan Carol was thinking the same thing he was thinking: if the threat of exposing Snow on air was gone, they weren't going to be getting any documents the next day. He'd out-maneuvered them.

Susan Carol took one last stab. "What if he keeps calling me?" she said.

"You come tell me and I'll deal with him," Vincent said. "Which is what you should have done in the first place."

He slid out of the booth. "You know something, Susan Carol? You've been a pain in the butt all week. I really don't need this teen drama. Trust me when I tell you, the people back in the office will hear about all this."

"Trust me when I tell you, I don't care," Susan Carol said.

Vincent stared at her for a second, started to say something, then turned and walked off.

"Now what?" Stevie said.

Susan Carol leaned back and sighed. "What choice do we have?" she said. "Drop back ten and punt."

By the end of dinner, they had an alternative to punting. As planned, they would bring Kelleher and Mearns into the picture. Only now they were hoping the *Washington Herald* and the *Washington Post* might both run a story about Susan Carol and her encounter with Snow. He'd deny it, but *she* was a credible source. And the newspapers weren't nearly as likely to scare off the story because of a phone call. They knew it was a long shot, but it was better than nothing.

They finished dinner, thanked Mike D'Angelo, and walked back outside because it was almost impossible to hear anyone on a cell phone from inside. Susan Carol got through to Kelleher and told him that she and Stevie needed to talk to them right away.

"An hour?" Stevie heard her say with a sigh. "Okay then. In the Marriott lobby at eleven o'clock."

She was starting to hang up when he saw her nod in response to something Kelleher had said. "As a matter of fact, we have."

Then she hung up.

"As a matter of fact we have what?"

"Gotten ourselves in trouble again," she said. "Come on, we can sit in the Canterbury lobby and have a hot chocolate while we kill time. They're at a party and can't get back to the hotel until eleven o'clock."

If the circumstances were different, Stevie might have enjoyed sitting in front of a fire sipping hot chocolate with Susan Carol sitting next to him, her legs curled up underneath her. The lobby was quiet, but they were both jumpy, looking at their watches every five minutes, except when Stevie started to look every two minutes.

Finally, at 10:45, Susan Carol said, "Come on, let's get a cab. It's too cold to walk."

"What about your car?" Stevie said.

"I told Dave to take the rest of the night off."

The doorman got them a cab. Downtown was still packed and they probably could have walked to the Marriott as quickly as they got there in the cab, but they would have been icicles by the time they arrived.

They walked into the lobby at precisely eleven o'clock and found it jammed—just as it had been all week. Kelleher and Mearns were standing right near the door, both looking concerned.

"I hope you were joking about being in trouble again," Kelleher said. "But something tells me you weren't."

"Nope," Susan Carol said. "We need a quiet place to talk."

"Follow me," Kelleher said.

He led them up the escalator to the second floor. They walked past radio row—quiet now, except for a couple of West Coast stations that were still on the air—around the corner, and past a room marked MEDIA HOSPITALITY, which was packed. They walked all the way down the hall, until Kelleher opened the door to one of the many conference rooms.

"They never lock these rooms," he said. He felt around on the wall until he found a light switch. The room was set up for some kind of meeting the next morning but was completely empty at the moment. They pulled four chairs into a circle and sat down.

"Okay," Bobby said. "What have you two gotten into this time?"

Susan Carol walked them through the story, with Stevie throwing in details along the way. Every so often Kelleher and Mearns looked at each other and shook their heads in disbelief. Neither one of them interrupted until Susan Carol had finished her description of Vincent interrupting their dinner after Snow's frantic phone call to Mike Shupe.

"You guys are amazing," Bobby said. "You remind me of that *Peanuts* character Pigpen, who had dirt following him wherever he went. You guys have stories—messy stories no one would believe—following you around."

Tamara stood up. "Too true," she said. "But what are we going to do? We need a cleanup plan."

Kelleher nodded. "It's your story," he said, looking at Stevie and Susan Carol. "What do you think we ought to do?"

Susan Carol looked at Stevie. "Go ahead," he said. "This all started because you wore high heels."

"Nice," she said. Then she turned to Kelleher and Mearns. "Bobby, I think you should call Dr. Snow," she said. "For one thing, that'll let him know the circle has widened and that there are adults involved now. Tell him the *Herald* and the *Post* are planning to do stories on Saturday in which I will describe our conversation at the party on Tuesday night—in detail. But if he'd like to go on the record, or if he can produce the documents we asked for, we'd prefer to run with the real story and not make him the focus."

Mearns looked at Susan Carol. "I want you to think seriously about this for a minute," she said. "We believe you, of course. But if we accuse this guy of coming on to you, the team and maybe even the league are going to come *after* you. They're going to call you a liar; they're going to try to say you encouraged him in some way, that you lied about your age—whatever it takes to undercut you and your story. They will call you names that will make your parents very unhappy—no matter how untrue they are."

"And there will be people who will believe them," Kelleher added.

Susan Carol looked a bit stunned.

"We aren't trying to talk you out of anything," Mearns said. "But you need to understand what the possible consequences of going forward are. You already found out tonight how quickly someone working for an NFL team can get to a big-time TV executive. They'll come after you with every bit of power they have—and they've got plenty."

"What if we can get Brennan to go on the record?" Stevie asked.

"You've already explained why it would be suicide for him to go on the record," Bobby said.

"But if they try to smear Susan Carol and he knows they're lying, I'll bet he'd come to her defense."

"Are you willing to bet her reputation, and maybe her future as a reporter, on it?" Mearns asked.

Stevie took a deep breath. "Obviously, that's not my decision to make," he said.

They all looked at Susan Carol. It was now her turn to take a deep breath.

"How about this," she said finally. "Bobby, you make the call first thing in the morning. See what Dr. Snow says. Then we can decide what to do next."

Kelleher stood up. "I think that sounds like a plan," he said. "Let's all get some sleep. Tomorrow could be a long day."

He smiled. "Friday is usually the easy day at the Super Bowl. No access to the players, or even the Dome. Just a press conference here in the Marriott with the two coaches and then one with the commissioner."

"Yeah," Mearns said. "They call it his 'state of the game' address. Too bad he's got no idea what the state of his game is right now."

15: INTERCEPTED

STEVIE NORMALLY DIDN'T HAVE TROUBLE SLEEPING. But he found himself tossing and turning, and when he did fall asleep, he kept dreaming that Dr. Snow was trying to kidnap Susan Carol and he'd snap awake again. When he woke up a third time and saw that it was just a few minutes before six a.m., he decided to give up.

He took a long shower, got dressed, and went downstairs to the lobby, where he bought a copy of the *Indianapolis Star* and then poured himself a cup of coffee from the lobby table that offered free coffee and little pastries. He plopped down on a couch, wondering if Susan Carol had gotten up to swim.

He was reading a story on why Don Meeker had surpassed Dan Snyder as the least-liked owner in the NFL when he sensed someone standing over him. "Couldn't sleep either?" He looked up and saw Susan Carol, sipping her own cup of coffee.

"You didn't swim?" he said.

She shook her head. "Day off. I told Jason I would meet him tomorrow morning instead."

"He seems nice. Good swimmer too."

She nodded. "Yeah, for an old guy." She sat down next to him on the couch. "He told me he swims back home with Clay F. Britt."

"Who is Clay F. Britt?"

Her eyes went wide. "You don't know who Clay F. Britt is? He's a legend. Back in the—"

She was mercifully interrupted by the arrival of Bobby and Tamara. "I guess no one slept in this morning," Kelleher said.

"Did you make the call?" Susan Carol asked.

"I thought I would wait until after seven o'clock," Kelleher said. "Don't want the guy to claim he told me something because I woke him up. Why don't we get some breakfast, then I'll call him."

They all agreed on that. The coffee shop was virtually empty. "Not too many early risers during Super Bowl week," Tamara commented.

"You see someone at this hour, they're as likely to be coming in as going out," Bobby agreed.

They ate quietly, Kelleher giggling as he read the story on Don Meeker. "According to this, people who work in his house are given written instructions on how to behave,"

Kelleher said. "Among them are: do not speak to Mr. Meeker unless spoken to, do not enter a room Mr. Meeker is in without permission, and *never* look Mr. Meeker in the eye unless he is speaking to you."

"Boss of the year," Tamara replied.

By the time they finished, it was almost 7:30. "Time to see if our boy is up," Kelleher said.

He took out his cell phone and walked to the front door, dialing as he went. "You guys wait inside," he said. "No need for you to freeze too."

He was back a few minutes later. "He's going to call me back," he said. "I told him he had until noon and then we would alert our editors the story was coming. I told him not to bother calling anyone at the newspapers because they weren't going to roll over and play dead like the TV guys."

"How did he sound?" Stevie asked.

"Pissed," Kelleher said. "Extremely pissed. Look, Tamara and I have to go to a radio studio for a show back home. We'll call you when we hear something. Where will you be?"

"I don't have anything until the coaches' press conference at eleven," said Stevie.

"I have to be at the Dome at eight-thirty," Susan Carol said. "We're supposed to interview someone for tonight's show."

"Who?" Stevie asked.

"I have no idea. I think they were trying to get one of the general managers. No players are available today, and we've already had both coaches."

"Well, keep your cells on," Kelleher said. "I'll call as soon as I hear something."

He and Mearns headed for the door along with Susan Carol. Stevie was left alone to either sit in the lobby and worry or sit in his room and worry. He opted for the room. Even after two cups of coffee, he was exhausted. It wasn't quite eight a.m.

✦ ✦ ✦

Stevie didn't even realize he had fallen asleep until the phone woke him up. He looked at the clock and was surprised to see it was almost ten. He had finally slept without having a bad dream. He picked up the phone hoping it was Kelleher. It wasn't.

"Meet me in the lobby in five minutes."

It was Susan Carol. "What? What's going on?"

"I'll tell you when I get there. Bye."

Stevie was tempted to take another shower to clear the cobwebs from his head, but the sound of her voice made him decide not to keep her waiting. He splashed some water on his face and grabbed his coat and phone.

Susan Carol was walking in the door when he got downstairs. The lobby was now back to normal—packed—and she waved him in the direction of the door as soon as she saw him.

"What's up?" he said as they walked outside.

He noticed she was shivering, even though it was a bright, sunny day and it felt much warmer than any day since their arrival.

"He c-called," she said. "He s-says he'll m-meet with us and only us and g-give us the documents."

"What?! Where? When? Why?" Stevie sputtered.

"Walk me back to my hotel and I'll explain."

They set off, and Susan Carol began slowly. "There are two stories to tell," she said. "I'll go in order because it's easier."

Stevie nodded, so she continued.

"When I got over to the Dome, Tal was all excited about who he'd gotten to be our guest for tonight."

"Let me guess," he said. "Dr. Snow."

She shook her head. "Better. Don Meeker."

Stevie almost tripped. "What?! Little Donny doing a TV interview?"

"It's better than that," she said. "Apparently the deal they made was that he had approval over all the questions. Remember how we used to do our interviews? We'd just ask whatever came into our heads, right? Not today. The questions were all set up for us on the prompter when we got there. And if you ask me, Meeker didn't just approve the questions, he *wrote* them. My first question—I am *not* making this up—was 'Mr. Meeker, why do you think the media refuse to write or talk about all the work you've done for charity over the years?'"

"Oh God," Stevie said. "What else?"

"Everything was like that. Jamie had to ask one about the media being jealous of him because he's a self-made billionaire, and I had to ask about his 'brilliant' free-agent signings that people kept giving credit to Eric DaCosta for."

"Why credit the general manager when you can credit the owner, right?"

"Exactly. I mean, it was sickening. Meeker was practically cuddly, talking to us like we were a couple of little kids and explaining just how mean all these people have been to him. When he left, I told Tal that I thought the whole thing was a disgrace."

"What'd he say?"

"He said we had an exclusive no one else in town had and that I should spare him my teenage righteous indignation."

"What an idiot. Did you point out that an infomercial hardly qualifies as an exclusive?"

"Hang on, I'm coming to the important part. I go and get my makeup off and I'm thinking I need a long bath just to get all the slime off me, when I turn on my phone and there's a message from Snow."

Stevie had almost forgotten there was a part two to this story.

"I call him back, and he says to me he won't deal with Bobby because Meeker really hates him and he doesn't trust him."

"Well, that's a bunch of—"

She held her hand up. "I know. Just listen. He said he'll only meet with us, that if Bobby or Tamara show up, he'll walk and take his chances."

"That sounds like a trap if I ever heard one," Stevie said. "Keep the adults away."

"That's what I said to him. He said he doesn't want to

risk being seen with Bobby or even talking to him again. He said there was no point giving us proof *and* being pegged as a source. He'll give us the test results, but Bobby can't mention him in the story."

"Huh—there's a certain weird logic to that. . . ."

"Yeah. So he'll meet us at eleven o'clock at this place called Union Station. It's one of those old train stations they built into a mall. It's only a couple blocks from the Canterbury. It will be crowded, which means I've got to go put on a big coat and a cap or something so people won't recognize me. You probably should wear a hat too just to be safe."

"Hang on a minute," he said. "We need to at least tell Bobby what's happening."

They were walking into the lobby of the Canterbury. Susan Carol nodded. "You're right. Why don't you call Bobby while I go upstairs and change. See what he thinks we ought to do to cover ourselves."

She left him in the lobby. Stevie walked back outside to call Kelleher. When he explained the latest plot twist, Bobby let out a long whistle. "That definitely sounds like a setup," he said. "Even in a crowded mall, I don't like it. He's clearly up to something. Problem is, Tamara and I are tied up here for another hour. Maybe you should call Snow back and postpone the meeting."

Stevie was shaking his head, even though Bobby couldn't see him. "We do that, he'll figure we're on to him and he might bail out completely," he said. "We need to go, but we need to go with some protection because—" He stopped. A light had just gone off inside his head.

"Stevie?" Bobby said.

"Yeah, sorry. I've got an idea. Let me call you back."

He hung up and thought for a second about waiting for Susan Carol to come back downstairs. He decided against it—time was of the essence—and quickly dialed Eddie Brennan's cell phone number. Brennan picked up on the first ring. "Stevie, what's up?" he said.

"A lot," Stevie answered. "No time to really explain now, but we may have a way to get this story without needing you as a source. But we could use some help."

"Name it."

Stevie quickly explained to Brennan about the meeting with Snow and their suspicion that it was a trap.

"Don't go," Eddie said.

"We have to," Stevie said. "Maybe he has the test results on him. Maybe if he makes a mistake of some kind, then he'll have to give them to us. If we don't go, we're nowhere."

"What do you need me to do?" Brennan asked.

"Is there any way you can send a couple of your security guys to Union Station? Have them follow us in, and if they see anything going on, they can jump in and stop it."

"Bad idea," Brennan said. "Snow will recognize them, and then he'll figure that I sent them since he knows I've been talking to you during the week. What you need are some security types he *won't* know. Hey, wait a minute. . . ."

"What?" Stevie asked.

"I've got an idea," Brennan said. "It may be a little risky, but it could work."

"I'm listening," Stevie said.

Susan Carol came back downstairs just as he was hanging up with Eddie Brennan. "You reach Bobby?" she asked.

"Yes, and he can't come," he said. "But we've got backup. Come on, I'll tell you about it while we walk over."

They walked briskly in the direction of Union Station. With the sun out, even though the temperature was still in the low forties, people were clogging the streets. They walked up the steps to the shops level of the mall, which was teeming with people too.

Snow was waiting near the pizza place he had mentioned, looking a little out of place in a dark sports coat. He wasn't wearing a tie, but he was wearing a scowl. There were no hellos and no small talk.

"Okay, Dr. Snow. We're here," Susan Carol said. "Where are the documents?"

"You can't possibly expect me to just hand something like that to you right here in front of all these people, can you?" he said.

Stevie's trouble antenna went up. "You're the one who picked this place."

Snow was looking around as if he were afraid he had been followed.

Susan Carol said firmly, "Look, doctor, if you were bluffing or something . . ."

"I'm not bluffing," Snow said, dropping his voice to a

whisper that could barely be heard above the din. "One of my partners is here with me." He looked around again. "He's on the other side of the mall, near the movie theaters. It's quieter there. He's got the documents. Let's walk."

"After you." Stevie walked as slowly as possible. "This place is enormous," he called up to Snow. "Where are the movie theaters?"

Snow glared at him and kept walking. Even with her cap on, Stevie noticed that Susan Carol drew some curious glances, the kind that said, "I think I know that person, but I'm not sure why. . . ."

They rounded a corner, following a sign that said UNION STATION CINEMAS—PARKING GARAGE.

The crowds thinned noticeably. They came up on the movie theater area—which was empty since, according to the sign out front, the first shows weren't until one o'clock. There was no one in sight.

"He probably walked down the hall or something," Snow said. "He paces when he's nervous."

"Well, then he'll pace back here by the theater soon, right?"

"Let's just walk around the corner and see if he's there," said Snow.

As they rounded a corner, Stevie saw two men step from the shadows. They were both huge and looked familiar. In a split second, he knew just who they were: Don Meeker's bodyguards.

"About time," one of them said.

He took Stevie firmly by the arm, while the other one did the same to Susan Carol.

"Okay," Snow said. "Just stay calm and you'll be out of here in about five minutes."

16: GOAL-LINE STAND

THE TWO BODYGUARDS led Stevie and Susan Carol a few yards farther down the hall to a door marked NO ADMITTANCE. One of them opened the door and pushed them inside.

The room was dimly lit with packing boxes on the floor and more boxes stacked on shelves around the room. There was a small table in the middle. It looked to Stevie like a combination storage/break room for the people who worked at the mall. There was no one inside.

"Have a seat," one of the bodyguards said, shoving Stevie in the direction of a chair. Stevie sat. Susan Carol was seated in much the same manner an instant later. Snow walked around to the other side of the table looking very smug.

"What's going on here?!" Stevie said loudly.

"Calm down, no need to shout."

"Oh, I think we have plenty of reason to be worried. You walk us through the mall, past the empty theaters, and down an empty hall, where two of Don Meeker's bodyguards grab us and shove us in a room marked NO ADMITTANCE!"

"Well, not so cool when someone else has the upper hand, are you? Now you listen to me. This is the last conversation we're going to have. You are going to stop threatening me and stop blackmailing me." He nodded at the two bodyguards standing behind them. "Mike and Moe are here this time to get your attention. You don't want to cross paths with them again."

"So I guess it's fair to say that you're now threatening *us*," Susan Carol said.

"It's not a threat," Snow said. "It's a promise. Here's the deal: you want to tell your silly story—go ahead. I did a Google search on you, sweetie. Your daddy is a minister, isn't he? What do you think Reverend Anderson will think when he hears his little angel was drinking and throwing herself at a married man?"

Susan Carol waved her hand at him. "My dad would never believe something that ridiculous."

"Maybe not. But other people will. Especially when Mr. Meeker admits you were flirting with *him* at the NFL party the other night. Mike and Moe were there—right, boys?"

"Absolutely," said one.

"I was there too," Stevie said.

"Ah, yes," Snow said. "But who will people believe?

A respected doctor and an NFL owner or two teenagers?"

"Oh please. Look at *her* and look at you two old guys. *No one* would believe she was interested in you."

"Hmmm—you could have a point there, Steve. But sadly, Susan Carol, your boss at USTV also mentioned to Mr. Meeker this morning that you've been all over your new partner this week."

"What?!" Susan Carol said, jumping out of her chair. "That's crazy, and Jamie will say so too."

Snow just smiled his oily smile. "Mr. Whitsitt is very popular with the tabloids—he's denied a lot of things lately."

Mike or Moe put a hand on her shoulder and pushed her back into the chair.

"Kill the story and none of this ever comes up," Snow said. "For now, just so you understand that I'm not kidding, you two are going to spend some time here with the boys."

"You said this would be over in five minutes," Stevie said, now starting to get scared.

"I lied," Snow said. "I'll be going now. . . ."

The door suddenly opened, pushed hard from the outside. Stevie swiveled his head just in time to see Darin Kerns bolt inside followed by two well-dressed men. Before Mike or Moe could make a move to defend themselves, the two men in suits had grabbed their arms and twisted them behind their backs. A second later, Mike and Moe were on the floor, facedown, squirming.

One of the men in suits leaned down and said, "If you stop fighting, you won't get your arm broken. Lie still—*now!*"

Darin Kerns had Snow with his arm behind his back as well. Snow was grimacing in pain. "Same for you, doctor," Kerns said. "I'm not a pro like these boys, though, so I might hurt you even if I don't mean to. So do yourself a favor and stay very still."

"Who the hell are you?" Snow said.

Kerns smiled. "We're the good guys. We come to the rescue of kids being bullied by sleazebag doctors and oversized bodyguards who work for a punk like Donny Meeker.

"Did you get what you needed here?" Kerns asked.

"Not so far," Stevie said. "I'm betting he doesn't have any documents on him either."

Kerns quickly checked Snow's pockets. He shook his head. "Nothing."

"I can have the Indy police here in about five minutes," said one of the men in suits. Stevie now recognized him as Vernon Holley—the Ravens' security guy he'd met while interviewing Steve Bisciotti. "At the very least, they'd all be charged with detaining two minors. Maybe kidnapping too."

Susan Carol was shaking her head. "We don't want that. We don't need to answer any questions about this right now."

"Your call," Kerns said.

He gave Snow a shake. "Here's the deal. You threaten these kids again and you will go to jail. All three of us can testify you were holding them against their will. And given who these two thugs work for, it won't be hard to prove *he* was the one who set this up. How would that look—Mr. Meeker in jail, maybe on Super Bowl Sunday."

Snow's shoulders sagged. "Fine. Let us go now and we'll call it all even. You keep quiet, sweet thing, and we'll keep quiet too."

"Go to hell!" Susan Carol said, surprising Stevie with both her use of the word and the emphatic tone with which she used it.

"Let 'em up," Kerns told Vernon and the other man.

"Fair fight, you wouldn't have a chance," Mike or Moe said.

"I was in homicide for twenty-three years," said Vernon. "Take your best shot."

Mike or Moe looked carefully at Vernon. He had at least a seventy-five-pound weight advantage, but clearly, Vernon was not someone to be messed with.

"Come on, Doc," he said. "We've done what we came to do. Let's get out of here."

The three of them headed for the door.

"Remember," Kerns said. "Come near them again . . ."

"Yeah, yeah," Snow said. "Believe me, I have *no* desire to see either one of them ever again."

He slammed the door on the way out.

"Great guy, huh?" Stevie said. He pulled his cell phone from his shirt pocket and pressed the disconnect button. Within seconds, the phone started to ring. Stevie smiled when he saw the number come up on the screen.

"Hey, Eddie, everything went great," he said. "Thank goodness for modern technology. I guess you could hear us loud and clear?"

"I could," Eddie said. "Whatever kind of phone you've

got, they could make a commercial about the sound quality."

"Oh yeah—I'm sure lots of cellular customers will be signing on for the anti-kidnap plan. Just keep the line open, hide the phone in your pocket, and keep shouting out your location!"

Eddie laughed. "So, I'm guessing the good doctor didn't have anything for you."

"No. Don't worry, though—we'll figure something out. You go to practice and worry about the game."

"We're on the bus right now," Eddie said. "I'll check with you guys later."

◆　◆　◆

Kerns insisted on giving them a ride back to the Marriott, where Bobby and Tamara were no doubt waiting impatiently.

On the way, Kerns filled in the rest of the story: "I was in the locker room doing paperwork when Eddie called. He said you two were in trouble and might need backup. So I grabbed Vernon and Joe and we headed over to the mall, and Eddie called us with your location. Eddie said you guys were hoping to get some documents. Are they very important?" asked Kerns.

"Extremely," Susan Carol said. "Do you want us to tell you what it's about?"

"Actually, given that it apparently involves the team we're playing on Sunday, I guess I'd rather *not* know. I'm no good at keeping secrets."

The ride to the Marriott only took a couple minutes. Stevie and Susan Carol thanked Kerns and Joe and Vernon profusely as they got out. "Do us a favor," Vernon said. "Try to stay out of trouble the rest of the weekend."

They both said they would do their best. But as they watched the car pull away, Stevie couldn't help but laugh. "What do you think the chances are," he said, "that we're going to stay out of trouble the rest of the weekend?"

"Given our history?" Susan Carol said, laughing now too. "I'd say pretty close to zero."

Susan Carol paused in front of the doors. "You know why I like you so much?" she said.

"Because I help you get into trouble?"

She shook her head. "No. Because you can always make me laugh, even when I'm scared half to death."

He looked up at her. "I didn't think you ever got scared," he said.

She kissed him and then wrapped her arms around him. He hugged her back and they stood there for several seconds, Stevie not wanting to stop. She finally pulled back, her arms still loosely around him, and said, "I feel better now."

"Good enough to face Bobby and Tamara?" Stevie asked.

"That might require another kiss."

◆　◆　◆

Kelleher and Mearns were waiting for them inside the media workroom. Tamara was reading the *New York Times* and Bobby was on his cell. He hung up when he saw the two of them approaching.

"I *promised* your dad that I'd make sure you stayed out of trouble!" he said.

He was smiling, but he made it clear he wasn't happy with either of them. "I'm all for aggressive reporting, you both know that," he said. "But that was an unnecessary risk. What did you gain?"

"Well, we know Meeker is really deeply into this if his bodyguards are involved."

"Yeah—and it's possible that someone at USTV is involved too. Or maybe Dr. Snow was just lying when he said Tal told Meeker I was into Jamie," added Susan Carol.

"Okay," said Tamara, "we need to figure out what to do next. We're a little more than forty-eight hours from kickoff and not close to having enough proof to write a story. As of this moment, the bad guys win this one—the cheaters get to play, and Meeker gets away with his cover-up."

"What if," Stevie said, "we talk to the commissioner after his press conference. He's in a much better position to investigate than we are."

Bobby looked at Tamara. "I'm not sure that's a good idea," he said. "Given all the constraints put on the league by the union, even he might not be able to get the information before game time. To be honest, he might not want to try too hard. I mean, what an embarrassment."

"You think he'd cover it up?" Susan Carol said.

"No. No, I don't," Kelleher said. "But he's an official— he'd have to go through proper channels on something as big as this. He's not really in a position to move quickly."

"Well, then," Stevie said, "where does that leave us?"

"We could try another bluff," Kelleher said. "Susan Carol, you got Meeker's cell phone number the other day, right?"

"Yeah."

"I could call him and tell him I've got evidence of the positive test and the cover-up. He's so hot-tempered, he might bite."

"Except he knows we're onto the whole thing already," Stevie said. "He'll probably be careful."

"Maybe," Kelleher said. "Might be worth a try, though. . . ."

Stevie heard the Duke fight song. Susan Carol pulled out her cell and looked at the number. "Well," she said, "this might be something."

"Who is it?" Stevie asked.

"Eddie Brennan," she said, flipping the phone open.

Susan Carol had to walk out of the room to get better phone reception, so Stevie, Kelleher, and Mearns couldn't hear the conversation.

It was almost one o'clock. A PA announcement was telling people the commissioner's press conference would begin in five minutes in ballroom C.

Susan Carol came back in, closing her phone. "Stevie, I think your phone is off," she said. "Eddie said he got voice mail. He wants us to meet him at the Dome after practice," she said.

"Why?" Stevie asked, checking his phone and seeing he *had* accidentally turned it off.

"I'm not sure exactly," Susan Carol said. "He just said, 'Enough is enough, we need to settle this.' He wants to meet us in one of the owner's boxes so we'll have complete privacy. He says he can set it up."

"We might have trouble getting in the building," Kelleher said. "It's off-limits to the media until Sunday."

"He's making arrangements for us to get in through the back loading dock," Susan Carol said. "Power of being a star. But . . ."

"What?" Tamara said.

"He doesn't want you guys there. He's afraid if the four of us show up it will draw too much attention."

Kelleher was shaking his head vehemently. "We just had this conversation," he said. "I already feel guilty about what happened this morning. I can't let you guys go off on your own again."

"This is different," Susan Carol said.

"Bobby, relax. I don't think Eddie Brennan is laying a trap for them," Tamara said. "Why would he?"

Kelleher sighed and looked at Mearns. "Are you sure we want to have kids?" he said.

"Cats aren't a lot of trouble, you know," she said.

"Let's go listen to the commissioner," he said. "We've got two hours to figure out what to do."

Stevie had read that Roger Goodell was only forty-seven when he was named commissioner. He looked younger, with his wavy blond hair and snappy, perfectly fitted blue suit. His comments were pretty predictable: selecting Indianapolis to host the Super Bowl had been a masterstroke on the part of the owners; the new dome was spectacular; he anticipated a great game and was proud of the fact that an expansion team had reached the Super Bowl in only its third season. The questions were, for the most part, ho-hum. The local TV people wanted him to talk about what he had enjoyed most in Indianapolis. "Today's weather!" he replied enthusiastically, then went on to talk about the "remarkable" hospitality everyone had experienced all week.

It was Mark Maske of the *Washington Post*, someone Tamara had introduced Stevie to during one of the media sessions in the Dome, who finally asked a question that got Stevie's attention. There were rumblings, Maske said, that the new drug-testing system was less than perfect, that positive tests might be "slipping through the cracks."

Goodell had obviously been prepped that such a question might be coming. "No system is perfect right out of the chute, Mark," he said. "We knew and the union knew that once we got into blood testing, especially with the need to confirm any positive test with a B sample, there would be complications. But I think the fact that we've tested every player in the league, some on several occasions, and had only twenty-seven suspensions since training camp is proof the system is working—and also proof that the HGH problem may not be as widespread as some people feared. Twenty-seven positives out of close to two thousand tests isn't awful."

Stevie and Susan Carol looked at each other. Did Maske know something that would cause him to ask such a question? Mearns read their minds. "Mark's good," she said. "But there's been talk about trouble with the new system. He's just on top of that—nothing more."

When the session was over, they filed out with every other media person in the city and then made plans to go get the real story.

Kelleher agreed Stevie and Susan Carol could go alone, but he extracted a promise.

"If you check in with us every fifteen minutes, I won't call your parents and tell them what's going on."

Stevie wondered if he was joking. It didn't look like he was. "How about every thirty minutes?"

"Nope," Kelleher said. "Every fifteen. If you go past fifteen minutes once, I call Dome security or the cops or both. You can take turns making the call."

"Okay then, Dad," said Stevie.

Tamara snickered.

"Fine, laugh—but *call* me."

They left the hotel shortly after three o'clock. Stevie and Susan Carol circled to the far side of the Dome in search of the loading dock as directed by Eddie. Stevie was very happy that the day was relatively warm because the walk took a good fifteen minutes. As they approached the dock, they saw several police cars with their lights flashing and three buses.

"Whoa," Susan Carol said. "Let's wait until they pull out of here. No need to take a chance on running into Snow getting on one of those buses."

They angled over to stand in the shadow of the building while the players, still in uniform but with their cleats off, trudged out to the bus.

"This is the only day they actually practice in the Dome—but I guess they shower back at the hotel," Susan Carol said. "Why don't you call Kelleher while we're waiting."

Stevie nodded, dialed Kelleher, and told him they were about to walk into the Dome.

"Call me again in fifteen minutes," Kelleher said. "You were a minute late this time, but I cut you some slack because I know it's a long walk around the building."

Stevie recognized Coach Skyler Kaplow, dressed in a Dreams sweatshirt, walking to the bus. If Snow was with the group, they didn't see him. They waited until the police escort pulled out with the buses following and then walked the last few yards to the loading dock entrance. As soon as they reached the bottom of the ramp, they found several security guards.

"Can we help you?" one of them asked.

"I'm with CBS," Stevie said, flashing his credential. "I think you have our names there anyway—Steve Thomas and Susan Carol Anderson?"

"Uh-uh," the guard said. "There are no names and no list today. If you're CBS, you have to go back around to the front entrance. . . ."

Stevie was about to become exasperated when another guard walked up from behind. "Actually, they're okay, Frank," he said. "They're with Brennan. He told me about them coming in." He smiled. "Sorry, kids, I had to go inside to show Ed to the elevator. Follow me, he's waiting for you."

Relieved, Stevie and Susan Carol followed the guard into the hallway.

"So, couple of kid reporters getting an exclusive with Eddie Brennan, huh?" the guard said. "Boy, is he a good guy."

"Great guy," Susan Carol said, turning on the smile.

"Yeah," the guard said. "He told me the team has the rest of the day off, so he had some extra time for you."

They had reached an elevator bank. The guard pushed the UP button and the door opened immediately. He stepped onto it, turned a key of some kind, and hit 6.

"Just turn right when you get off on six and go about a hundred yards," he said, stepping out of the elevator. "It's box twenty-four. It'll be Meeker's box on Sunday."

Stevie shuddered just a bit at the thought of walking into Don Meeker's box. But Susan Carol boldly knocked on the door.

"Come in!" a voice said.

They opened the door. As promised, Eddie Brennan was waiting for them. But he wasn't alone.

"Come on in, guys," Brennan said. "I want you to meet someone."

17: HAIL MARY!

FOR A MOMENT, Stevie semi-panicked. Brennan was wearing a friendly smile, though, and he decided he would look like a fool if he grabbed Susan Carol and made a run for it.

"Stevie, Susan Carol, this is Bob Arciero," Brennan said, nodding at a man with jet-black hair, graying at the temples, and wire-rimmed glasses. He was smiling too as the four of them met in the middle of the box to shake hands. Stevie noticed that the box was spacious, but nothing like the one he had met Steve Bisciotti in a couple of days earlier. "Bob is another one of our team doctors. He's the orthopedic surgeon who fixed my shoulder a couple years ago."

"Did a hell of a job too, if I say so myself," Arciero said, laughing.

"He's known for his modesty," Brennan said. At that point he stopped smiling. "And unlike Dr. Snow, he's also known for his honesty. So when I saw him here today, I told Coach Kaplow that I needed to stay behind this afternoon so he could look at my shoulder."

Arciero shook his head. "I feel so bad about this. Eddie just filled me in on what's gone on this week. What Meeker and Snow are doing is beyond inexcusable. To be honest, I'm shocked the coaches are allowing it, but I'm sure Meeker told them all they'd be fired if they opened their mouths."

"You mean you didn't know anything about it?" Susan Carol said.

Arciero shook his head emphatically. "Not until just now. Like Eddie said, I'm the orthopedic surgeon. So I'm not around every day. But now that I *do* know, I'm not going to sit idly by and allow this to happen."

"What can you do?" Stevie said.

"I can get you the results of the drug tests," Arciero said calmly.

Stevie and Susan Carol looked at each other.

"I should have gone to Bob with this sooner," Brennan said. "I wasn't thinking straight until Darin filled me in on the details of what Snow did to you two. Then I got mad."

"*How*," Susan Carol said to Arciero, "can you get the drug tests?"

"The test results should be on file at the team's training facility. One of the other doctors in my practice is still in L.A. and can go over there this afternoon and pull the records."

"They'll just let him walk in and do that?"

"Of course. We all have access to the medical files of all our players. They probably won't even ask him why he needs to get into the files, but if they do, he'll just say he needs to pull some information on game-day meds that I need."

"And the drug tests will be in the files?" Stevie said.

"I suspect that's the *only* place they'll be. If they're trying to hide them, they'd get someone to 'lose' the results at the lab, where they don't know who has access to files and who doesn't. But at the training facility, the only people who have access to the files are the team's medical staff. Gus, that's my partner, can fax them to me today and then bring hard copies with him when he flies in tomorrow."

Stevie looked at Susan Carol. "That would be perfect," she said. "If we've got the documents, you don't need to go on record, Eddie."

Brennan nodded. "Which, to be honest, is important. If the other players knew I was involved in this, I might not survive the game on Sunday."

Arciero agreed. "That's for sure," he said. "Cheaters aren't the bad guys in professional sports; the ones who expose the cheating are."

"But if we write the story to run on Sunday, what do you think will happen?" Stevie asked.

"I don't know," Brennan said. "I doubt the league will suspend the guys on the day of the Super Bowl. It will be a bombshell, but I think we'll still play the game."

"How will you feel if you win?" Susan Carol said.

"I'm not sure," Brennan said. "I mean, I want to play. I

want to *win*. But all I've been able to think about this week are the drugs that *I* didn't even take! I feel like I've got to help you to clear my own head. I couldn't do nothing. But I can't go on record. . . ."

"Because your teammates would hate you?" asked Stevie.

"Oh yeah."

"But how do you feel about *them*? Your teammates who tested positive?" Stevie asked.

"I'm torn," Brennan said. "They're my friends. I like them all. I even understand why guys feel like HGH could help their careers. The chance to make big money in this sport doesn't usually last long. But I can't condone this. I just can't."

They were all silent for a moment. "If we're going to do this," Arciero said, "I should call Gus right away."

Stevie and Susan Carol looked at Brennan.

"Make the call," he said.

Arciero pulled out his cell phone and started dialing.

In the end, they decided faxing the reports was a bad idea. The fax would have to go to the hotel, and it was too dangerous to have some hotel employee looking at the test results and deciding he had important information that should be shared with, say, ESPN or USTV.

Arciero agreed to have his partner take a red-eye out of Los Angeles. He would land in Chicago early Saturday morning and be in Indianapolis in time for breakfast. That would give Arciero plenty of time to get the documents to

Stevie and Susan Carol and allow them to write something for Sunday's paper.

"I will drive downtown with the documents myself," Arciero said.

They were all shaking hands when Stevie's cell phone started ringing. Seeing the number, he smiled. "Whoops. Forgot to call Bobby."

He could hear Susan Carol explaining their deal with Kelleher to Brennan and Arciero while he talked. "We'll be back in a few minutes," he said. "Everything is okay."

But even still, Stevie caught himself looking over his shoulder a couple times as they circled back around the Dome.

"What are you looking for?" Susan Carol asked.

"Not sure," Stevie said. "Mike and Moe? Snow? Anyone? I just keep thinking something is bound to happen."

"I know what you mean," Susan Carol said. "Look, we're still a long way from getting this done. Even if we do get those documents, you can bet the lawyers at the *Herald* are going to have a lot of questions."

"Lawyers?" he said. "Why would a newspaper have lawyers?"

She gave him the "you are too stupid to live" look. "Every newspaper has lawyers," she said. "The TV networks do too. You can't just print a story accusing someone of something like this without being a hundred percent sure you've got it right. Newspapers don't like getting sued. There's an old saying in the newspaper business that if you lose a lawsuit, you might lose a printing press."

"How do you know everything about everything?"

She smiled. "I think it's called reading? You may have heard of it while you were watching *Daily News Live*, once upon a time."

"Now you sound like my mother."

"Remarkably smart woman, your mother."

A minute later, they walked into the Marriott and found Kelleher and Mearns waiting for them. They sat down in the lounge and Stevie and Susan Carol filled them in.

"Brennan is really out on a limb here," Kelleher commented. "Anyone finds out he's involved in this, his career could be over."

"But why?" Susan Carol said. "He's doing the right thing."

"According to you and me and most reasonable people," Bobby said. "But in the culture of the locker room, he'd be nothing but a snitch."

"The drug-test results will come out eventually anyway," Stevie said. "He's not turning his teammates in as much as he's exposing Meeker's cover-up."

"You're being logical, Stevie," Tamara said. "You can't apply logic in situations like these."

They had to figure out a plan to get a story written the next day when the documents were in hand, and decide where the story should run. There was no way the *Post* and the *Herald* were going to agree to run the same story written by the same writers. "My editors won't be at all happy with this story breaking in the *Herald*," Tamara said. "But Stevie's here for the *Herald* and Susan Carol isn't here for the *Post*. You should write it for the *Herald*."

"What's going to happen when the story breaks?" Stevie asked.

Kelleher sat back in his seat. "Honestly? I don't know," he said. "All hell will break loose, that much I guarantee. The league will have to decide whether to try to suspend the players for the game. They probably can't, really, since the rules require a second test to be positive too."

"True," Tamara said. "But the league can't just sit back and do nothing. An owner has manipulated the rules—completely ignored them, actually. There's no way Goodell will want to hand the Lombardi Trophy to Meeker on Sunday night after this story breaks on Sunday morning."

Susan Carol, who had been staring at a TV screen over Kelleher's shoulder, snapped back into the conversation. "You want to know the truth?" she said. "At this point, I don't care what the league does on Sunday. I don't know what the solution is. But I know what the problem is, and I want everyone else to know too so something—anything—can be done."

Tamara smiled. "Remember when I told you a few months ago you weren't cut out for TV?" she said. "This is why. You have the heart and soul of a reporter. You're not an entertainer. You're a reporter."

"Well," Susan Carol said, "I'm ready to do some serious reporting tomorrow."

✦ ✦ ✦

The rest of the afternoon was spent doing background research. One statistic Kelleher came up with was fascinating:

the five accused linemen had started the season weighing an average of fifteen pounds more than when they first came into the league.

Susan Carol had no USTV obligations until after the game on Sunday. The network would devote Saturday to coverage of the Hall of Fame announcement and endless analysis of the game, so *Kid-Sports* was off the hook and off the air until after the game.

Stevie and CBS were another story. Stevie called Andy Kaplan to find out if he was expected to do anything for the pregame show. "Right now I think the answer's no," Kaplan said. "It isn't because they didn't love what you did, but because we have so many people down here jockeying for airtime. Sean's got to try to keep his stars happy."

Stevie wasn't disappointed to hear that news. He wondered if he owed CBS any kind of tip-off. After all, they had been very good to him, and this story would certainly affect their game coverage—not to mention the pregame show. But he doubted they'd believe him without proof, and they didn't have that yet, so he told Kaplan nothing at all.

They ate dinner at St. Elmo again because it was easy— thanks to Mike D'Angelo. Stevie didn't think it was possible, but there were more stars in the place than on the previous nights.

"City is really starting to get crowded," Kelleher commented as a wave of security people led Matt Damon to a private room. A few minutes later, Stevie saw another wave of security people coming: Dan Snyder, the owner of the Washington Redskins, was coming in along with Tom Cruise.

"Place is really crawling with celebs tonight," Mearns said.

"Ever since Snyder signed that deal with Cruise, he trots him out every chance he gets," Kelleher said. "He must be pretty sick of the whole thing."

"Sick of it?" Mearns said. "Look at him—he's wearing sunglasses indoors in February. The guy's nuts anyway."

"I liked *Mission: Impossible*," Stevie said.

"Oh please," Susan Carol said. "The last good movie he was in was *Rain Man*, and Dustin Hoffman was the reason that worked."

Stevie had never seen *Rain Man*, so he decided not to argue.

They dropped Susan Carol off at the Canterbury after dinner and walked back to the Marriott. Stevie was crashing after his ridiculously eventful day and passed on the chance to hang out in the media hospitality room. Normally, spending time with writers was both entertaining and educational for him. But now he couldn't keep his eyes open.

Unlike the night before, tonight he had no trouble sleeping. It seemed like only minutes later when the phone woke him. Thinking it was Susan Carol, he rolled over and picked it up, saying, "What possible reason can there be to wake me up?"

"It's Bob Arciero," was the answer he got.

"Oh my God. Sorry, doctor. I thought you were—"

Arciero cut him off. "Gus just got here. I've got what you need. I'll be at the Marriott in twenty minutes. Can you and Susan Carol meet me there?"

"I'll call her right now."

He was tingling as he dialed the phone. Susan Carol was right. What happened after they wrote the story didn't really matter. Their job was to get it written and get it out there.

18: ALL~OUT BLITZ

KELLEHER HAD POINTED OUT at dinner that Saturday was usually the longest and most boring day of Super Bowl week. Other than the announcement of the Hall of Fame vote, which wouldn't come until two o'clock, there was nothing going on. There was no access at all to the teams, who would be moving to different hotels that day to ensure that no one would know where they were or bother them the night before the game. For most reporters, there wasn't much doing, so the Marriott lobby was still pretty empty at 7 a.m. Which meant Stevie could pace without attracting too much attention.

Susan Carol arrived about five minutes before Dr. Arciero.

If Arciero was nervous, he didn't show it.

"We need to go someplace private so I can walk you guys through what's in here," he said, holding up a thick manila envelope. "You're going to need to take some notes."

"My room is a mess, but it's quiet," Stevie said.

"That works," Arciero said.

Once they were in the room, Arciero opened the envelope. Stevie cleared off the desk where his computer had been, and Arciero spread out the documents.

"I haven't even looked at these myself," he said. "I just took them from Gus, sent him to bed, and called you. Give me a minute."

As it turned out, Gus Mazzocca had brought the test results from all twenty-three players who had been tested after the conference championship game. Arciero walked them through how to read the reports. "Here, look at Eddie's," he said. "See the notation that he has traces of allopurinol in his system? He has a tendency to run high levels of uric acid, and allopurinol controls that. He's registered with the league as taking it for medical reasons. So when it shows up in his system, the league looks at it, sees he's been cleared to take it, and he's fine.

"Okay, now we get to the serious stuff. Here's Bill Bryant. Look at the notes at the bottom: 'Clear traces of HGH appear in patient's blood work. Hormone level is raised. Testosterone levels raised synthetically.'"

"What exactly does that mean?" Susan Carol asked.

"Different men have different levels of testosterone. Some are naturally higher than others. What the tester is saying here is that Bryant's raised testosterone level isn't caused naturally, that it is the result of something he put in his body."

"HGH," Stevie said.

"Based on this—yeah," Arciero said.

They went through the remaining reports. The five starting offensive linemen were almost identical. Only Steve Sanders, the left tackle, had a notation saying his high testosterone level might be natural, based on prior testing. "Looks like he might have suspected they'd be tested again and was trying to get off the stuff," Arciero said. "His levels are lower than the others."

"But he was still taking it?" Susan Carol said. "We don't want to accuse anyone unfairly."

"He was taking—see, it says so right there. It just appears he may have stopped at some point. The others apparently didn't."

He shut the files with a disgusted look on his face. "Idiots," he said. "Even if you put aside the fact that they're cheating and breaking the rules, they're probably killing themselves."

"You know that for sure?" Stevie said.

"We don't know anything for sure," Arciero said. "But the more we know about steroids, the more dangerous they appear to be. That's why you're starting to see players from the 1970s and '80s suddenly die in their forties and fifties."

"Scary," Susan Carol said.

"Not scary enough, apparently," Arciero answered.

He stood to go. "I hate being a part of this," he said as he walked to the door. "I'd rather you not use my name in the story, but if you have questions during the day, you can reach me on my cell."

They thanked him at the door and watched him walk down the hall.

"He's a brave man," Susan Carol said. "Deep down, he has to know he'll be fingered as a source and that the team will come after him."

"What about Eddie?"

She sighed. "They'll probably figure that out too. They know we both know Eddie—you wrote about Eddie and Darin, interviewed them both on CBS. And it was Darin who came to our rescue yesterday. Maybe Snow didn't recognize him, but . . ."

Stevie hoped she was wrong. Problem was, she was almost always right.

❖   ❖   ❖

They woke Kelleher and Mearns soon after to tell them about Arciero's visit.

"We need a quiet, private place to work on this," Kelleher said. "Let's meet in the media workroom."

"Won't there be people in there?"

"Not at this hour," he said. "I'll bet we can even order room service and just charge it to one of our rooms."

He was right. There was no one in the huge room when Stevie and Susan Carol arrived. They showed the documents to Bobby and Tamara and showed them the parts Arciero had pointed out as being crucial. By lunchtime, they had written close to 2,000 words explaining the saga. Their lede was direct:

"Five members of the California Dreams tested positive for human growth hormone (HGH) after the Dreams' victory over the Washington Redskins in the NFC Championship game, according to medical documents acquired by the *Washington Herald*.

"Although the positive tests should have triggered a second set of confirming tests, Dreams owner Donald Meeker engaged in a widespread cover-up to ensure that the players—all of them starting offensive linemen—would not face suspension for tonight's Super Bowl game. Under league rules, players are automatically suspended from their next game if both an A and B blood sample test positive for HGH. But because of the cover-up, second samples were not taken from the players in question.

"Asked what the chances were that the second samples would *not* have come back positive, one doctor familiar with the tests said, "about 100-to-1 against. The players union has tried to portray this test as having a high false-positive rate, but I've found it to be almost completely accurate. It's pretty clear these guys were taking HGH. The second test isn't much more than a formality."

They talked about whether that quote—from Arciero—would unmask him as a source. Not necessarily, they decided, since they could have showed the results to any doctor familiar with HGH and he would have drawn the same conclusion.

"The issue is going to be who gave you the test results,"

Kelleher said, "not what a doctor thinks looking at them."

The rest of the story laid out the backstory of the new NFL drug-testing system and why the league had felt it necessary to adopt it, and how it had played out during this first season. They worked in a quote from the commissioner from his press conference, but stated clearly that the league hadn't anticipated the potential for manipulation of the tests. Then they went into what might happen and the penalties the players, the team, and Meeker might face.

Kelleher and Mearns went through the story in detail and rewrote a number of paragraphs. It was almost one o'clock. People were starting to trickle into the room.

"Okay, our room should be clean by now and it's pretty big," Kelleher said. "Let's go up there and get this to the paper and the lawyers in Washington. Then we'll decide when we're going to call Goodell and when we're going to call Meeker."

"Call Goodell and Meeker?" Stevie said. "What for?"

Kelleher smiled. "Story like this, you have to give people a chance to comment. Goodell will express shock and say the league will investigate—that's about all he can say. Meeker may hang up on us or may curse at us—who knows? But you have to give him a chance to say something."

"But won't the story get out once we call them for comment?" Susan Carol asked.

"Absolutely. The *Herald* will post a bulletin online this evening, and the story will be in our first edition, which hits the streets about nine o'clock tonight. Sunday's news really breaks Saturday night.

"One other thing," Kelleher said.

"What's that?" Stevie said.

"You guys need to call your parents. They need to hear about this from you."

"Oh God," Susan Carol said. "Not again."

Kelleher smiled. "Yes, Susan Carol," he said. "Again."

✦　✦　✦

The session with the lawyer was both serious and funny at the same time. Kelleher put her on the speakerphone in the room, and she began asking questions.

"This shouldn't take more than an hour," said the lawyer, whose name was Heather Matlock.

"An hour?" Kelleher said. "This is a newspaper story, not a book."

"A very controversial news story with all sorts of legal implications," Matlock said.

She had a point. Many of her questions were understandable. Without asking for names, she wanted to know how reliable the sources quoted in the story were. There were also questions that were borderline silly: "Are you sure this doctor is a doctor?" she asked about Arciero at one point.

"If he's not, all the people he's done surgery on are in for quite a shock," Kelleher said.

Heather Matlock didn't even giggle.

She also asked at one point if Stevie and Susan Carol had actually seen the test results.

"Heather, the story says 'according to documents obtained by the *Washington Herald*,'" Kelleher said.

"Oh, that's a reference to the test results?" Matlock said.

Stevie could see Kelleher biting his lip. He knew he was thinking the same thing: *No*, it's a reference to today's *Indianapolis Star*. Kelleher resisted. "Yes, that's what that is."

Matlock proved to be right. The session took a little more than an hour. As if to prove she was somehow in charge, she concluded by saying, "I'm going to sign off on this on the condition that you get responses from the owner—what's his name, Meeker?—and from the commissioner."

Kelleher sighed. "Heather, I've been doing this a few years now. I know how to be a reporter."

"Your name isn't on the story, Bobby," Matlock replied. "We're running a story about a major scandal written by a couple of fourteen-year-olds. If I'm not cautious, I'm not doing my job."

"Yeah, I hear you, Heather. But they've got this nailed, I promise."

They signed off with Heather Matlock. Tamara had gone downstairs to cover the Hall of Fame press conference.

"When do we talk to Goodell and Meeker?" Susan Carol asked.

"When the press conference is over, Tamara is going to tell Goodell's main PR guy that it's going to be vitally important we talk to the commissioner at around six o'clock. After we talk to him, we'll call Meeker on that cell phone number you got, Susan Carol. Deadline is six-thirty, so we'll phone the quotes in fast. There will be a bulletin about the story on our Web site at eight o'clock and the full story will be out there at nine. Then the bullets will start flying."

Stevie shuddered a bit. In the other stories he and Susan Carol had broken, the bad guys had all been caught before the papers hit the stands. To him, the writing of a story like this should mean the adventure was over, that the bad guys were out of circulation. But this time the bad guys would still be out there. And they would be very, very angry.

✦   ✦   ✦

The next few hours crawled by. They rewrote a few paragraphs and took a few calls from the editors at the *Herald* asking questions. Susan Carol went briefly to the Canterbury to pick up some things—they'd agreed she should stay with them at the Marriott after the news broke. Tamara came back to report that the highlight of the Hall of Fame press conference had been the announcement that Tony Kornheiser, one of Stevie's heroes in journalism, had been voted into the writers and broadcasters wing.

"I guess *they* know who he is," Stevie said, remembering an incident in New Orleans when a hotel clerk had not known who Kornheiser was—much to Tony's dismay.

"More important, I talked to Joe Browne," Tamara said. "He was pretty baffled by the whole thing, but he promised that the commissioner would call here at six o'clock. He said he'd only have about five minutes."

"When he hears what the story is, he'll have more than five minutes," Kelleher said.

"How are we going to do this?" Stevie asked.

"We'll put him on speaker—and we'll do the same thing if we get Meeker—and let him know there are three *Herald* reporters on the call. I will simply read the first few paragraphs of the story, and then we'll let them comment."

"It's all a little bit scary, isn't it?" said Susan Carol, making Stevie feel better about his case of nerves.

"Uh-huh," Kelleher said. "I hope you aren't having second thoughts, because it's too late to back out now."

"Second thoughts?" Susan Carol said. "No way. We're reporters. We have a story. We have to tell it."

"Even if it *is* frightening," Stevie said.

"That's exactly right," Kelleher said. "You guys will be fine. We're the good guys. Always remember that."

Stevie didn't feel like such a good guy when he got his parents on the phone. He tried to downplay the story, telling them he and Susan Carol had stumbled on another scandal—a cover-up involving the Dreams—and that the story would be in Sunday's *Herald* and they would probably be hearing their names on TV again later that night.

"What kind of scandal?" his father wanted to know.

"It involves HGH," Stevie said.

"Guys testing positive?"

"Yes."

"And the team is covering it up? And you can prove it?!"

"Yes."

"Oh my God. Let me talk to Bobby."

He passed the phone to Kelleher, who was alternately apologetic and firm, telling Bill Thomas he should be very proud of Stevie and assuring him he would be in good hands until he got home to Philadelphia. A few minutes later, he had a similar conversation with Don Anderson.

"When the two of them talk to one another, which they will," Susan Carol said, "we're both going to be in a lot of trouble."

"I suspect we'll *all* be in a lot of trouble," Kelleher said. "But we'll deal with that in a day or two. For now, we still have to get the story into the newspaper. We can deal with the fallout later."

They took a walk to get some fresh air and then watched a college basketball game between Indiana and Illinois on TV.

"I love that orange jacket that Bruce Weber wears," Tamara said when the Illinois coach came on camera wearing a jacket that looked a lot like an orange Creamsicle to Stevie.

Beyond that, there wasn't much chatter, except for Susan Carol saying quietly, "Thank goodness," when the Duke–Florida State score flashed on screen, showing that Duke had pulled out a 77–73 victory at home.

Stevie had just looked at his watch for perhaps the thousandth time when the phone rang. Even though it was exactly six o'clock and the phone was supposed to ring, the sound was almost jarring.

Kelleher picked up the phone. Joe Browne had placed the call for Goodell. "We're ready to go on this end, Joe," Kelleher said.

Goodell was obviously standing right there, because a

second later Stevie heard Kelleher say, "Commissioner, I know how busy you are tonight, so I'm going to put you on speakerphone right away and let Steve Thomas and Susan Carol Anderson say hello to you too."

Kelleher laughed. "No, not ganging up on you. But they actually wrote the story we need to ask you about. I'm just sort of the on-site editor."

Stevie was consistently amazed by Kelleher's willingness to give up the spotlight. All week he had been setting Stevie up with stories that he easily could have written himself, and now, on a story that would no doubt make huge headlines, he was doing everything he could to make it happen—while taking none of the credit for it himself.

Kelleher hit the speaker button and said, "Roger, can you hear me?"

"I can hear you," Goodell said. "Steve, Susan Carol, I've been watching your work all week—it's been terrific."

Stevie and Susan Carol both said thank you and brief hellos.

"You might not enjoy this piece of work as much," Kelleher said. "But they've done a great job nailing this story down, and I think it's important you be aware of it before it breaks in a few hours, because you're going to be bombarded once it's out."

"Joe told me it was something like that. I'm listening."

"I think the easiest thing to do is to read you the first few graphs. You'll understand where we're going pretty quickly."

He proceeded to read the first five paragraphs to

Goodell. At one point, Stevie thought he heard Goodell say, "Oh holy . . ." When Kelleher got to the point where he was going to start explaining how the NFL's drug-testing rules worked, he stopped. "Do you want more?" he asked.

"No," Goodell said. "I've heard enough."

There was a lengthy silence on the other end of the phone. Stevie was going to say something, but Kelleher put a finger up to indicate he should stay quiet. Stevie noticed Kelleher was looking at his watch. He realized what he was doing—timing how long it took Goodell to say something.

"I'm honestly not sure I can say anything or should say anything," Goodell said finally. "Bobby, can we go off the record for just one minute?"

"Why?" Kelleher said.

"I just want to ask you one question."

Kelleher was silent for a second. "Okay," he said. "But you know we need an on-the-record response from you."

"I know that," Goodell said. "My question's simple: Are you absolutely, one hundred percent certain about this? The story's been lawyered—everything?"

Kelleher smiled. "That's a reasonable question. Yes, we're sure. And so are our lawyers."

"You've seen the test results, then. Someone didn't just tell you what was in them?"

"Commissioner, the story says 'documents obtained by the *Washington Herald*.' We've got them here with us right now."

Goodell sighed. "Okay. You know I'd like to consult with Joe before I answer."

"And you know we don't want an answer crafted by Joe. We want your answer. You're the commissioner."

More silence. "Ready?" Goodell said.

"Been ready," Kelleher said.

"The allegations made in this story are, of course, stunning and frightening for a number of reasons. Clearly, we must undertake a full and thorough investigation, and I can only hope that the story proves to be untrue. If it is true, the league will act swiftly and thoroughly to punish anyone found guilty of wrongdoing."

He stopped. They waited for more.

"That's it," Goodell said. "That's all I've got."

"But what about the game?" Susan Carol asked, echoing the exact five words flashing through Stevie's mind.

"What about it?" Goodell asked.

"You're going to let them play?"

"As of this moment, I've got absolutely no proof that anyone is guilty of anything," Goodell said. "I can't take action against people based on a newspaper story—all of you know that."

"What if someone turned over the documentation to you?" Kelleher said.

"That's still just the first sample. Until there's a B sample, no one can be considered guilty."

"But there *is* no B sample *because* of Meeker's cover-up," Stevie said, then realized he was yelling when Susan Carol and Kelleher shot him looks.

"That's your allegation, Steve," Goodell said. "It may prove true. It may not. But again, I can't take any action based on it."

"So the five guys play tomorrow night," Kelleher said.

"I've got no evidence that could lead to a suspension."

"I've got a question, Commissioner," Susan Carol said. "Hypothetically, if someone took a drug test the day after the conference championship games and tested positive, would there be time to get results back from a second sample before the Super Bowl?"

"Absolutely," Goodell said.

"And if someone came back positive on both samples, you would suspend them for the Super Bowl?"

"I would have no choice under the collective bargaining agreement," Goodell said. "They would be suspended— period."

Kelleher followed up. "So, if an owner or a coach had a player test positive, and he wanted him to play in the Super Bowl, covering up the A sample and stalling on the B sample would be the way to go."

"You know I didn't say that, Bobby. What I will say is this: we can't suspend a player until we get both samples back. It's exactly the same as the Olympic drug rules."

Kelleher looked at Stevie and Susan Carol to see if they had any more questions. "Commissioner, thank you," he said.

"Bobby, Steve, Susan Carol, you just ruined my weekend."

"That's on the record," Kelleher said.

Goodell laughed. "That's fine. It happens to be true."

He hung up.

"Okay," Kelleher said. "One more call to make."

"I suspect this one won't be nearly as pleasant," Susan Carol said.

"That may be the understatement of the week," Kelleher answered.

He picked the phone back up and started dialing.

19: TOUCHDOWN!

STEVIE WAS HALF HOPING they would get voice mail on Don Meeker's cell phone, although Kelleher had already said that if they did, they would have to call Dewey Blanton, the Dreams' PR guy who had been so helpful to Stevie earlier in the week. Stevie knew he was right.

There was no need, as it turned out. Meeker picked up on the second ring.

"Donald Meeker," he said.

"Mr. Meeker," Kelleher said, intentionally being formal, Stevie knew, because of the gravity of the situation. "This is Bobby Kelleher. I'm here with Steve Thomas and Susan Carol Anderson."

He had put the call on speaker when dialing because he knew that, unlike with Goodell, courtesy would be pointless.

"What the hell can you three possibly want?" Meeker said. "How did you get this number?"

"You gave it to me the other night, sir," Susan Carol said, jumping in.

"I'll have it changed about five minutes from now," Meeker said.

"All well and good," Kelleher said. "But we're calling you as a courtesy because Steve and Susan Carol have written a story that is going to appear in tomorrow's *Washington Herald*, which will be on the streets in about three hours.

"I'm just going to read you the first few paragraphs and let you comment. Then we'll be done."

"We'll be done when I say we're done," Meeker said.

"That's fine," Kelleher said. He started to read.

He was two paragraphs in when Meeker began screaming. "You ———! Why, you little ———! Are you ——— kidding me! I will sue your asses for so much money, I'll not only own the newspaper, I'll own you and your families for the rest of your lives! No way can you prove a word of that, you lying little ———!"

Stevie had heard a fair amount of profanity at school, but nothing quite like this. Kelleher's voice was as soft and calm as Meeker's was shrieky and out of control. "Mr. Meeker, I'm going to remind you we're on the record, and on tape—which is legal since this call is not across state lines. I will then point out to you the phrase 'has obtained documents.' We've got the test results. We've got not one source, but three. So, if you want to leave your profane rant as your comment, that's fine, but be aware of what you're dealing with here."

There was silence for a moment. "When exactly are you publishing this crap?"

"The first edition of the Sunday papers will be out in a little less than three hours. The *Herald* will publish a bulletin alerting people to the story on its Web site at eight o'clock."

"That means I have ninety minutes to get a court order stopping you."

"Good luck."

"—— you, Kelleher, and your two little friends too. I'll take you all down—I guarantee it."

"Thanks for your time, Don."

The phone clicked on the word *for*.

Stevie looked at Kelleher. "Can he get a court order?"

"On what grounds?" Kelleher said. "Even if he could find a judge on a Saturday night, no one can order us not to publish a story unless national security is at stake. The only one whose security is at stake here is Meeker."

"And ours," Susan Carol said. "At least judging by his tone."

"Don't worry," Kelleher said. "We'll make sure there are plenty of people around you at all times.

"Okay," Kelleher continued. "We need to phone these quotes in for the story. It'll be closing on the desk in about fifteen minutes. So. First person to dig a printable quote out of what Meeker just said wins a prize."

When neither Stevie or Susan Carol laughed, Bobby studied the two of them. "Are you okay?"

They both nodded.

"Good," he said, picking up the phone. "Because there's no turning back now."

✦   ✦   ✦

Once Kelleher had phoned in the quotes from Goodell and Meeker, telling the desk where to put them in the story, they decided they were entitled to a fast trip to St. Elmo. They called Mike D'Angelo, who said he had one table left that could handle them if they came over right away. "Perfect," Kelleher said. "We should have just enough time to eat and get back here before the story breaks. I want you both under wraps by eight."

They all put on their coats, but before they left, Bobby put the drug-test results back into their envelope and slipped them in his pocket. "We should keep these with us at all times."

The sun was down and the air had that pre-snow feel again when they walked outside. They decided to take a cab to save time and to stay warm. The restaurant was, of course, packed. D'Angelo looked a little tired. "It's a great week having the whole world in town," he said as he walked them to a booth. "But I can't say I'll be sad when everybody leaves."

"You've probably done enough business that you can shut down for the next month," Kelleher said.

D'Angelo smiled. "More like a year. The amount of money some people spend is mind-boggling."

The food was delicious, but Stevie noticed that Susan Carol wasn't eating very much.

"Nervous?" he asked.

"Yes," she said. "But I'm not sure why. We know the story is right."

"Perfectly natural," Tamara said. "You've written a very, very explosive story that the people accused *have* to try to deny. They have to try to make you and Stevie the bad guys. Everything will be fine in the end, but they're going to take some shots at you and you know it's coming."

Kelleher's cell phone rang. He looked at the screen and then at Tamara. "It's Wadkins," he said.

"Whoo boy," Tamara said as Bobby flipped open the phone.

"Who is Wadkins?" Stevie whispered.

"He's the executive editor of the paper," Tamara said. "He doesn't call a reporter unless he's unhappy about something."

Wadkins was talking and Kelleher listening.

"Mr. Wadkins, the story couldn't be more solid," Kelleher finally said. "We have the test results in hand. And they were given to us by one of the team's own doctors."

There was a pause while Wadkins talked some more. "What would you expect him to say? That's his MO anyway, trying to intimidate people."

Stevie could now hear Wadkins's voice coming through the phone. "No, sir, I'm not saying you can be intimidated. I'm saying this is what Don Meeker does."

Wadkins talked some more. "Put it this way," Kelleher said in response. "I'd trust them with my job and my reputation. That's what we're talking about, right?

He paused again. "Yes, sir, I understand. And I'm comfortable with that."

He closed the phone. "Wyn getting cold feet after a call from Little Donny?" Tamara asked.

"The problem with Wadkins is he's more one of them than he is one of us," Kelleher said.

"What's that mean?" Susan Carol asked.

"He sees himself as part of the Washington elite. He likes to run with the rich and the famous a lot more than with any of his reporters. So when Meeker calls screaming that his reporters are unfairly trying to do him in, Wadkins would be inclined to listen."

"But he's running the story, right?" Stevie asked.

"He's running it, but he said if one word is wrong, he'll expect my resignation."

"Sounds like a wonderful guy to work for," Susan Carol said.

"A peach," Kelleher said. "A real Georgetown peach."

"Don't you mean Georgia peach?" Susan Carol said.

"No, I meant Georgetown peach: spoiled and rotten. All you need to know about the guy is that he loves sitting in Dan Snyder's box at Redskins games."

"I bet he won't be sitting there much next season after this story," Stevie said.

"I bet he's thinking exactly the same thing," Kelleher said. "Come on, let's get out of here. It's coming up on eight o'clock."

They walked back to the hotel even though it was cold, because Tamara pointed out they probably weren't going to get much chance to go out the next day once the story broke. When they walked into the lobby, Stevie was immediately blinded by the lights of a TV camera.

"Uh-oh," Kelleher said. "We didn't get back here soon enough."

Stevie counted at least a half dozen camera crews and, from what he could see, a number of radio reporters, coming in their direction. He looked at his watch. It was 8:15. Could the news have traveled that quickly?

"Steve, Susan Carol!" he heard several voices calling.

Kelleher put his arms around both of them. "All you say is, 'We're going to let the story speak for itself,' okay?" he said.

They nodded. The cameras rushed toward them.

"Are the two of you aware that Don Meeker has put out a statement categorically denying the charges in your story?" someone in the crowd said as the cameras and lights shone on them.

Stevie was still trying to put on some semblance of a poker face when he heard Susan Carol respond coolly, "What would you expect him to say? We'll just let the story speak for itself."

"Are you aware he says he'll sue the paper and the two of you?" someone else asked.

Susan Carol smiled this time. "As I said before, would you expect anything different from Mr. Meeker?"

Stevie noticed his legs were shaking. Susan Carol's voice could not have been calmer.

"So you still say that five Dreams tested positive for

HGH and Meeker is covering it up?" another voice said.

This time Susan Carol looked disgusted. "Why in the world would we write a story saying that if we weren't one hundred percent sure it was true?"

Stevie heard Kelleher's voice behind him. "Okay, guys, I think you've got what you need. We're going now."

"Who died and put you in charge, Kelleher?" someone holding an ESPN microphone said.

"No one. But I'm their editor on this and I'm responsible for them." He smiled at the guy with the microphone, whom Stevie had seen before but didn't recognize. "I can't wait to see how you guys try to somehow take credit for this story."

He and Tamara began pushing Stevie and Susan Carol in the direction of the elevators. People were still shouting questions. It reminded Stevie of something out of a movie. He heard one voice shout, "You kids better have it right!" That made him shudder.

"Why would they doubt us like that?" he said once they were safely at the elevator bank and the horde had turned away.

"Because *they* didn't break the story," Kelleher said. "Happens all the time. Be prepared. It will be like this all day tomorrow."

Stevie took a deep breath. Judging by the last ten minutes, tomorrow was going to be a very long day.

✦　✦　✦

Kelleher's cell phone rang incessantly for the next couple of hours. He answered it a couple of times when he saw a number or a name he recognized. "The story's right," he kept repeating. "Read it; they've got it nailed."

They were all in Mark Maske's room, figuring that was the safest place to be for a while since no one was apt to look for them in the room of a *Washington Post* reporter. Bobby and Tamara agreed that Susan Carol should stay with Tamara in their room and Bobby and Stevie would stay with Mark, who had graciously offered to share his room with colleagues in need.

Stevie answered his phone twice. The first time it was his parents, saying they were being bombarded with calls from people wanting to know how to get in touch with him.

"*Meet the Press* called," his dad said. "They're ready to replan their whole show if you and Susan Carol will come on in the morning."

"What'd you tell 'em?" Stevie asked.

"I told them my sense was you wanted the story to stand on its own merit."

"Perfect. We want to lay as low as possible tomorrow."

"That might not be easy."

"I know."

Susan Carol fielded a similar call from her father. And she chose not to answer a couple calls each from Tal Vincent and Mike Shupe at USTV. But she did take the call from Jamie Whitsitt.

"Susan Carol! Dude, what a story! No wonder I haven't seen you in a while! You should lay low, though—reporters are totally staked out in the hotel lobby. And Tal's about ready to pop a blood vessel. . . ."

"Thanks for the warning, Jamie," Susan Carol replied. She listened for a minute more, laughed, and then clicked off.

"What did he say?" Stevie asked.

"He said, 'Rock on, dude!'"

Stevie's next call was from Sean McManus. Stevie was afraid for a moment that he was going to be upset Stevie hadn't given the story to CBS. If he was, he didn't mention it. "We can't ignore the story, even though I'm sure the league would like us to," he said to Stevie. "Don Meeker is going to come on the pregame show to give his side. I'd like you and Susan Carol to come on and give yours."

"*With* Meeker?" Stevie asked.

McManus laughed. "Absolutely not. For one thing, Meeker insisted on coming on alone. For another, we don't want a riot on our hands."

Stevie asked McManus to hang on for a moment and explained the situation to Kelleher. "That's the one you should do," Kelleher said. "Meeker's going to spend all day shooting you guys down. That's the spot to respond. Plus, you owe it to CBS. Tell Sean there's just one condition."

"What's that?"

"You go on *after* Meeker."

Stevie nodded. McManus agreed. "What we'll do is read the basics of the story on the air and let Meeker respond. We'll play you the tape of what he says and you can respond to it."

"What time do we do this?" Stevie asked.

"Meeker is coming to our compound at three o'clock,"

McManus said. "So I need you both to come at about four so we'll have time to get you set up to tape with Jim."

"Nantz?" Stevie said. "Doesn't James Brown host the pregame show?"

"He does. But this is a huge story and Jim's our number one guy. In fact, given the hard-news implications, I may bring Bob Schieffer in to do the interview. We're still talking about it."

"Okay," Stevie said. "I guess we'll see you at four."

"Sounds good," McManus said. Stevie thought he was about to hang up, but then he apparently had another thought. "Stevie?"

"Yes."

"This is really a bad thing for the NFL if it's true," he said. "We're partners with the NFL—I'm sure you understand that."

"I do."

"We're obligated to be skeptical."

"I understand."

"I know you do. But I want you to know something."

"What?"

"I hope you've got it right."

Stevie nodded, even though McManus couldn't see him nodding. "Mr. McManus?" he said, realizing he couldn't be seen.

"Yes?"

"We've got it right."

20: FUMBLING

BY ELEVEN O'CLOCK THAT NIGHT, every TV channel was reporting the story and Meeker's denials, many of them putting excerpts from the story on their screens, while mentioning that the bylines on the story belonged to the two fourteen-year-old kid reporters who had become famous for helping break major stories at both the Final Four and the U.S. Open tennis tournament in the past year. There were quick flashes from the impromptu lobby press conference and a lot of tape of Stevie and Susan Carol on camera together back in what now felt like the long-ago days of their co-employment on USTV.

Both USTV and ESPN had on experts who shook their heads sadly and said they thought perhaps the two kids had overreached this time, that they could see no way the

Dreams could have successfully covered up five separate players testing positive for HGH.

"I've been in a lot of locker rooms in my time," said an ex-NFL player on USTV. "This kind of thing can't stay secret for long. I actually feel sorry for these kids. I think they're going to be in a lot of trouble when the truth comes out."

Kelleher said, "These TV guys will just keep shooting the story down until they've got no choice but to admit that it's right."

Tamara had been in contact with her desk early in the evening and had written a column quoting the *Herald* story, saying the story was undeniably true and it was a shame that the league couldn't stop the five players from playing.

"The bottom line," she had written, "is, of course, the bottom line. The NFL doesn't want to see its showcase event turned into a rout because the entire Dreams' offensive line is suspended—even though they would have been suspended if not for the cover-up. If the Dreams win the game it will re-prove a sad truth about professional sports: frequently, crime *does* pay."

When they couldn't stand to watch the TV any longer, Bobby and Stevie walked Susan Carol and Mearns upstairs. "I just want to make sure no one's lurking outside the door," Bobby said when Tamara tried to insist they didn't need an escort. "And Stevie needs to pick up his toothbrush."

Mark Maske arrived in the room soon after Kelleher and Stevie had returned unscathed and reported that everyone in the business was trying to either find a way to confirm the story or shoot it down.

It was after midnight when they all tried to go to sleep. Stevie tossed and turned on the cot they'd had brought in, conjuring up different scenarios for the next day. Finally, exhausted, he fell asleep. He woke up to the sound of the phone ringing. He squinted at the clock on the bedside table. It was just after eight. Maske answered the phone.

"Susan Carol," he said, pointing the phone at Stevie. "She says she needs to talk to you right now."

Stevie's first thought was that her father had called to order her home right away. Undoubtedly, the Andersons had been subjected to the same kinds of calls his parents had received.

Stevie crawled out of bed and took the phone. "What's up?" he asked.

"Plenty," she said. "Eddie just called."

"Whaa? Why?"

"He says Meeker pegged him as our source."

"How?"

"I don't know. He just said, 'I'm dead. Gotta go—watch your backs.' Look, Tamara and I will be down there in fifteen minutes. We'll fill you in."

She hung up before Stevie had a chance to object.

"What was that?" Kelleher asked, sitting up and blinking sleep from his eyes.

"Eddie Brennan called Susan Carol and it sounds bad. She and Tamara are going to be down here in fifteen minutes."

"I'll take a fast shower," Kelleher said.

Mark Maske had gone to the door and picked up the

local newspaper. "Late edition," he said. "You guys are stars."

Stevie looked at the front page and gasped. A huge banner headline proclaimed: "Super Scandal?" Underneath were photos of Meeker and all five accused linemen. Below that were photos of Stevie and Susan Carol with a caption that said "Kid reporters accuse players, owner." The story was basically a rewrite of the *Herald* story, beginning with the words, "According to a story in this morning's editions of the *Washington Herald,* tonight's Super Bowl will be tainted by both a drug scandal and a cover-up."

"Cuts right to the heart of the matter, I'd say," Maske said, reading aloud to Stevie.

Mark left a few minutes later, saying he'd let Tamara represent the *Post* on this one. Stevie got dressed and read the paper while Kelleher showered. He was just pulling his shirt on when Susan Carol and Tamara arrived.

Each of them was carrying two coffees. "Figured you guys would need these," Mearns said.

They all found places to sit.

"Eddie called our cells first, but they were turned off," Susan Carol said. "He said he asked for Bobby's room, figuring he would know where we were."

"Yes, yes," Kelleher said. "Cut to the chase."

She nodded. "Right. He said his coach showed up in his room at seven o'clock and told him Meeker *knew* Eddie was the source of the story and that he was going to come to the team breakfast and tell everyone Eddie had ratted out his teammates."

"But how could Meeker know?" Stevie asked.

"Eddie said someone from USTV was feeding Meeker information about the time we spent with Eddie during the week."

"Tal Vincent?" Stevie said.

"I think so. Someone must have sucked up to Meeker big-time to get that interview Friday. And now he's getting back at you by telling Meeker we were spending time with Eddie."

"But that doesn't prove he told us anything," Stevie said.

"He doesn't have to prove anything," Tamara said. "And it doesn't really matter how he knows. All he has to do is make the accusation and Eddie's in trouble."

The room phone rang and everyone jumped.

"I told Eddie to call us back here," Susan Carol said. "I bet that's him."

Kelleher answered. He nodded to Susan Carol. "Eddie, it's Bobby Kelleher. Stevie and Susan Carol and my wife, Tamara, are all here. You mind if I put you on speaker?"

Eddie sounded a little bit breathless as he started to talk. "Meeker told the team it was me, that I had ratted out the o-line. He said he wouldn't tell the coach what to do, but as the team owner, he didn't want a snitch playing quarterback in the Super Bowl."

"Did anyone bother to point out that if the o-line hadn't been using HGH and if Meeker hadn't been covering it up, there would have been nothing to tell?" Susan Carol said, her voice indignant.

"I told you guys earlier in the week how this would go if they thought I was your source," he said. "They're not the bad guys right now—I am."

"So what happens next?" asked Stevie.

"Kaplow told me I'm not starting. He said it's for my own protection. He's afraid the o-line might pull a club rush and I'd get killed."

"Club rush?" Susan Carol asked.

"It's when you purposely don't block," Stevie said quickly. "They do it to rookies sometimes in training camp if they don't like them—right, Eddie?"

"You got it," Brennan said. "Only this isn't training camp, where guys will hold back a little to keep someone from getting hurt. This is the Super Bowl."

"Do you think Kaplow's right?" Stevie asked.

"Probably, yes. But here's the thing: they can't win this game without me. That may sound cocky, but it's true. Meeker signed Jeff George as our backup quarterback even though he's about a hundred and has been through a half dozen teams. Meeker's paying him a ton because he thinks he has big-game experience while I'm just a kid. But really, George is *way* over the hill."

"Don't the guys know that?" Susan Carol said.

"I think they do. But Meeker has them convinced I'm the devil."

"What did *you* say to them?"

"I said Meeker was crazy—which he is. But I didn't want to say too much—I didn't want to lie to them. But I'll tell you who will lie: Meeker. He's going on USTV and CBS today to say that he knew nothing about any positive tests, and if there are reports with positive results, they must be either fakes or bad tests. He's going to ask for a brand-new round of tests tomorrow."

"But that wouldn't prove the guys weren't positive two weeks ago," Susan Carol said.

"I know," Brennan said. "He's a weasel. You two need to be careful. This guy is going to play serious hardball. He'll do anything to try to make you look bad, to make me look bad, to make the testers look bad. Anything to get out of this."

"He won't get out of it," Stevie said.

"I hope you're right," Brennan said. "But right now, I'm not convinced that you are. When it comes to being evil, this guy is on another level." He sighed. "I gotta go," he said. "I have a game to not play."

Stevie felt a wave of guilt, thinking if he and Susan Carol hadn't persuaded him to help them, none of this would be happening. "I'm really sorry, Eddie," he said.

"Don't be," Brennan said. "You did the right thing. So did I. We all did. Don't feel bad about doing the right thing." He paused. "Someone has to do it—right?"

They hung up and just looked at each other. They'd run their story—told the truth—and the wrong player wasn't playing.

◆　◆　◆

"Oldest story in sports," Bobby said. "It's the Code. I see it in college basketball all the time. It's worse to be accused of turning someone in for recruiting violations than to commit them."

"He's right about Jeff George too," Tamara said. "They can't win with him playing. I can't believe Meeker would go through all this to keep the linemen on the field, then throw it all away to spite Eddie."

"He doesn't think he's throwing it away," Susan Carol said. "He's the one who signed George. This is his chance to prove that Kaplow's been playing the wrong quarterback all year."

"Even though that quarterback got the team to the Super Bowl," Stevie added.

"I feel helpless about all this," Susan Carol said.

"We've done all we can do for the moment," Bobby said. "This is like any game we cover—we have nothing to do with the outcome when all is said and done."

"Except we do," Stevie said. "We're responsible for getting one team's quarterback benched."

"You aren't responsible for that," Tamara said. "He's a grown man. He made a decision. And he just told you guys he didn't regret it—you shouldn't either."

Stevie still felt queasy about the whole thing. They couldn't leave the room without getting bombarded by media again, so they read the papers and ordered room service and stewed.

21: REVIEWING THE PLAY

STEVIE WAS RELIEVED when Sean McManus finally called to say he was going to send his car to pick them up outside the hotel. "He'll drive you right under the stadium so you can avoid the crowds," he said. "I don't think you want to wade through the Dreams' fans right now."

That was a good point. Stevie had been so focused on not wanting to talk to any more media people, he had almost forgotten about the fans. Great—thousands of people all ticked off at him were now heading into the stadium.

So they all gathered their laptops and their courage and set out to the Super Bowl. "Gee, I guess it pays to know important people," Kelleher said as they climbed into Sean's car. The drive took no more than five minutes. They were stopped briefly at the loading-dock entrance they had used the other day so the police could check under the car, then they pulled up at the back of the CBS compound.

"Now this," said Tamara as they got out, "is living."

"First Super Bowl I've been to in years where it didn't take an hour to get inside the building," Kelleher said.

Stevie was just relieved to be inside and in an area that was off-limits to the public. They walked around the CBS compound to the downstairs media workroom and arrived just in time to see Don Meeker's face on TV sets all over the room. The sound was apparently turned up on all the sets because they could hear him quite clearly as soon as they walked in.

"These are kids who got carried away," Meeker was saying. "They're not professionals. The people who should be ashamed are the so-called pros at that paper. The story's wrong—just wrong."

"The story says there is documentation on these positive tests. . . ."

"We're aware of that. We're investigating right now. I was given a report that all our players tested clean. It's my belief that someone, perhaps someone in our organization, doctored the test results, then found the only two reporters gullible enough to believe this phony story."

"Why would someone in your own organization do that?"

"Let me just say that we've had some competency issues with at least one of our doctors. I don't want to say anything more about that right now."

Kelleher took a deep breath. "I hate to tell you guys

this," he whispered, "but he's setting Arciero up. This whole interview is a setup."

"Big surprise," Susan Carol said. "Look where it's airing."

Now Stevie noticed the USTV logo at the bottom of the screen.

The interviewer said he had one last question. "Can you see any reason why these two young reporters would want to produce a story like this on the day of the Super Bowl?"

Meeker almost smiled. Kelleher was right, Stevie decided. This *was* a setup.

"Well, you know, Chris, the obvious answer is to call attention to themselves," he said. "They've certainly been everywhere this week."

"How do you mean?"

"Well, I'm hesitant to bring it up, but the young girl . . ."

"Susan Carol Anderson."

"Yes. I read now that she's only fourteen. But if you'd seen her behavior at some of the cocktail parties this week . . . Well, there would be any number of men who would be as shocked by her age as I was. . . ."

Stevie heard Susan Carol gasp. Protectively, he put an arm around her.

"Ask the SOB exactly what he means by that, you TV weasel!" Stevie heard Kelleher shouting.

The TV weasel asked nothing else. Instead, he said, "Mr. Meeker, we're grateful to you for coming on under such difficult circumstances and speaking with so much candor."

"I need to sit down," Susan Carol said. "My father's going to see that."

As soon as Meeker disappeared from the screen, a number of reporters in the room turned in the direction of Stevie and Susan Carol. Stevie, arm still around Susan Carol, was guiding her to a chair.

Microphones began to surround them.

"Ms. Anderson, any comment on what Mr. Meeker just said?" someone asked.

Kelleher jumped in front of them like a human shield. "Here's the deal, guys," he said, his voice raised so people could hear him. "Don Meeker is a lying dirtbag—you can quote me on that. I happen to know both these kids, and not only is the reporting they've done impeccable, they are completely above reproach as people."

"Aren't you a little biased, Bobby?" someone said. "The story's in your paper."

"What I am is *right*," Kelleher said. "Now give the girl some room to breathe, will you? She's just been slandered on national TV."

People began backing off. "We can't stay here," Kelleher said. "You'll be mobbed again soon."

"We can go to CBS," Stevie suggested.

Kelleher nodded. "Good idea. It's three-thirty. Meeker ought to be done in there by now. I guarantee you CBS didn't throw softballs at him like USTV did."

"I have to call my father," Susan Carol said.

"Call him when we get to CBS," Kelleher said.

They walked out of the room—all eyes on them. They were about to walk under the CBS SPORTS sign when Stevie saw Don Meeker walking toward them with Mike and Moe on either side of him and three yellow-jacketed security guards leading the way.

"I'm going to kill him," Stevie said, not caring about the security coterie.

"Easy," Kelleher said. "Keep walking. Don't talk to him."

But as they got closer, in spite of Kelleher's warning, Stevie heard himself shout, "You won't get away with this, Meeker! You're going down—everyone is going to know you're a liar and a cheat!"

Meeker was smirking. "You want to repeat that, kid?" he said. "I don't think Mike and Moe heard you clearly."

"Oh, aren't you brave," Kelleher said. "What're you going to do, sic five hundred pounds of bully on a hundred-and-thirty-pound kid?"

"—— you, Kelleher," Meeker said. "Keep walking, fellas, there's no one here worth talking to." He looked at Susan Carol. "What're you doing, sweetie, looking for a date?"

That was it for Stevie. He didn't care about Mike and Moe. He put his head down and charged at Meeker. Fortunately, Kelleher took a quick step forward and cut him off. "Easy, Stevie," he said, almost catching him in midair. "This guy will get what he deserves. Just not here and now."

Stevie wanted to get to Meeker, but he knew Kelleher was right. "Okay," he said. "Okay."

Meeker and company departed, Meeker saying something Stevie couldn't hear as they left.

Stevie looked at Susan Carol. She was beet red and looked like she might cry. He wanted to put an arm around her, but Kelleher was still holding on to him. Now Kelleher took him by both shoulders and forced his attention back to him. "I want you to listen to me, Stevie," he said. "I understand why you would react that way. But you *cannot* go around here the rest of the day all wound up and ready to blow. You need to take a deep breath and not let anything anyone says get to you. You've done your job. Let your reporting do the talking for you."

"But he shouldn't be allowed to get away with saying that stuff. . . ."

"He won't be. I'll bet the CBS people didn't let him say any of it. The calmer and more rational you are, the crazier he looks. So keep your cool. Got it?"

Stevie nodded. "Okay, got it. But I'd still like to kill the guy."

"I think you'd need to get in line," Susan Carol said. Her voice was calm but her face was still flushed.

Andy Kaplan came to greet them. "Someone just told me Meeker was being a jerk going out," he said. "When you see the interview we did with him, you may understand why he was in a bad mood."

He led them back to a studio setup Stevie hadn't seen earlier in the week. Jim Nantz was waiting. Introductions were made all around.

"That was a great piece of reporting you guys did this morning," Nantz said.

They all sat down to look at the Meeker interview. Andy Kaplan hadn't been kidding. Nantz was gentle at the start, but when Meeker started into all the conspiracies against him, Nantz—unlike USTV—wouldn't let him get away with it.

"Hang on, Don," he said. "You are asking us to believe that someone in your own organization, people working in a lab, and two reporters at a highly respected newspaper *all* conspired to sabotage you and the Dreams? Isn't that far-fetched?"

On the screen, Meeker's face tightened. After the softballs at USTV, he hadn't expected this. "I'm here to tell you the truth," he said. "If CBS chooses to side with a two-bit newspaper and some bitter, incompetent people working for me . . ."

"Two-bit newspaper?" Nantz said. "We aren't talking about the *National Enquirer* here, Don. And if these people were so bitter and incompetent, why were they still working for you—"

"They won't be for long," Meeker broke in. "And I've heard that USTV is firing Susan Carol Anderson as well. This kind of smear campaign won't work."

Nantz smiled. "Well, we'll all be eager to have the truth come out here. Let me ask you this, if the test results prove to be true, what action will you take? Will you apologize to everyone involved?"

"I don't apologize," Meeker said. "Not to you. Not to anyone. You're against me too, aren't you?" He was starting to really scream now. "Everyone knows CBS wants the Ravens to win this game! You're no different from the rest of them!"

"Mr. Meeker, thank you for your time," Nantz said.

"Wow," Kelleher said when the screen went blank. "All he needed was to reach into his pocket for some steel balls."

Everyone laughed. Stevie was baffled, Susan Carol could tell. *"The Caine Mutiny,"* she said. "It was summer reading for us last year. The paranoid captain of the *Caine* always played with two steel balls whenever he was convinced someone was trying to get him."

"Humphrey Bogart played Queeg in the movie," Nantz added. "So, are you both ready to go? I don't want to rush anyone, but I need to get up to the booth pretty soon."

Stevie and Susan Carol were miked and, as the cameras rolled, Nantz asked them in detail about the story. When they'd walked him through it, Nantz nodded and said, "As I'm sure you know, Don Meeker tells quite a different story. Why should we believe you?"

Stevie fielded this one. "Well, we have no reason to lie. We have nothing to gain and nothing to lose but our credibility—which is why Mr. Meeker is doing everything he can to undermine that now by making ridiculous personal remarks about Susan Carol. Anyone who's met her knows how crazy his comments are. But Mr. Meeker, on the other hand, has every reason to lie."

Nantz continued to question them. "So, these lab reports, you actually have them?"

"Oh yes," Susan Carol answered.

"And you believe them to be authentic?"

"Without a doubt," she said. "We would never make this kind of accusation without being one hundred percent sure, and neither would the *Herald*."

"Now, Susan Carol, Mr. Meeker told us you were being let go by USTV. Is that correct?"

She gave him her best smile. "No one's told me about it if it is."

"So, bottom line," he said finally, "you and the *Herald* stand by everything in the story?"

"Every word," Susan Carol said. "We know some people don't like to hear the truth—especially this kind of truth. They want to believe all their athletic heroes are wonderful guys. Some of them are. Probably most. But our job is to tell people the truth—whether it's good news or bad news."

And that was a wrap.

"Hard to believe either of you is fourteen," Jim Nantz said when the stage lights went out and they un-miked. "I'd like to have your futures."

"Wouldn't we all," Kelleher said, walking up.

Nantz thanked them and shook hands all around and headed up to the booth.

"Less than two hours until kickoff," Kelleher said.

"Finally," Stevie said.

"Amen to that," Susan Carol added.

✦　✦　✦

At Andy Kaplan's invitation they lingered in the CBS compound for a while, not wanting to deal with any more media queries than they had to.

Stevie and Susan Carol both turned their cell phones back on once the interview was over. Stevie had one message—from his parents. Susan Carol gasped when she saw she had nineteen messages. "How did all these people get my number?" she asked. She looked through the calls on the "received calls" page, shaking her head no at each number she didn't recognize. She stopped at one, looking surprised.

"Wonder what this is about?" she said.

"What is it?" Stevie asked.

"Jamie," she said. She had already pressed the button to call the number back, which, in spite of everything she had said all week, still made Stevie feel a little queasy.

"Jamie," she said. "It's Susan Carol. I see you've left three messages for me the last couple of hours. I'm sure you know I've been a little bombarded here, but if you really need something, I'll have the phone on for a while. Otherwise, I'll see you postgame—unless the rumors that I've been fired are true."

She looked at Stevie as she hung up. "What's that look for?"

"Why would you call him back?" he asked.

She shrugged. "I'm telling you he isn't a bad guy. It might be that he's just concerned about me."

Stevie wasn't buying. "Yeah, concerned about you."

"Stop it, Stevie," she said. She moved closer to him and said quietly, "There's only one boy I've kissed this week, and you know who he is. Okay?"

Stevie nodded, feeling a little embarrassed and a little weak in the knees. "Okay," he said. "I'm sorry."

He still wished she hadn't called Whitsitt back.

About thirty minutes before game time, they decided to

go upstairs to the press box. There were two—the main box halfway up in the stands and an auxiliary box at the very top of the building. Stevie and Susan Carol were in the auxiliary box, Bobby and Tamara in the main box.

"You guys should be okay up there," Kelleher said. "Anyone asks you anything, just say, 'We stand by our story and we'd just like to watch the game now.'"

They took the elevator to the auxiliary box level and stepped into a place that was so far from the field it made Stevie almost dizzy to look down. "Good thing they have TV monitors all over the place," Susan Carol said. "We wouldn't see much from up here."

The auxiliary press box was huge. It stretched from one 20-yard line to the other 20-yard line and had three rows of chairs lined up with desks in front of them. Some writers had already set up their laptops at their seats. Others were in their seats working, no doubt on pregame notes. There were TV sets hanging over the desks, each of them about three seats apart, meaning everyone had a good view of a TV even if the field was in another time zone.

"I wonder if the regular press box is as big as this one," Stevie said.

"I think Bobby told me it's bigger," said Susan Carol. "There are more seats down there than up here, if you can believe that."

Kaplan had told them downstairs that he would be working throughout the game, so Susan Carol could sit in his assigned seat next to Stevie. CBS had gotten him a seat, which was actually a good thing because it was in the front row, as opposed to the seat assigned to him for the *Herald* in the back row. They worked their way to their seats and, for the first time in twenty-four hours, no one seemed interested in talking to them. The focus—at last—was on football.

The player introductions and the pregame ceremonies seemed to take forever. The NFL brought in a different singer to sing every patriotic song ever written. "Oh God, not him," Susan Carol said when Lee Greenwood came out to sing "God Bless the U.S.A."

"You're not 'proud to be an American'?" a voice said behind them.

Stevie turned and saw Pete Alfano, a columnist for the *Fort Worth Star-Telegram* he had met at the U.S. Open, sitting one row up with a smile on his face.

"I am," Susan Carol said. "I just can't stand that song."

"Used to be, the national anthem was enough," Alfano said. "The only one they haven't done so far is 'America the Beautiful.'"

"That'll be halftime," Stevie said.

Finally, at 6:25—seven minutes after the designated kickoff time of 6:18—the game began. The Ravens' Matt Stover kicked into the end zone and the ball came out to the 20-yard line. When the Dreams' offense trotted onto the field, a loud buzz went through the crowd. Jeff George was the quarterback.

People in the auxiliary press box immediately began shouting at one another. "Is that George? What in the world is going on? Someone turn the sound up on the TV— see if CBS knows anything."

The sound came up on the TV hanging just over Stevie and Susan Carol's heads.

". . . complete surprise to us," he heard Nantz saying. "We will try to get a report from the sidelines on what is wrong with Eddie Brennan as soon as possible."

The Dreams had told no one of the quarterback change. With Jeff George in charge, they quickly went three and out: two running plays picked up three yards, and then George had to throw the ball away with Ray Lewis bearing down on him on third down. So they punted, and Steve McNair, the Ravens' veteran quarterback, began moving his team down the field.

The Ravens had just picked up a first down at the Dreams' 22-yard line when an announcement came over the press box PA: "Jeff George is starting at quarterback for the Dreams due to a coach's decision. The Dreams have not reported any injury to Eddie Brennan."

That didn't really tell anyone anything. Reporters began leaving their seats, no doubt to go downstairs and see if Dewey Blanton or someone from the league could shed more light on the situation. "I bet anyone with money on the Dreams isn't too happy right now," Susan Carol said. "The NFL would never admit it, but one of the reasons they're so obsessed with making all injuries public is that they know it affects the betting lines."

Stevie hadn't even thought in those terms, but it made sense. The Dreams clearly were a different team—no matter what Don Meeker thought—with George at quarterback instead of Brennan.

The Dreams' defense was still solid, though, and they held the Ravens out of the end zone. Then Matt Stover came on and kicked a twenty-eight-yard field goal to make it 3–0. "Hasn't he been in the league for like a hundred years?" Stevie said.

"Since 1990," Susan Carol said.

"*How* do you know that?" he asked.

"I read the media guide," she said. "Do you ever read anything?"

"I'm going to read *The Caine Mutiny* as soon as I get home."

She shot him a look, but said nothing.

The Dreams had the ball again, but when Jeff George was sacked at the 6-yard line, the Dreams had to punt again. The Ravens returned the punt to the Dreams' 41-yard line on a great run from B. J. Sams. From there, it took McNair only six plays to get his team into the end zone. He ducked a blitz on third-and-four from the 13, raced to his right, and, on the run, threw a strike to tight end Todd Heap in the back corner of the end zone. With 2:44 left in the first quarter, the Ravens were up 10–0.

"This game will be over before halftime if this keeps up," Susan Carol said.

"Couldn't happen to a nicer guy," Stevie said, thinking of Meeker.

The first quarter ended with George overthrowing a wide-open receiver and being intercepted at midfield. Someone tapped on Stevie's shoulder as the teams were changing ends of the field. It was Andy Kaplan.

"Our guys want to know if you can shed any light on the Brennan situation," he said. "No one from the Dreams is saying anything. We're wondering if it has anything to do with your story."

Stevie and Susan Carol looked at each other. It was up to Brennan—not them—to decide what to tell people about why he had been benched.

"Andy, we just can't talk about that," Stevie said awkwardly. "You guys really need to ask Eddie that question when the game's over."

Kaplan nodded. "I understand. But your answer leads me to believe that the story may have something to do with it."

"It wouldn't be fair to Eddie to speculate that way," Susan Carol said.

"Don't worry," Kaplan said. "We won't say anything specific. But at halftime, our guys will be talking about the story, and we're certainly going to have to wonder if there's some connection, since the Dreams are being so close-mouthed about it."

That was fair. Right now about 100 million people were wondering why Eddie Brennan wasn't playing. CBS had to at least throw out the HGH story as one possible reason. Kaplan departed.

The second quarter began. A thought flashed through Stevie's mind: he would be glad when this was over and he could get back to school. Never in his life would he have believed that such a thought would cross his mind smack in the middle of the Super Bowl. Now it made perfect sense.

22: COMEBACK

THE GAME WOULD HAVE BEEN OVER by halftime except for the fact that the Ravens' offense wasn't much better than the Dreams' in the second quarter. After the interception, the Ravens moved the ball to the 31 and stalled. Matt Stover came in and kicked another field goal. George turned the ball over twice more—on another interception and a fumble—but the Dreams' defense was totally locked in and the Ravens were only able to convert that into another three points. As a result, the halftime score was 16–0. It could have been so much worse.

Bobby and Tamara came upstairs during the break. "Might as well have something to eat," Kelleher said. So they worked their way through a food line at the back of the auxiliary box that included hamburgers and hot dogs.

"There's never been a Super Bowl halftime that lasted less than forty-five minutes."

Stevie had almost forgotten about the endless halftimes at the Super Bowl. The big entertainment act this year was U2. Stevie remembered reading an NFL press release earlier in the week trumpeting the fact that U2 was the first act *ever* asked to *return* to perform at halftime of the Super Bowl. Such drama!

Stevie had just taken a bite of his hamburger when his cell phone buzzed inside his pocket. Thinking it would be his parents, he pulled the phone out and opened it without looking at the number.

"Stevie," a voice hissed, "I've got another scoop for you."

"Eddie?" he said, nearly choking and drawing a surprised look from Kelleher. He lowered his voice. "Is that you? *Where* are you?"

"Yeah," he said. "I'm just outside the locker room. There's a lot of time to kill. Listen, I'm starting the second half."

"*What?!* You are? What happened?"

Brennan's voice was barely a whisper, and it was hard for Stevie to hear with all the noise around him. "What happened was the first half," he said. "You saw it. The o-line guys went to Kaplow and said, 'Look, we're probably going down when this is over. We want to at least win this game before we do.' Kaplow went for it."

"Did he check with Meeker?"

"I have no idea. But given that Meeker will do anything

to win—lie, cheat, steal—I don't think he's going to object at this point."

He was right about that. "Good luck" was all Stevie could think to say.

"Yeah, thanks. I've gotta go." He hung up.

Susan Carol, Kelleher, and Mearns were all looking at him. "Let me guess—Eddie's starting the second half," Susan Carol said.

"Uh-huh."

"Why do you think he called you?" Bobby asked.

Stevie shrugged. "I have no idea."

"He probably just had to tell *someone*," Susan Carol said. "He couldn't let his buddy Darin Kerns in on it because that would give the Ravens a little more time to prepare for him. So he called you."

"You're the only one who truly understands right now," Kelleher said.

Bono and U2 were reaching the end of their halftime performance, so Bobby and Tamara headed back down to the main press box.

"Game should be more interesting now," said Kelleher in parting.

"Yeah, but do we really want the Dreams to rally?" said Tamara.

No one knew what to say to that. . . .

Stevie thought he heard Bono singing "God Bless America." "Isn't he Irish?" he asked Susan Carol.

"Forget that. Do you know what you should do now?" Susan Carol said.

Stevie shook his head.

"Let CBS know about Eddie. They've been good to you. Give them a heads-up so they look good."

Stevie liked that idea. So when Susan Carol headed off to the ladies' room, he dialed Andy Kaplan's cell phone number and told him that Brennan would start the second half.

"You sure?" Kaplan said. "How do you know?"

"Can't tell you how, but believe me, it's happening."

"Thanks," Kaplan said.

Stevie turned his attention back to the field for a moment. A huge stage had been set up for U2 to perform on and a couple of thousand fans had been brought down to the field to stand around the stage and create a rock concert atmosphere. Stevie thought it was all pretty hokey. His mother was a big Bono fan and he tried to picture her near the stage, waving her arms to the music. No, he thought, not my mom. At least he hoped not.

He noticed that he was sweating a little bit. Nerves? Certainly possible. But it was also considerably warmer in the Dome than it had been on the practice days when the building was almost empty. He looked at his watch. It had already been thirty-five minutes since the half had ended, and they still had to take down the stage and clear the fans off the field before the teams could come back from the locker rooms. No wonder Eddie had called him, Stevie thought. He had plenty of time to kill.

On the TV overhead, Jim Nantz and Phil Simms were back on screen. Stevie grabbed a remote and turned up the sound.

"What we don't know," Nantz was saying, "is why Brennan didn't start in the first half. The Dreams gave no reason for the last-second switch to Jeff George."

"Jim, what we *do* know is that the switch failed miserably, and now Eddie Brennan is going to be asked to rally his team against one of the best defenses in football."

"You would think," Nantz said, "that just having him back in charge will give the Dreams a boost—and they most certainly need one." The score went up on the screen and Nantz began taking the network into commercial. Stevie reached for the remote to turn the sound back down.

"You seem to know everything. What do you think is going on?" a voice said behind him.

He turned and, to his surprise, saw Tal Vincent standing there.

Stevie almost gagged on the swig of Coke he had just taken. "Yeah, as if you don't know why Brennan was benched," he said.

Vincent gave him a funny look. "Me? Why would I know anything about that? You're the one who had the one-on-one with him earlier in the week, did the big feature for CBS on him and his buddy from the Ravens. . . ."

"Yeah, and because of that you ran to Meeker and told him that he was our source on the HGH story."

"Whaa? Me?" Vincent moved a step closer to Stevie, and for a minute Stevie thought they were finally going to have the fight they had been heading toward all week. "Listen, Steve," he said softly. "I understand why you hate me. I'll even admit I haven't behaved very well this week—I've behaved really badly, in fact. There's been a lot going on you don't know about, which doesn't excuse it, but . . . Look, you're way off base on this. I spoke to Don Meeker once this week—when we did our interview with him. I said hello and thank you and that was it."

"Oh sure. So no one from USTV made contact with him to set up that bogus interview, not to mention that attack on Susan Carol you guys let him get away with today. . . ."

"God, that was awful," Vincent said. "So embarrassing. That was something I might have quit over if everything weren't ending already."

"What? You mean because Susan Carol's going to be fired anyway?"

"No, because Meeker's boy at USTV is going."

"Who?"

Vincent shook his head. "I can't tell you that," he said.

"Why the hell not?" Stevie said. "Why bother giving me all this crap about how bad you feel about what happened if you won't tell me who's really working for Meeker?"

"You make a good point," Vincent said. "And one much truer than you know." He looked around to see if anyone else was listening. Then he shrugged and said, "What do I care—he won't be my boss anymore in a week."

"Boss?" Stevie said. Then it hit him. "Shupe? Mike Shupe?"

Vincent smiled. "Technically speaking, I never told you anything."

Stevie was about to charge off to find Susan Carol when

he remembered what Vincent had just said. "What do you mean he won't be your boss in a week?"

"You're a reporter," Vincent said. "Figure it out." Then he turned on his heel and left.

Stevie was now desperate to find Susan Carol and happily spotted her walking back to her seat. "I just talked to Bobby and Tamara," she said. "They said they would meet us in the interview room when the game is over to decide who's going to write what."

"You'll never guess who was just here," he said.

"Tal Vincent?"

"How—?"

"He met me on my way out before—he came to tell me I'm fired. So you're stuck with me again as a writing partner."

"You seem awfully calm about this."

"Oh, it's a relief, really. And Tal was almost apologetic. He said he was sorry about the way he'd behaved all week and that this wasn't his decision."

"Yeah, well, I know whose decision it was," Stevie said. "Come on, we've got work to do."

"Now? The game's about to start."

"Now," Stevie said firmly.

He took out his cell phone and dialed Andy Kaplan.

"Did that tip help you guys out?" Stevie asked. "Good. Now I need your help."

✦　✦　✦

"What is this about?" Susan Carol said as they rode downstairs in the elevator.

"Andy's getting a CBS credential for you," he said. "They give you access to the entire building, except maybe for the owners' boxes. But that's not where we need to go."

"Where do we need to go?"

"First we need to find the USTV luxury box," he said. "After that—we'll see."

"*Why?*" she asked. "I don't have any interest in seeing any of those people."

"Oh yes, you do," he said. "You need to see Mike Shupe."

"Because?"

"Because he's the one who fired you. He's the one who told Meeker that Brennan was one of our sources."

"How do you know that?"

"Believe it or not, from Vincent. I accused him of being the one who went to Meeker and he denied it."

"And you believe him why?"

"I'm not sure. But he said something about Shupe not being his boss anymore."

They had reached the press box level. Andy Kaplan was waiting a few yards from the elevator. When he saw Susan Carol, he smiled. "Should I be giving a CBS pass to a star from another network?" he said.

"Not anymore," Susan Carol said.

"What? Did they really fire you?"

"Yup—at halftime. And I've never been happier."

Andy laughed and handed over the credential. "This doesn't have a photo on it because it is only good for game day. Fortunately, this is game day, so it will work just fine."

Stevie heard a roar in the background. He looked up at one of the TV monitors and saw Dreams wide receiver Troy Slade spiking the ball in the end zone.

"I've got to get back to the truck," said Andy. "Maybe I'll see you guys after the game."

Stevie and Susan Carol stood and watched the replay. Brennan had made a beautiful play fake to running back Andrew Thompson and then thrown a fifty-eight-yard strike to Slade, who caught the ball in stride, with a Ravens defender practically glued to him.

"Looks like we could have a game here," Susan Carol said. "Sixteen to seven now and lots of time left."

"Yeah, maybe we'll get to watch the fourth quarter," Stevie said. "Right now, we have to find Shupe."

"Why? Even if he is the one who went to Meeker, what good will it do for us to find him?"

"You think we should just let the league handle this from here on out?" Stevie pressed the elevator button. "Who knows what Meeker has done to try to cover his tracks. He's already claiming the results have been doctored somehow. We know it's a lie, but if the league doesn't have absolute proof . . ."

"They might not be able to take any real action."

"Exactly."

They rode the elevator down to the luxury box level. A guard waited there, but when he saw the CBS passes, he moved aside. They walked past the owners' boxes—Stevie couldn't help but note that there was one security guard outside Bisciotti's, five outside Meeker's.

They walked past boxes with corporate names on them and finally saw one marked USTV. There was no security guard anywhere in sight.

"Okay," Stevie said. "What now?"

She laughed. "You're looking at me? You were the one who wanted to come down here."

"Yeah, but you're still the smart one."

She shook her head. "If I were smart, we'd just be watching this game, minding our own business."

"We don't do that," he said.

"No. Not usually, do we? Okay," she said finally, "we'll go in, find Shupe, and tell him we want to talk outside."

"And if he says no?"

"I pitch a fit in front of all their clients."

"I like it," Stevie said with a grin. "I hope he says no."

He pulled the door open and followed her in. The box was packed. Some people were sitting in the bar and seating area, eating and drinking and watching the game on a large-screen TV. Others were up front in the seating area, watching the actual field. Stevie could see the scoreboard. There were under seven minutes to play in the third quarter and the score was still 16–7.

"Hey, Susan Carol," Stevie heard a voice say from the corner of the room. He almost groaned when he saw who it was: Jamie Whitsitt. He walked over to the two of them, a smile on his face. He put out a hand to Stevie. "Hey, dude, I read what you guys wrote this morning. Awesome stuff." He looked at Susan Carol. "Been calling you all day." He was whispering, as if not wanting to be heard.

"I called you back," she said.

He shook his head impatiently. "I'll bet you're looking for Shupe. He's standing over in the corner of the box watching. He's a nervous wreck."

Now Stevie was really baffled. How could Whitsitt possibly know they were looking for Mike Shupe? He could tell Susan Carol was thinking the same thing. "How . . . why would you think we're looking for . . ."

"Because you're smart," Jamie said. He smiled—dreamily, no doubt—and looked around again. "Go talk to him. Before you leave, though, come talk to me. He's the reason I've been calling you."

"I already know he fired me. Is that what you want to talk to me about?"

"No," Jamie said. "I need to talk to both of you. Trust me. I'm not wasting your time."

That was strange. Both of them? They looked at each other.

"Let's go talk to Shupe," she said. "There's a time-out."

Stevie saw the clock had stopped at 4:41. The Dreams had just stuffed the Ravens' floundering offense again and had returned a punt to their own 36.

"I'll be here when you're done," Jamie said as they started to walk toward Shupe.

Stevie had no clue what Whitsitt could want. For now, they had to focus on Shupe. He was standing in a corner of the box by himself. When he saw Susan Carol and Stevie coming, he threw up a hand as if to say "stop."

"Not now, Susan Carol," he said. "Have your father contact Tal Vincent tomorrow. I'm not having this conversation in the middle of the Super Bowl."

"That's not what this is about," she said. "We want to talk to you about Don Meeker."

Stevie saw Shupe's face flush. They had hit a nerve.

"What the hell would I have to say about Don Meeker?" he said, his voice hushed because there were people close by.

"Maybe you could explain why you told him that Eddie Brennan was a source on our story," Stevie said, deciding to take a chance. "When we write about it, you'll be outed for changing the course of the Super Bowl, not to mention for being in the pocket of a team owner. How do you think the other thirty-one owners will feel about that?"

"Not to mention never being able to set foot in Los Angeles if the Dreams lose this game because Eddie didn't play the first half," Susan Carol added.

Another roar went up. Stevie looked down at the field and saw Troy Slade being pushed out of bounds on the Ravens' 19-yard line. The Dreams were close to scoring again.

"Walk outside with me," Shupe said. "I'll give you sixty seconds."

He walked quickly through the box and out onto the concourse. When he started talking, his face was red.

"You have it wrong," he said. "You can't prove a thing. You accuse me of anything like that, I'll sue you and so will Meeker."

"We've got sources. . . ."

"Screw your sources. I didn't tell Meeker a thing."

"You *did* talk to Meeker, though," Susan Carol said. "You were the one who set up the two interviews."

"So? What does that prove?"

"Why are you leaving USTV?" Stevie blurted.

"What?" They had caught him off guard again. "Who told you that?"

Susan Carol could also see they had surprised him. "Doesn't matter," she said. "We know it's true."

Shupe stared at them for an instant. Then he waved his hand at them. "You've got nothing," he said. "Screw you both. I'm going back to watch the game."

He yanked the door open and walked back into the box.

Stevie and Susan Carol looked at each other. "Now what?" Stevie said. "He's right. All we've got is Tal Vincent implying Shupe was the one who told Meeker. That's not even on the record. There's no way to prove what he and Meeker discussed."

The look in Susan Carol's eyes said he was right.

"Actually, there is a way."

Stevie looked up and saw Jamie Whitsitt standing there. He must have come out right after Shupe left.

"*What?*" they both said.

"Follow me," Whitsitt said. "We need to find someplace quiet."

23: GOING FOR TWO

"THERE *IS* NO PLACE QUIET," Susan Carol said. "This entire building is packed."

"Except for our studio downstairs," Whitsitt said. "There's no one in it right now."

He was right. But what in the world could he possibly tell them? What could he know about all this? And yet he had somehow known they were looking for Shupe.

"If we're going, let's go fast," Stevie said. Another hanging monitor showed the Dreams' kicker lining up a field goal from the 25-yard line. If he made it, the score would be 16–10.

"Can you give us some idea what in the world this is about?" Susan Carol said as they walked to the elevator.

"Patience," he said. "Trust me, it will be worth your while."

They rode in silence down to the locker room level. Because the hallway leading to the locker rooms had been blocked off in anticipation of the game's end, they had to circle the long way to get to the USTV studio.

"You know I'm quitting after the game," Jamie said at one point.

"You are?" Susan Carol replied.

"Yeah," he said. "I'm not cut out for this. I don't know sports, and if it wasn't for you, I'd look like an idiot every show."

Stevie thought that sounded pretty accurate but just managed to stop himself from saying so.

There was a guard at the door when they finally reached the USTV studio, but he moved aside when he saw Jamie and Susan Carol.

"You guys aren't watching?" he asked in surprise.

"Just have to do something real quick," Susan Carol answered.

The guard shrugged. They walked into the dark, empty room and Whitsitt found a light switch. There was a round table just to the left of the set. They all pulled up chairs.

"Okay, Jamie, please tell us now, what gives?" Susan Carol said.

"Hang on, sweet girl, let me tell you the story," he said. "Only take me a minute. You're gonna hug me when I'm done."

"Not if I have anything to say about it," Stevie said—on this he couldn't hold back.

Jamie laughed. "Easy, dude. I know she's your lady. And

no offense, Susan Carol, but you're too young for me."

"Okay, okay," Susan Carol said impatiently. "Where is this going?"

Whitsitt nodded. "You weren't around when Tal first heard we had to interview Meeker. He wasn't happy because he had that list of questions we had to ask—you remember that?"

"Of course," Susan Carol said.

"Anyway, I asked him why we had to do it, if the questions were going to be so dumb. He just said, 'That SOB Shupe.' I was like, 'What? What's Shupe got to do with this?'

"He laughs and says to me, 'Dude, he's got everything to do with this. Five million bucks a year worth.'"

"He said 'dude'?" Stevie asked.

"Shut up, Stevie," Susan Carol said.

"Anyway, I didn't ask him what that meant. To be honest, I wasn't all that curious. We did the interview, and after you left I said to Vincent that I didn't know much about TV, and I know less about football, but that was awful. He said, 'You got that right' and just walked away.

"So, Saturday, I was here doing my 'Rockin' Look at the Big Game' piece—you know, Susan Carol?"

"Yes."

"And when I left here Saturday, I forgot my tape recorder—left it sitting right on this table. This morning, I woke up and realized I'd left it here. I use it a lot to record bits of songs, or lyrics. Plus—as you've noticed, I'm sure—I have a bad memory, so I can use it to remind myself of stuff.

I just turn it on and say, 'Call Susan Carol at ten.' Or, 'lunch with Steve at noon.'

"So today, when I realized it was gone, I came over here to get it. Got into the building no problem—told them where I was going and what I was doing. Got in here, the tape recorder was sitting right where I left it. Someone had delivered the morning papers on the table and I saw all the headlines about your story. So I sat down to read."

He paused and smiled at Stevie. "Dude, you probably don't think I know how to read, do you?"

Before Stevie could answer, he plowed on. "Sorry, I digress," he said. "I'm almost done reading the story, sitting right here when the guard—Josh, he's a good guy—comes in and says, 'Jamie, Mr. Shupe and Mr. Meeker are headed in here. You might want to clear out.'

"I'm like, no kidding, I better clear out. Then I think, hang on, Jamie, this has to be connected to the story you're reading. Shupe is clearly *real* tight with Meeker, I already know that from Tal. So I look at this tape recorder, and I have this crazy idea. I turn on the player to record and leave it on a chair. I figure, why not? From what I just read, Meeker is a *bad* dude, and it seemed kind of suspicious that he and Mike Shupe were skulking down here to talk. . . ."

Stevie and Susan Carol were both wide-eyed now. "That was . . . unbelievably quick thinking," Susan Carol said.

Whitsitt smiled. "I have my moments. So I ducked out the back way and took a walk. I waited like half an hour, then came back. Josh said they'd been gone for ten minutes."

"And?" they both said.

He reached into his pocket and pulled out his micro-recorder. "There's twenty minutes of stuff, but there's only about two minutes you need to hear."

He put the recorder on the table and pressed a button. They could hear Don Meeker's voice loud and clear.

". . . So there's no doubt it was Brennan. He didn't even try to deny it when I outed him at breakfast. Good tip on that. I'm sure his doctor pal Arciero's the one who got them the test results."

"He would have access?" Mike Shupe's voice was just as clear.

"Yeah. That was my mistake. But it's taken care of. The doctor who heads up the lab will explain that there was a mix-up in the samples and the testing was faulty."

"That's great. So can we use that in the interview today?"

"No, Adamson will talk on Monday."

"Why?"

"Because the banks are closed on Sunday. God, Shupe, are you planning on questioning me once you come to work for me?"

Stevie and Susan Carol both gasped.

"No, no—I've got five million reasons to be agreeable."

"Don't forget it," Meeker snarled. "So we're clear, then? On what I need to say in the interview with you?"

"Yeah, I've got the questions."

"And you'll fire the girl today."

"Yes."

"Good. She'll be hiding under a bed for the next five years."

"What about Brennan? You bench him, he's bound to talk publicly."

"Fine. We'll just say poor Eddie got bad information from the docs. He believed it and made a terrible mistake. After George wins the game for us today, no one will care about him anyway."

"You really think Jeff George can win the game?"

"You kidding? The only reason Kaplow didn't play him all year was to prove he knows more about football than I do. George can still throw it eighty yards in the air."

"Huh. What about CBS? You going to do them too?"

"Have to. They told me they were going to interview the kids, so I need to defend myself, keep them honest. Then tomorrow, this Dr. Adamson at the lab says it was all a terrible mistake. The league has no choice but to drop it, and the Lombardi Trophy sits in my office."

"The kids' story is completely shot down."

"And the kids with it," Meeker added.

Whitsitt leaned forward and stopped the tape. "The rest is them making plans for after the game," he said. "You heard the important part."

Susan Carol jumped out of her chair and hugged Whitsitt. Even Stevie had to admit he was entitled.

"Told you you'd hug me," he said, smiling.

"We need that tape," Susan Carol said.

"All yours," Whitsitt said, pulling it out of the recorder.

"And you highbrow journalists always protect your sources, right? I just want to go back to L.A."

Susan Carol nodded and laughed and then hugged him again. Stevie shook his hand and even put an arm around him in thanks. Jamie Whitsitt was about as unlikely a hero as he could imagine, but he was—without question—the hero of the day.

"I'm going back upstairs to watch the end of the game," Jamie said, looking up at the muted TV monitor in the corner. "Looks like it might be a wild finish."

Stevie had almost forgotten the game. He looked at the monitor. They were just going to commercial. The teams had apparently traded field goals. The Ravens were leading 19–13 with just 4:21 to go in the game.

They walked back into the hallway, and Whitsitt said his goodbyes and headed for the elevator.

"Let's go watch the end from the field," Stevie said.

"We can do that?"

"Uh-huh. Andy Kaplan told me CBS personnel can go out for the last five minutes."

They made their way to the tunnel, which was now filled with security people. The CBS badges were magic. No one said a word. They came out of the tunnel into a wall of noise. Stevie had been on the field throughout the week, but that had been with no one in the stands. Now the building was full and the noise seemed to be coming straight down at them from all sides.

"Let's go over on the Dreams' sideline," Susan Carol said over the din.

"Will we be safe there?" Stevie asked, following her anyway.

"They won't even notice us at this point."

She was right. Everyone's focus was on the field.

Play had been stopped for the two-minute warning. Stevie could see that the Dreams had a first down on the Ravens' 31-yard line. It felt as if the pregame show had ended about fifteen minutes ago. Only it hadn't. The game was three and a half hours old and it now appeared likely it would be decided on this drive. The Dreams needed a touchdown—and the extra point—to win. Anything short of that and the Ravens could run out the clock. According to the scoreboard, the Dreams had one time-out left.

The sideline was crowded with photographers and security people, but they all had to stay five yards back from the playing field. Stevie and Susan Carol were able to slip just in front of them and had a perfect view of the field.

They walked to about the 25-yard line and could see Eddie Brennan consulting with Coach Skyler Kaplow a few yards away during the time-out. Loud as it was, Stevie could hear Kaplow, who was yelling to be heard.

"Check at the line," he was saying. "See what you've got, make your call. If you *don't* like it, we've got a time-out left. Don't be afraid to use it."

"'Check at the line' means Eddie calls the play at the line of scrimmage," Susan Carol said. That was what Stevie had figured. Normally he would have made a wise-guy comment about having been to a football game before, but

Brennan was trotting back out and the noise had gone to another level, so he didn't bother.

Brennan stepped into the huddle, said about three words—Stevie guessed they were "check with me"—and the Dreams came to the line. Brennan looked the defense over and shouted instruction in both directions. Stevie could see his center, Bill Bryant—one of the HGH Five—pointing in several directions. Brennan took the snap, started to drop back, then slipped the ball to tailback Omar Nelson. It was a draw play.

Nelson had a huge hole. He motored to the 16 before he was taken down. Somehow the noise got louder. The clock ticked away. The Dreams appeared to be in no hurry. "What they want to do is score and not give the Ravens time to come back and get a field goal," Susan Carol yelled. This time he *was* annoyed. He knew *that*. What he didn't know was what he wanted to see happen. Part of him couldn't help but root for Brennan. But he knew he should root against the cheaters. And the thought of Meeker holding the trophy almost made him ill.

Brennan was shouting another play. This time he dropped straight back and waited for the Ravens' rush to come. Just as Terrell Suggs and Ray Lewis looked as if they were going to bury him, Eddie lofted a screen pass to Nelson in the left flat. The play had sucked the Ravens in perfectly. Nelson had blockers in front of him. For an instant, Stevie thought he would score. But Ravens linebacker Bart Scott came sprinting across the field and somehow pulled Nelson down on the 3-yard line.

It was first and goal. Four tries to go three yards. The clock ticked to under fifty seconds. Still no time-out called by either team. Stevie wondered if the Ravens might call one to give themselves a chance if the Dreams scored. But he could see they only had one left too, and they clearly wanted to save it in case they needed it for a last-second desperation drive.

Brennan checked at the line again. Ben Fay, the team's other tailback, was now in for Nelson. Brennan took the snap, stepped left, and then pitched the ball to Fay running wide. Again, Stevie thought he might score. But two Ravens chased him down and wrestled him to the ground just outside the 1-yard line. The clock continued to run, ticking toward twenty seconds. Coolly, Brennan came to the line, took the snap, and spiked the ball to stop the clock with sixteen seconds left.

"Two plays to try and go one yard," Susan Carol said.

"They have a time-out, so they can run or pass," Stevie said. "That helps them a lot."

Brennan looked quickly to the sideline. Kaplow merely circled his finger as if to say, "Keep doing what you're doing." Brennan nodded and brought his team to the line. Brennan shouted to his teammates, struggling to be heard over the noise. This time he faked to Nelson, who dove into the line as if he had the ball, and then lofted what looked like a perfect pass to tight end Marcus Arlington in the back of the end zone. Brennan's arms were in the air as soon as he released the pass. But just as Arlington gathered the ball in,

Ravens cornerback Chris McAlister slammed into him. The ball popped loose.

Did he hold on long enough for it to be a catch? The back judge signaled touchdown. Bedlam broke out around Stevie and Susan Carol. Brennan was being mobbed by his teammates, who had left the bench. The score was tied at nineteen. Five seconds were left. Only the extra point stood between the Dreams and the Super Bowl title.

"Hang on a second," Susan Carol said, shouting into Stevie's ear to be heard. She pointed at the referee, who was huddling with the other officials. The Ravens were screaming that the call was wrong, that the ball had never been caught. The referee turned on his mic: "The play will be reviewed," he said. "The ruling on the field is a touchdown."

From behind where they were standing, boos erupted from the blue-and-gold-clad Dreams fans. On the other side, where most of the crowd was dressed in Ravens purple, there were cheers. Stevie could see people pointing at the replay board as if to say, "Look at this replay."

"Wow," Susan Carol said. "Can you imagine if they overrule this call? There might be a riot."

The referee trotted almost directly past where they were standing, with security people all around him, to get to the camera position where he would look at the replay. "Has to be indisputable evidence that the call on the field is wrong," Stevie said.

"Check it out," Susan Carol said, pointing at the giant board. The replay showed Brennan's pass landing in Arlington's hands just as McAlister collided with him. The ball popped loose instantly. The fans on the Ravens' side began screaming as soon as they saw the replay.

"Oh my God," Susan Carol said. "I don't think he ever had possession."

"If he did, it was for about point zero, zero one seconds," Stevie said.

They showed the play over and over. Each time, the crowd on both sides screamed. The referee remained under the camera hood, looking at the play over and over.

"Maybe he's hoping if he stays under there long enough, everyone will go home," Susan Carol said.

Stevie, whose stomach was tied in knots, though he wasn't sure why, smiled. "Brian Billick hates replay," he said. "He calls this a 'peep show.'"

"He's either going to really hate it or change his mind in the next few seconds," Susan Carol said.

The ref finally emerged, trotting slowly back onto the field. The stadium buzzed, then went almost quiet when he opened his mic and began talking. "After further review, the receiver did *not* have possession of the ball. . . ." Stevie couldn't hear the rest because the stadium had erupted. All of the Dreams people were going crazy, screaming.

Stevie saw Kaplow signal for time-out. It was now fourth down. The Dreams had one last chance and he wanted an extra moment to calm his players and talk to Brennan about what play he wanted to call. It would probably be too loud to check at the line. They would make their choice and then either win or lose the game on this play.

Stevie took a step to try to get close enough to hear Kaplow, but it was impossible. He was talking directly into Brennan's ear, and Brennan was nodding. He started toward the field and Kaplow pulled him back to say one more thing. Inside the helmet, Brennan was smiling.

The ref signaled that the time-out was over, so Brennan stepped into the huddle and called the play. Stevie looked around and saw that everyone in the stadium was standing. One play to decide a Super Bowl.

"I really don't know who to root for," Susan Carol said, voicing the same conflict Stevie felt.

The Dreams broke the huddle. Brennan pointed a finger at Troy Slade and made some kind of signal. A decoy, perhaps? He pointed both right and left, ducked under center, took the final snap of the season, and dropped back. He held a moment, seemingly looking for a receiver. The Ravens had rushed wide—trying to force him out of the pocket before he had time to set up and pass. The middle was wide open except for Ray Lewis, but just as Lewis started toward Brennan, Slade came in from the side and knocked him off his feet. Brennan tucked the ball under his arm and raced into the end zone completely untouched.

Touchdown!

Stevie looked at Susan Carol. She had an "are you kidding me?" grin on her face.

"They ran E-D Special!" Stevie screamed. "I can't believe it!"

Brennan was being mobbed—this time for real. Around

them, players and coaches were hugging one another. The clock was at zero.

"Extra point, extra point!" Kaplow was screaming. The Dreams still had to kick the extra point. The score was 19–19. The Dreams' kicking team trotted onto the field. Billick used his last time-out. No sense saving it now. Extra points were pretty much automatic, but Billick could at least try to shake the kicker's confidence by making him think about what was at stake.

"How crazy would it be if he missed," Susan Carol said.

"That last play was beyond crazy," Stevie said. "I don't know what this would be."

The teams lined up, the ball was snapped, and Jason Covarrubias kicked it right down the middle.

Fireworks began exploding the minute the ball hit the net behind the goalpost. The Dreams had won, 20–19. Everyone on both sides was moving toward the center of the field for handshakes and hugs.

Stevie saw Eddie Brennan heading for Darin Kerns. Cameras were everywhere.

They saw Kerns, dressed in Ravens purple, race up to his friend. "You ran E-D Special, you crazy SOB!"

"Still works!" Stevie heard Eddie yell. "I didn't even tell Kaplow!" he screamed. "Just Troy! I knew it would be open."

He had tears in his eyes. So did Kerns. Stevie understood. The media had now been allowed on the field, and cameras and microphones began to descend on both of them.

"Let's get out of here," Susan Carol said. "I have no desire to see Meeker with the trophy."

"I know," Stevie said. "But he won't get to enjoy it for long."

They headed to the tunnel. They had work to do.

24: GAME OVER

IT TOOK THEM SEVERAL MINUTES to work their way to the massive interview room because security checkpoints had been set up every ten yards—or so it seemed—along the hallway. Kelleher was waiting for them at the back of the room.

"Where's Tamara?" Susan Carol asked.

"She went straight to the locker room," he said. "She's going to write about the HGH Five, and none of them are going to be brought in here, that's for sure."

"You think they'll say anything?" Stevie asked.

"No, but sometimes a column about people not saying anything is just as good."

"Bobby, we need to talk—alone," Susan Carol said.

"That may be difficult right now," Kelleher said. He

pointed to the back corner of the room. Most of the media people pouring in were trying to find seats close to the front. There had to be at least fifty camera crews set up on a riser that was two-thirds of the way back in the room.

They got as far away from other people as they could. "What's up?" Kelleher said.

"We've got Meeker nailed," Susan Carol said.

"I thought you nailed him pretty good this morning. . . ."

They both shook their heads emphatically. "No, *really* nailed," Susan Carol said.

She took the tiny tape out of her pocket and held it up for Kelleher to see. "On this tape, we've got Meeker and Mike Shupe talking about Eddie's benching and, more important, Meeker admits to paying off the head of the lab to say there was a problem with the testing and that the documents we have aren't valid."

Kelleher's mouth was hanging open. "How . . . ?"

"We'll tell you the whole thing later," Stevie said before Susan Carol could start to answer. "I think right now we need to let Meeker and the commissioner know we have the tape."

Kelleher nodded. "Is that the only copy?" he asked. They nodded. "Okay, then we need to get copies made right away." He paused, clearly trying to decide what to do. Then he snapped his fingers. "Okay. My column is going to be on all of this anyway. It's the only story—especially with what you've got here. I'm going to take the tape upstairs to the media work area, listen to it, and see if I can make copies. Someone must have a dual tape recorder. Lots of guys use these micro tapes.

"Stevie, you're going to the Dreams' locker room. Meeker will be in there taking bows. When you get an opening, you tell him exactly what you've got."

"What if other people are listening?"

"Don't worry about it. It's already after ten o'clock on the East Coast, and we're the only ones with the tape. Everyone's going to have to write off our stories. In fact, make sure there *are* people around. Who knows what Meeker may do when he hears you've got him."

"I'm ready for him," Stevie said.

"Yeah, well, keep your cool, slugger," Kelleher said. "You aren't in there to fight, you're in there to report. If he's crazy enough to take a swing at you, you step out of the way, let others intervene, and report it that way. You understand?"

"Yes," Stevie said, knowing Kelleher was right.

"Susan Carol, I'm going to get you to Joe Browne, who can take you to Commissioner Goodell. He should know about this and we need a response—even if it's a 'no comment.'"

"What about Eddie?" Susan Carol asked.

"Eddie will be in here. He's going to be asked about the first-half benching. So will Kaplow. I'll try to be back in time to see what they say. Worse comes to worst, we'll call Eddie later on his cell to tell him what happened and get a comment from him that way. Okay, let's meet back in the main press box and decide what else we need when we've got all this."

He paused and looked at them both. "Are you sure you've got this right?" he said.

"We're sure—go listen."

Kelleher nodded. "You're right. Stevie, you need to get moving to the locker room. It's a long walk from here. Look for Tamara when you get there."

Stevie had to wait behind a barricade with other media members while the triumphant Dreams came through their tunnel following the awards ceremony that had just ended on the field. He spotted Brennan but couldn't catch his eye. Once all the Dreams had gone by, security people pulled the barricade back and the media began charging toward the victors' locker room. Stevie hung back, not wanting to get whacked on the head by a stampeding cameraman. He walked in a couple of minutes later and saw complete bedlam. Champagne was being sprayed everywhere. Players were pouring champagne, beer—anything they could get their hands on—on their own heads, on the heads of the media, on any heads they could find.

Eddie Brennan, Troy Slade, and Skyler Kaplow were being led by security and NFL personnel out the door to be taken to the interview room. Stevie knew the Ravens would already be there by now. The losers went first while the winners were on the field for the awards ceremony.

Brennan spotted Stevie, said something to one of the NFL people, and sprinted over to him.

"Can you believe it?!" he said. "Did you see? We ran E-D Special! Kaplow is actually upset!"

"Just like in high school!" Stevie said, and Brennan laughed.

"Eddie—we've got a tape," Stevie said, shouting to be

heard even though he was talking right into Brennan's ear. "We've got Meeker on tape, talking about the whole conspiracy. We've got him, Eddie."

"You're *sure?*"

"One hundred percent."

Brennan let out a whoop and hugged Stevie, drenching him in sweat and champagne. "My God," he said. "What started as the worst day of my life may end as just about the best."

"Except the o-line guys shouldn't have played."

He sobered for a second. "You're right. But ruining this for Meeker helps a lot."

He was gone then, pulled away by someone in a blue blazer. "People waiting for you on the golf cart, Eddie," he said.

"Talk to you later," Brennan said as he left.

Stevie took in the locker room scene for a moment. He spotted Tamara in a corner with several other writers, talking to Bill Bryant. He decided not to interrupt.

"You looking for someone specific?" asked a helpful person wearing an NFL PUBLIC RELATIONS credential.

"Meeker," Stevie said.

"All the way in the back," he said.

Stevie squared his shoulders and walked through the locker room, getting sprayed as he went. Not surprisingly, Meeker was surrounded by cameras, tape recorders, and notebooks. Even in the chaos, he could hear Meeker clearly.

". . . This is the last time I'm going to say this. All the

questions raised by that story will be answered in the next day or two. The people who wrote it will end up apologizing to us—or they can apologize to our lawyers. We've done nothing wrong."

"I don't think that's true," Stevie said, shouting to be heard.

Almost by magic, the cameras in front of him seemed to pull back, giving him a clear path to Meeker, who was still holding the Lombardi Trophy. Meeker's face turned into an angry snarl when he saw Stevie.

"Here's one of the reporters who got duped into writing a story that's one hundred percent wrong," he said. "Why don't you ask him about it?"

Stevie noticed several cameras turned in his direction. He was now pouring sweat—or maybe it was champagne. "I came down here to give you a chance to comment on the story we're writing for tomorrow," he said.

"Dreams win the Super Bowl? Kid reporters exposed as fools?" Meeker asked.

"Not quite," Stevie said. "More like, 'Herald acquires tape recording of Meeker explaining cover-up plot to Mike Shupe of USTV.' Would you like to comment?"

Meeker stared at him for a second. "You're a liar."

"We'll find out soon who the liar is," Stevie said.

For a moment, he thought Meeker was going to lunge at him. "There's no way you have a tape," Meeker said, his voice now shaking. "Shupe and I were the only ones in that room. . . ."

He stopped, realizing what he had said. The cameras were

now turned in his direction. Meeker's voice was getting very high-pitched. "I met with Shupe to discuss my interview today. You all saw it. That's all it was. The kid is bluffing."

"Fine," Stevie said. "If that's your comment, I've got a story to go write."

"Get him out!" Meeker screamed. "Get him out of *my* locker room right now!"

"Don't worry, Little Donny," Stevie said, feeling very secure now. "I'm leaving. I've got all I need."

Stevie could hear Meeker still screaming—on camera, no doubt—as he turned and walked away.

✦   ✦   ✦

Susan Carol and Kelleher were already writing when Stevie returned to the main press box. There was plenty of room to work, since a lot of the other writers had opted to write from the downstairs workroom.

"I just thought I should get us started since it's so late," Susan Carol said.

Kelleher filled him in on the plan. He had transcribed the key parts of the tape—"never heard anything like it in my life"—and sent it to the paper. He was writing a column calling for the league to force Meeker to sell the team. "They won't call the game a forfeit, so the win stands," he said. "But Goodell told Susan Carol that if it was all true, the other owners could vote to compel Meeker to sell the team."

Tamara returned just after Stevie and they brought her up to date too. "Just beyond amazing," she said, shaking her head.

Once Stevie and Susan Carol started writing—she sat at the computer, he made suggestions over her shoulder—Stevie understood the term "a story that writes itself." Kelleher had told them to just write and not worry about length, and they wrote close to 3,000 words. Kelleher, who finished his column just as they were wrapping it up, read it through quickly before they sent it to the *Herald*.

"Unbelievable," Kelleher kept saying. "I thought New Orleans was unbelievable. This is beyond that. And the best part is, you've got 'em cold. This story almost doesn't need to be lawyered. It's all right there on tape."

He folded his arms and looked at the two of them. "Okay, now tell me just how you got this tape," he said.

Susan Carol smiled. "We have to protect our source on this, Bobby," she said.

Kelleher's eyes narrowed. "Come on. Just tell me enough so I can tell the lawyers I'm completely sure it's legit."

"Dude, it's all good," Stevie said, smiling. "Our favorite dude came through, okay?"

Bobby looked at them for a minute, then smiled. "If you're saying what I think you're saying, don't tell me any more," he said. "It will all be too strange for me to understand anyway."

"Works for us," Susan Carol said, flashing the smile. Stevie had almost forgotten what it looked like, it had been so long.

They still had to answer some questions from the lawyer and from the editors, but it was all pretty basic. It was hard to argue with a recorded confession.

It was well after one a.m. by the time they packed

up their computers and walked out of the press box.

Tamara had called Mark Maske, who was working downstairs, to alert him to the *Herald*'s story, which she had referred to in her column. "Scooped by children again," she said, laughing.

They walked back to the hotel with snow falling steadily. The streets were still crowded, mostly with Dreams fans, celebrating their victory.

"The amazing thing is, none of these people care that their team won a tainted Super Bowl," Tamara said. "None of them care that the team owner is an incredible sleazebag."

Bobby nodded. "We could write a million stories like the one you guys wrote tonight and most fans will just shrug and say, 'Yeah, but we won.'"

"So why do we bother?" Stevie said.

"Because the truth matters," Kelleher said. "The truth will bring the bad guys down. Meeker is going down, and the players will be penalized. And maybe other players won't think they can get away with cheating in the future. The truth always matters."

They contemplated that and what lay ahead as they walked. The story would take on a life of its own now, one with far-reaching ramifications. But Stevie and Susan Carol wouldn't be on the front lines of it anymore—they were going home.

Bobby and Tamara left Stevie and Susan Carol alone to say goodbye in front of the Marriott. Susan Carol was going to take a cab back to the Canterbury—she had a seven a.m. flight.

"You going to be okay on four hours' sleep?" Stevie asked.

"I'll be fine. I sleep well on airplanes," she said.

He was trying to figure out what to say or do next. After spending so much time together, it was strange to think he wouldn't see her tomorrow.

"Steven Richman Thomas," she said finally. "Have you not yet learned how to kiss your girlfriend goodbye?"

"Are you really my girlfriend?" he asked. "It's not like we see each other that often. There must be other guys at home. . . ."

"And plenty of girls in Philadelphia," she said. "Do you *want* me to be your girlfriend?"

"Oh yeah," he said. "Oh yeah."

He leaned forward, standing on his toes just a little to kiss her, but she had a silly grin on her face.

"What?" he said.

"You know, Jamie Whitsitt did turn out to be a much better guy than you gave him credit for," she said.

"You want to call him?" he said. "I'm sure you've got his cell. . . ."

He had to stop at that point because she was kissing him. He put his arms around her, not really caring about all the people walking in and out of the hotel, and held her for quite a while.

"Wow," Susan Carol said. "Pretty good for someone so young."

"Yeah—fourteen isn't so bad."

They still had their arms around each other. "I know,"

she said. "I think you've got great growth potential."

He laughed. "When will I see you?" he said.

"Duke is playing at Temple in two weeks," she said. "Maybe I'll come up for the game."

"Bad idea," he said.

"Why?" she said, a surprised look on her face.

"You *like* Duke. And if *we're* both at the game, there's bound to be trouble of some kind."

"We are kind of a jinx, aren't we?"

"Yup. Basketball, tennis, football . . . What sport shall we ruin next?"

"How do you feel about baseball?" she asked.

"No! I like baseball. And we can't wreck swimming either."

"Oh, hey—think of the damage we could do at the Olympics!"

They both laughed for a long time, hanging on to each other a little crazily, the snow swirling around them.

After a while, Susan Carol said, "So, I shouldn't come to Philly for the game?"

Stevie kissed her again. "Of course you should," he said. "Trouble is what we do."

"And we do it well, don't we?"

"We sure do, Scarlett. We sure do."

1: SUDDEN VICTORY

EVEN THOUGH HE WAS ONLY FOURTEEN YEARS OLD, Stevie Thomas considered himself a veteran of sports victory celebrations. He had been to the Final Four, the Super Bowl, the NBA Finals, and the U.S. Open—in both tennis and golf. He had seen remarkable endings, miracle shots, and improbable last-second heroics.

But he hadn't seen anything quite like this. He was standing just outside the first-base dugout inside Nationals Park, the home stadium for the Washington Nationals, and even though the game had been over for several minutes, the noise was still so loud he couldn't hear anything Susan Carol Anderson was shouting in his ear.

"Mets . . . clubhouse . . . press box . . . ," he managed to make out over the din. Since she was starting to pick her way through the celebrating Nationals and the media swarm surrounding them, he guessed that she had told him that she was going to make her way to the clubhouse of the New York Mets and then meet him back in the press box. She was taking the harder job—talking to the players on a team that had just suffered a shocking defeat. His job was easier: talking to the winners.

The ending of the game had been stunning. With the National League Championship Series tied at three games all, both teams had sent their star pitchers out to pitch game seven: Johan Santana for the Mets, John Lannan for the Nationals. Both had pitched superbly, and the game had gone to the ninth inning tied at 1–1.

Nationals manager Manny Acta brought Joel Hanrahan, his closer, in to pitch the ninth, a bold move in a tie game. And it seemed to have backfired when Carlos Beltran hit a two-out, two-run home run to give the Mets a 3–1 lead. In came the Mets' closer, Francisco (K-Rod) Rodriguez, to get the last three outs needed to give the Mets the pennant.

He got two quick outs, and it wasn't looking good for the Nats when shortstop Cristian Guzman hit a weak ground ball. But somehow Mets all-star shortstop Jose Reyes booted it, allowing Guzman to make it safely to first base. Clearly upset and distracted by the error, Rodriguez then walked Ronnie Belliard, bringing Ryan Zimmerman, the Nationals' best hitter, to the plate.

Guzman began dancing off second base, stretching his lead each time Rodriguez looked back at him. Second baseman Luis Castillo kept flashing toward the bag, as if expecting a pickoff throw from Rodriguez. Sitting in the auxiliary press box, Stevie was wearing headphones that allowed him to hear the Fox telecast.

"Rodriguez and Castillo need to forget about Guzman," he heard Tim McCarver say. "Right now K-Rod has one job, and that's to get Zimmerman out."

"But if the Nats double-steal, the tying runs would both be in scoring position," play-by-play man Joe Buck said.

"True," McCarver said. "But I'm telling you, there is *no* way Guzman is risking making the last out of the season trying to steal third. He's not that much of a base stealer to begin with."

Rodriguez finally focused on the plate and threw a 97-mph fastball that Zimmerman just watched go by for strike one. Again Guzman danced off second base. This time Rodriguez whirled and did make a pickoff throw as Castillo darted in to take it. Guzman dove back in safely.

"That tells me Guzman has gotten inside K-Rod's head," McCarver said. "You don't risk a pickoff throw in this situation. The only man in the ballpark he should care about right now is Zimmerman."

Rodriguez threw another fastball, and Zimmerman fouled it straight back to the screen.

"That one was ninety-seven too," Buck said. "He doesn't seem *too* distracted."

"Zimmerman was about two inches from crushing that ball," McCarver said. "You see a batter foul a fastball straight back like that, it means he *just* missed it."

Rodriguez came to his set position again. Guzman was

off the bag once more and Rodriguez stepped off the rubber. Everyone relaxed for a moment.

"Zimmerman has to look for a fastball here, doesn't he?" Buck said.

"Absolutely."

Rodriguez set again, checked Guzman one more time, and threw. Stevie glanced at the spot on the scoreboard that showed pitch speed, and saw 98. Rodriguez had thrown a fastball, and Zimmerman had in fact been looking fastball. This time he didn't miss it. He got it. He got *all* of it. The ball rose majestically into the air and sailed in the direction of the left-field fence. Mets left fielder Daniel Murphy never moved. The ball sailed way over the fence, deep into the night, and complete bedlam broke out in every corner of the stadium. The Nationals had won the game 4–3 and the series 4–3. Shockingly, they were going to the World Series.

The auxiliary press box was down the left-field line, and Stevie and Susan Carol had seen Zimmerman's shot go right past them heading out of the park. As 41,888 people went crazy, they had joined other members of the media who were scrambling to get down to the field and the clubhouses.

There had been no point trying to squeeze onto the elevators, so they had dashed to the ramps—which weren't too crowded, because most of the fans were still standing at their seats, celebrating. The Nationals were on the field, spraying one another with champagne—which someone had brought out from their clubhouse to allow them to celebrate in front of the fans—so the media was directed down the tunnel to the home dugout and stood just outside it watching the celebration.

"I guess when you go seventy-six years between championships, you're entitled to go a little crazy," a voice shouted behind Stevie.

He turned and saw Bobby Kelleher, his friend and mentor, standing there with a wide grin on his face. Kelleher, a columnist for the *Washington Herald*, had been sitting in the main press box and had apparently just reached the field.

"Is Walter Johnson smiling somewhere?" Stevie asked Kelleher, referring to the Hall of Fame pitcher who had been the Washington Senators' star in the 1920s and their manager when a Washington baseball team last played in the World Series—in 1933.

"My guess is someone will claim to have *spoken* to him by tomorrow morning," Kelleher said, still shouting because the noise had abated only a little bit. "It's hard for people to understand how remarkable this is. Washington's always been a town that either had no baseball or played *bad* baseball."

Not one but two teams had left Washington—the original Senators left town in 1961 to move to Minnesota; then an expansion version fled to Texas ten years later.

"Where'd Susan Carol go?" Kelleher asked.

"Mets clubhouse," Stevie said.

"Figures," Kelleher said. "She's always willing to take on the tough jobs. That's where Tamara went too. I have to write the Nats. I mean, seventy-six years without a pennant. Not to mention that this team lost a hundred and two games a year ago."

Tamara Mearns was Kelleher's wife, a columnist for the *Washington Post*. The two of them had taken Stevie and Susan Carol under their wing when the teenagers won a writing contest and were awarded press credentials to the Final Four in New Orleans.

That was a weekend that had changed Stevie and Susan Carol's lives forever. They had gotten off to a rocky start: the wise-guy kid from Philadelphia clashing with the seemingly wide-eyed Southern belle from a small town in North Carolina. But they had stumbled into a plot to blackmail a star player and had worked together to nail the bad guys, starting them on what had often been a bumpy road to media stardom.

Since then they had found trouble at the U.S. Open tennis tournament and the Super Bowl; been hired and fired by a cable TV network; and, finally, settled into part-time work as writers—Stevie working with Kelleher at the *Herald*, Susan Carol working with Mearns at the *Post*.

They had even managed to cover several major events in recent months—their second Final Four, the U.S. Open golf tournament, another U.S. Open tennis tournament—without ending up on the front page. That had been a relief—their parents had been threatening to never let them out of their sight again after the scandal at the Super Bowl—but also a little bit disappointing. Stevie didn't want to think himself jaded at the age of fourteen, but a couple of times he had found himself forgetting to tingle when he put on his press credential to cover a big-time event.

But now, standing in the sparkling new Nationals Park, surrounded by fans who were still screaming their heads off with joy, listening to what felt like the hundredth playing of "We Are the Champions," and looking at the happiness on the faces of the players, Stevie realized he was in the middle of a genuinely tingle-worthy moment. As he was soaking it all in, he heard Kelleher shouting at him again over the noise.

"Just work the clubhouse," he said. "See what you find. I've got to focus on Zimmerman. Anything else in there is yours unless Sally wants it—but I think she's writing a what-this-means-to-the-city piece."

Sally was Sally Jenkins, the *Herald*'s other sports columnist, whom the paper had stolen from the *Post* for big dollars a year ago. Jenkins was so good Stevie wasn't sure he was worthy of reading her stuff, much less working with her. He followed Kelleher and the onrushing cameras, notebooks, and tape recorders up the ramp into the Nationals clubhouse.

Not surprisingly, it was a mob scene inside. Stevie wasn't two steps inside the door before he was sprayed with champagne. He knew from experience that he didn't want to get hit in the eyes by the stuff, so he put his head down and tried to maneuver away from the mass of people in the middle of the room. The clubhouse was huge, with enough room for fifty lockers even though only twenty-five were absolutely needed. Stevie had noted earlier in the series that most players had two lockers to themselves, with ample space around each locker.

He headed toward some breathing space in the back corner of the room. From there he would be able to see who was still spraying champagne and who was moving away from the melee and making themselves available to talk.

"Pretty wild, isn't it?" Stevie heard a voice say behind him.

He turned and saw a player standing at a locker. He had a bottle of champagne in his hands but clearly wasn't involved in the celebration. After seven games Stevie thought he knew all the Nationals players, but he was drawing a blank on both the face and the number, which was 56.

Apparently, the player noticed the blank look on Stevie's face, because he stuck his hand out and said, "Norbert Doyle. You've never heard of me because I've never done anything."

Stevie laughed and shook hands with Norbert Doyle, whose name sounded only a little bit familiar.

"Steve Thomas," he said. "*Washington Herald.*"

Saying the name of the newspaper always made Stevie feel very grown-up. Doyle smiled and nodded. "Of course, I should have known it was you right away. You're one of the two kid reporters who keep breaking all those big stories. My twins are big fans of yours and your friend . . ."

"Susan Carol," Stevie said. "Susan Carol Anderson."

It would be a stretch to say that Stevie had gotten used

to being recognized, but it happened often enough that it no longer surprised him. This was a little bit different, though: an athlete knowing who he was when he didn't know who the athlete was.

"How old are your twins?" Stevie asked.

"I think the same age as you," Doyle said. "David and Morra turned fourteen in July. I'm pretty sure David's got a crush on Susan Carol."

"Who doesn't?" Stevie said. "You should see the fan mail she gets. . . ."

"Come on, Steve," Doyle said, smiling. "I'm sure just as many teenage girls have crushes on you."

"Not so much," Stevie said, shaking his head. "But Susan Carol likes me, which makes me pretty lucky."

"Norbert!" someone yelled from the middle of the room. "Get over here. You're part of this too, you know!"

Doyle smiled and waved his hand. "Be right there," he said. Turning to Stevie, he said, "That's a stretch to say I'm part of this."

"But . . . you're on the team," Stevie said.

"Well, yes and no," Doyle said. "They brought me in at the tail end of the regular season. Started three games, relieved in three others. Didn't get a win. I'm not on the postseason roster, but they let me hang around."

That was why Stevie knew the name. He remembered seeing Doyle's name in the postseason media guide he had paged through on the train down from Philadelphia. If he remembered right, Doyle was kind of an interesting story: the Nationals had traded for him at the end of August because two of their pitchers had been hurt and they needed someone to come up from the minors and make a spot start. What made the story interesting was that Doyle was in his late thirties and had never pitched in a major-league game prior to the trade. Then, suddenly, he'd been thrust into the middle of a pennant race.

"You didn't win a game, but you pitched really well, didn't you?" Stevie said, hoping he was right.

"I pitched okay," Doyle said. "I was thrilled to be here. I just wasn't quite good enough to make the postseason roster."

"Hey, Norbert, come on over here!" someone was shouting.

"Sounds like a lot of guys think you *are* part of this," Stevie said.

Doyle smiled. "They're good guys," he said. "I'll tell you one thing. I'll never forget a minute of this experience."

He shook Stevie's hand again. "Good luck with your story tonight," he said. "My kids will be thrilled to know I met you."

With that he was gone, and Stevie stood alone, still in search of a story. Too late, as Doyle was doused in champagne, it occurred to him that he had just let a terrific story walk away.

JOHN FEINSTEIN is the author of many bestselling books, including *A Season on the Brink*, *A Good Walk Spoiled*, and *Living on the Black*. His books for young readers—*Last Shot*, *Vanishing Act*, *Cover-Up*, *Change-Up*, *The Rivalry*, *Rush for the Gold*, and *Foul Trouble*—offer a winning combination of sports, action, and intrigue, with *Last Shot* receiving the Edgar Allan Poe Award for best young adult mystery.

He began his career at the *Washington Post*, where he worked as both a political and sports reporter. He has also written for *Sports Illustrated* and the *National Sports Daily* and is currently a contributor to the *Washington Post*, *Golf World*, the Golf Channel, and Comcast SportsNet.

John Feinstein lives in Potomac, Maryland, where he is hard at work on a new series: The Triple Threat. Visit him online at JohnFeinsteinBooks.com.

FOOTBALL.
BASKETBALL.
BASEBALL.

Whatever the sport, Alex Myers always has his game face on. . . . Here's a sneak peek at

THE WALK ON,

the thrilling first installment of John Feinstein's new series, THE TRIPLE THREAT.

As soon as the snap had hit his hands, instinct had taken over. He wasn't thinking about the score or all the eyes on him or the fact that he had called a play that contradicted a direct order from his coach. All he could see was Jonas, who was racing behind the King of Prussia cornerback and coming open just as Alex stepped up in the pocket and released the ball.

When the ball came off his fingertips, he knew he had thrown it just the way he wanted to. His momentum carried him in the direction of the line of scrimmage and he watched as Jonas, running full speed, raced under the ball at the KOP 25 yard line, gathered it into his arms, and cruised into the end zone.

Alex's arms went into the air and he could feel his teammates pummeling him as they all ran downfield to congratulate Jonas.

"*That's* the way to throw it, Goldie," he heard Allison say, a phrase repeated by several others as they all high-fived their way down the field. The Chester Heights sideline had exploded, stunned by the suddenness of the touchdown— and by the quarterback who had thrown the pass. Alex knew he still had a silly grin on his face as everyone trotted to the sideline while the kicking team went in for the extra point.

Matt was waiting. He took his right hand c̸ to give Alex a high five.

"I knew you could do it, Goldie," he said. "I j̸ Coach Gordon was right behind him.

"Was that an audible, Myers? It didn't look like here."

"No sir. I called it in the huddle."

"Was that what I told you to call?"

"No sir," Alex said, offering no excuse and waiting f̸ hammer to come down on his head.

"I called it," Matt said. "I called it because I knew A̸ could make the throw and we needed a quick score to chang̸ the momentum."

Coach Gordon stared at his son, then at Alex as another roar went up from the Chester Heights sideline as the extra point went through, making it 17–7.

"We'll discuss it after the game," he said finally, turning and walking away.

FOOTBALL.
BASKETBALL.
BASEBALL.

Whatever the sport, Alex Myers always has his game face on. . . . Here's a sneak peek at

THE WALK ON,

**the thrilling first installment of
John Feinstein's new series,
THE TRIPLE THREAT.**

As soon as the snap had hit his hands, instinct had taken over. He wasn't thinking about the score or all the eyes on him or the fact that he had called a play that contradicted a direct order from his coach. All he could see was Jonas, who was racing behind the King of Prussia cornerback and coming open just as Alex stepped up in the pocket and released the ball.

When the ball came off his fingertips, he knew he had thrown it just the way he wanted to. His momentum carried him in the direction of the line of scrimmage and he watched as Jonas, running full speed, raced under the ball at the KOP 25 yard line, gathered it into his arms, and cruised into the end zone.

Alex's arms went into the air and he could feel his teammates pummeling him as they all ran downfield to congratulate Jonas.

"*That's* the way to throw it, Goldie," he heard Allison say, a phrase repeated by several others as they all high-fived their way down the field. The Chester Heights sideline had exploded, stunned by the suddenness of the touchdown—and by the quarterback who had thrown the pass. Alex knew he still had a silly grin on his face as everyone trotted to the sideline while the kicking team went in for the extra point.

Matt was waiting. He took his right hand off his crutches to give Alex a high five.

"I knew you could do it, Goldie," he said. "I just knew it."

Coach Gordon was right behind him.

"Was that an audible, Myers? It didn't look like one from here."

"No sir. I called it in the huddle."

"Was that what I told you to call?"

"No sir," Alex said, offering no excuse and waiting for the hammer to come down on his head.

"I called it," Matt said. "I called it because I knew Alex could make the throw and we needed a quick score to change the momentum."

Coach Gordon stared at his son, then at Alex as another roar went up from the Chester Heights sideline as the extra point went through, making it 17–7.

"We'll discuss it after the game," he said finally, turning and walking away.

JOHN FEINSTEIN is the author of many bestselling books, including *A Season on the Brink*, *A Good Walk Spoiled*, and *Living on the Black*. His books for young readers—*Last Shot*, *Vanishing Act*, *Cover-Up*, *Change-Up*, *The Rivalry*, *Rush for the Gold*, and *Foul Trouble*—offer a winning combination of sports, action, and intrigue, with *Last Shot* receiving the Edgar Allan Poe Award for best young adult mystery.

He began his career at the *Washington Post*, where he worked as both a political and sports reporter. He has also written for *Sports Illustrated* and the *National Sports Daily* and is currently a contributor to the *Washington Post*, *Golf World*, the Golf Channel, and Comcast SportsNet.

John Feinstein lives in Potomac, Maryland, where he is hard at work on a new series: The Triple Threat. Visit him online at JohnFeinsteinBooks.com.